DIGGING UP THE DIRT

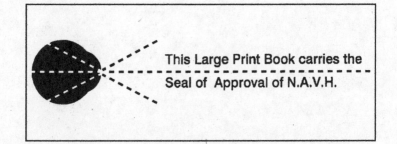

This Large Print Book carries the
Seal of Approval of N.A.V.H.

A SOUTHERN LADIES MYSTERY

DIGGING UP THE DIRT

MIRANDA JAMES

WHEELER PUBLISHING
A part of Gale, Cengage Learning

GALE
CENGAGE Learning·

Farmington Hills, Mich • San Francisco • New York • Waterville, Maine
Meriden, Conn • Mason, Ohio • Chicago

GALE
CENGAGE Learning®

LIBRARY OF CONGRESS CATALOGING-IN-PUBLICATION DATA

Names: James, Miranda.
Title: Digging up the dirt / by Miranda James.
Description: Large print edition. | Waterville, Maine : Wheeler Publishing, 2017. |
  Series: A southern ladies mystery | Series: Wheeler Publishing large print cozy
  mystery
Identifiers: LCCN 2016058023| ISBN 9781410495822 (softcover) | ISBN 1410495825
  (softcover)
Subjects: LCSH: Large type books. | GSAFD: Mystery fiction.
Classification: LCC PS3610.A43 D54 2017 | DDC 813/.6—dc23
LC record available at https://lccn.loc.gov/2016058023

Published in 2017 by arrangement with The Berkley Publishing Group, an imprint of Penguin Publishing Group, a division of Penguin Random House LLC

Printed in Mexico
1 2 3 4 5 6 7 21 20 19 18 17

In loving memory of my beloved aunts:

Mary Williams Woods (1945–2016)
Charlotte Naomi James (1928–2015)

ACKNOWLEDGMENTS

As always, my fervent thanks go to my wonderful editor, Michelle Vega, and her exceptional assistant, Bethany Blair. The art department at Berkley always manages to deliver beautiful, eye-catching covers for the original publisher's editions, and I am immensely grateful.

I didn't give my usual manuscript readers much of a shot at this one. I can only hope they won't be disappointed when they read the final version. But I thank them for their friendship and support, which always make the process easier. Amy, Bob, Julie, Kay F., Kay K., Laura, and Susie — I'm so glad you put up with me and allow me to participate virtually.

Finally, a great big thank-you to Nancy Yost and the amazing crew at Nancy Yost Literary: Adrienne, Natanya, and Sarah E. You're the best!

CHAPTER 1

Miss Dickce Ducote wanted a clear view of
her sister An'gel's face when she broke the
news. She wished there were a discreet way
she could set up the video camera on her
cell phone to record the moment. Then she
could threaten to show it to the rest of the
Athena Garden Club to annoy her sister.
An'gel needed to be wound up occasionally,
Dickce thought. Older sisters could get to
be a little too stuffy otherwise.

Miss An'gel Ducote looked up from where
she knelt at the edge of the flower bed,
trowel in one gloved hand, while the other
hand brushed back a stray lock of gray hair.
She grimaced. "What is it, Sister? You've
obviously got something to tell me. You're
practically bouncing on the ground."

Dickce gave her a sweet smile. "I've been
talking to Arliss McGonigal, and you'll
never guess what she told me." She paused
to make sure she had her sister's complete

attention.

"If you don't get on with it," An'gel said, "I'm going back to work on this bed." She brandished the trowel. "I have four more azaleas to plant here."

"Hadley Partridge is back in town." Dickce watched her sister's face with avid interest.

"That's not much of a surprise," An'gel replied, her tone cool and her expression unchanged. "Hamish died three weeks ago, and he had no other family besides his baby brother. Hadley's probably here to oversee the sale of Ashton Hall."

Dickce had felt sure that news of an old beau's return would rattle her sister at least a tiny bit, but An'gel remained as infuriatingly unflappable as ever.

"That's where you're wrong." Dickce had another round of ammunition to use. "Word is, Hadley has come home to Athena for good. He's going to restore Ashton Hall and the gardens. In fact, he's planning to be at the garden club board meeting *this very afternoon.*"

Whatever reply An'gel might have made to that news went unsaid, though Dickce did have the satisfaction of seeing a brief smile from her sister.

A reddish-brown streak on four legs

zipped through the space between the sisters. Hot on the cat Endora's trail came Peanut the Labradoodle. Endora came to a sudden halt about six feet away from where An'gel knelt, turned, and hissed at the dog. Peanut skidded to a stop an inch out of reach of Endora's swinging paw. Cat and dog stared at each other a moment, then Endora was off again with Peanut right behind.

"They've already been around the house at least four times." An'gel shook her head. "Where they find the energy, I have no idea."

"They're children, comparatively speaking." Dickce laughed. "Not old women like us." On a beautiful day like this, however, Dickce felt younger than her eighty years. An'gel, four years older, made as few concessions to the passage of time as possible, Dickce knew. That included ignoring overt references to her age.

An'gel turned back to the azalea she was about to transplant. "Hadley will be welcome at the garden club. Forty years ago he was one of our most active members."

"And the only man." Dickce chuckled. "I bet he'll be surprised to see his old harem gather around him."

An'gel snorted. "What a silly word. *Harem.*

11

You have a salacious mind sometimes, Sister."

Nettled slightly by An'gel's tone, Dickce snapped back. "Forty years ago you had one, too, Sister. I seem to recall you were pretty interested in Hadley yourself back then, despite the age difference."

An'gel's shoulders stiffened for a moment. She turned to glare up at Dickce. "Your imagination always did run wild. I seem to recall that *you* were the one who used to hang on Hadley's every word." She sniffed and turned back to her azalea. "Besides, you're older than he is, too."

"Only by five years," Dickce retorted. Then she couldn't help herself. She started laughing. She and An'gel sounded like teenagers squabbling over a boy.

An'gel continued to glare for a moment, then she, too, began to laugh.

When the merriment ceased, Dickce said, "Hadley was always too darn gorgeous for his own good."

"And everyone else's," An'gel said in a wry tone. "He's about seventy-five now, and he's probably lost all his looks. He liked the high life too much even then. Bound to be well past his glory days."

"Well, I guess we'll find out this afternoon." Dickce turned to head into the house but had to pause to let Endora and Peanut whiz by again. "Surely they'll get tired of that before long. See you at lunch, Sister." She walked away, and An'gel finished moving the azalea to its new home.

Dickce hit the brakes, and the Lexus skidded into a spot between a newish-looking BMW and a ragged-looking, elderly Jaguar. Dickce put the car in park and shut off the engine with a sly smile at her sister.

"Your driving is getting worse." An'gel unbuckled her seat belt, her hand a bit shaky.

"You said you didn't want to be late," Dickce retorted. She pointed to the digital clock on the dash. "We're actually ten minutes early."

"The way you drove, we could have been extremely late," An'gel said as she stepped out of the car. "As in dead."

Dickce ignored that little sally. "I don't recognize the BMW. Do you suppose that's Hadley's car?"

"Either that, or Reba's bought Martin a new car." An'gel shook her head. "The way she spends money on her son, they must be printing it in the attic."

"Maybe Martin has a job we don't know about." Dickce grinned as she followed

13

An'gel up the brick walk to the two-story colonial-style house that belonged to Barbie Gross, current president of the Athena Garden Club.

"If he has, it will be the first one in twenty years." An'gel stepped onto the small porch and rang the bell. "He seems allergic to work."

The door opened, and Barbie Gross nodded in greeting. Barbie, her hair as black as it was the day she had her first dye job at forty, exhibited her trim figure in a black Chanel pantsuit with a sleeveless top. Her tanned, firm arms had resulted from hours of gardening and lifting weights, Dickce knew. It didn't hurt, either, that Barbie was nearly twenty years younger than An'gel.

"Come on in, girls." She grinned. "Dickce must have driven, because you look a little shell shocked, An'gel."

"I always think she'll slow down a bit." An'gel grimaced. "I live in foolish hope, obviously."

Dickce paid no attention to them. "We saw Sarinda's car. Who's in the new BMW?"

"Arliss," Barbie said. "She picked up Lottie." She led the way into her spacious living room, where two women, one blond, the other a redhead, appeared absorbed in conversation.

". . . lay odds on who gets Hadley into her bedroom first." The redheaded woman snickered, and the blonde, evidently having noticed the new arrivals, poked her companion and shook her head slightly.

"Hello, Arliss." Dickce nodded at the redhead, and An'gel echoed her. Then they greeted the blond woman, Lottie MacLeod.

Dickce examined the two quickly. Arliss McGonigal had chosen a simple shirtwaist in polka-dotted blue silk. Her flame-red hair owed more to a bottle of henna than to nature, and strategic nips and tucks from a surgeon kept her looking at least a decade younger than her seventy-five years. Lottie MacLeod wore her blond ringlets short, and they framed a face with a pert nose, a generous mouth, and eyes that seldom missed anything. Lottie favored Chanel like her best friend, Barbie, but Lottie's shorter, plumper figure appeared better in a pencil skirt rather than a pantsuit. Dickce thought the pale blue dress flattered Lottie's coloring nicely.

"Where's Sarinda?" An'gel set her handbag on a table that stood in front of the wide picture window. Dickce did the same, and the sisters seated themselves in chairs that faced the sofa occupied by Arliss and Lottie.

"Touching up her makeup," Arliss said.

"With Hadley Partridge due here any minute she's determined to look as flawless as possible."

"You seem to have spent a good deal of time on your own." Barbie laughed, and Dickce thought the sound seemed tinged with malice.

Arliss tossed her head. "I require very little makeup. Unlike some women who put it on with a trowel." She glared at Barbie.

The claws are coming out sooner than usual. Dickce suppressed a giggle. Garden club board meetings always entertained her, and this one promised to be a corker. She wished Hadley would hurry up and get here.

Barbie regarded Arliss with a cool gaze. "You *must* give me the name of your plastic surgeon, dear. He seems to have worked absolute *miracles* for you."

Lottie chuckled, but quickly covered her mouth with one hand. Her gaze darted back and forth between her best friend and the manifestly peeved redhead.

"Can't you two rehearse a new scene once in a while?" An'gel glanced sharply at the two combatants.

Dickce looked toward the door to see Sarinda Hetherington, her ruby-red dress cut low to show off her ample cleavage, enter the room. Sarinda had her long blond hair

16

piled high in order to show off her elegant neck, the product of a top-notch plastic surgeon in Jackson. She, unlike Arliss, never hid the fact she'd had work done.

"Who's rehearsing?" Sarinda asked.

"Arliss and Barbie, who else," Dickce said with some asperity. "That's a gorgeous dress, Sarinda. Did you find it on your last trip to New York?"

"Thank you, Dickce." Sarinda ran her hands down the skirt. "Yes, I did. I found a wonderful new designer. Remind me later, and I'll give you her name." She eyed Dickce for a moment before she chose a chair nearby. "She can work wonders for small bosoms."

Dickce didn't bat an eyelash before she responded. "I see she works wonders with thick waists as well."

Both Arliss and Lottie chuckled at that remark, and An'gel shot her sister a quelling look. Dickce resisted the temptation to stick out her tongue at An'gel.

"I let myself in," a voice announced from the doorway. Everyone turned to greet the latest arrival.

Reba Dalrymple, Dickce noted with waspish amusement, had worn a short skirt today, the better to show off her long, beautiful legs. How a woman of nearly

17

eighty managed to keep her legs looking like that was a secret Reba never shared. Dickce wasn't in the least surprised to see the short skirt. Reba was obviously determined that Hadley Partridge would have a good look at her two best assets.

Reba approached the sofa and seated herself between Arliss and Lottie. "Isn't Hadley here yet?" She glanced around the room.

"He ought to be here any minute," Barbie replied. "As I recall, he was always punctual."

"Yes, he was," Arliss said. Lottie and Sarinda echoed her. Then they all glared at one another.

Dickce had to suppress another urge to giggle. She hadn't been far wrong earlier when she referred to Hadley's harem. They were all — including An'gel and herself — excited to see Hadley again. If he turned up bald and overweight, they would all probably faint from the shock.

The doorbell rang, and Dickce noticed that all heads turned immediately toward the doorway. Barbie hurried from the room. Dickce could hear the voices of Barbie and the latest arrival, and the newcomer sounded like a man. She could hardly bear the suspense while they waited for Barbie to

18

bring Hadley — surely it was Hadley — into the room. She closed her eyes for a moment, and when she opened them, there he stood.

CHAPTER 2

An'gel felt her heart flutter the tiniest bit at the sight of Hadley Partridge. Dickce had teased her earlier in the day about her attraction to Hadley, and she had tried to shrug it off as coolly as possible. She had to admit to herself, however, that she was eager to see the most handsome man she had ever known. He'd always had too roving an eye for An'gel to take him completely seriously when he flirted with her. According to the Athena rumor mill he'd had affairs with any number of women, some of them in this room. The moment she'd heard about his return, however, she began to speculate what he would look like after forty years, whether the old easy, notorious charm would have remained intact. Or whether he had come back to Athena a broken-down wreck of a man, after decades of dissipated living.

The flutter moved down to her stomach

as she stared at Hadley, who had paused in the doorway to observe the room. An'gel noted that the hair once jet-black had turned completely white, but the mane appeared as thick as ever. Hadley had never worn his hair to fit any fashion, and now the flowing locks brushed his neckline. He had obviously spent many years in the sun, and the tanned skin contrasted nicely with the hair. He wore black pants and a densely knitted, dark blue sweater that complemented his dark eyes and white hair perfectly. His slow, seductive smile emerged as he beheld the women who had waited so tensely for his arrival.

Hadley strode into the room, arms open wide. Barbie, her gaze firmly fixed on Hadley's back, stumbled in behind him and almost knocked over a table. She caught herself and the table in time, but barely, An'gel noted with amusement.

"Good afternoon, dear ladies." Hadley stopped about three feet away from the assembled group and treated them all to another expansive smile. His hands dropped to his sides. "You don't know how wonderful it is to be home again. And to be greeted by friends who by some miracle are just as gorgeous as they were the day I left Athena those many years ago."

An'gel heard several sighs, including one from her sister. She might even have sighed herself, but she would never admit it to anyone.

"Oh, Hadley, it's wonderful that you're back home." Sarinda propelled herself up from the sofa to leap into Hadley's arms. Evidently startled by the sudden movement, Hadley took a step back. Sarinda stumbled, and Hadley reached out to halt her fall. She ended up in his arms, her intention all along. An'gel suppressed a snort of irritation.

Hadley bestowed a quick kiss on Sarinda's cheek before he led her firmly back to the sofa. Sarinda resumed her place, but An'gel noted that the blonde's gaze never left Hadley's face. He kissed both Arliss and Lottie on the cheek quickly before he approached An'gel.

Was it her imagination, or did his eyes light up as he gazed into hers? An'gel couldn't remember the last time she had blushed over anything, but now she was convinced her face had flushed. Dickce would rag on her for the rest of her days.

Hadley extended both hands, and An'gel took them. Before she realized what he intended, Hadley pulled her up and into his arms. His lips grazed her ear when he

22

whispered, "Still as stunning as you were forty years ago." He hugged her for a moment and then released her. He grinned, and An'gel wanted to slap his face for making her feel so embarrassed.

"You're every bit as wicked as you were forty years ago." She spoke in a low tone in the hopes that no one but Hadley would hear, but when Dickce snickered she knew she had misjudged.

"Of course, An'gel," Hadley said, one eyebrow raised. "Would you have me any other way?"

He gave her no time to respond as he moved to stand in front of Dickce. He leaned down to give her a kiss, and An'gel heard her sister sigh. He moved on to Reba.

Feeling a sudden wave of hostility directed toward her, An'gel sat abruptly. She tried as coolly as possible to return the gazes of the other women. Hadley had singled her out, and they looked at her as if they could cheerfully strangle her. The first chance she had to speak to Hadley alone, she would give him a dressing-down he wouldn't soon forget.

Hadley found a chair and pulled it forward between Dickce and Reba. Barbie perched on the arm of the sofa next to Lottie once Hadley sat. Hadley leaned back, crossed his arms over his chest, and regarded them all. "Thanks for inviting me back into the fold, ladies. It's not often the prodigal son returns to such an open-armed greeting."

"We're all delighted you're back in Athena." Reba turned slightly in her chair to look at him. "We're all also hoping that you intend to remain and bring Ashton Hall back to what it ought to be."

"That is my plan." Hadley nodded. "I was appalled to see how my dear brother had let the gardens go." He grimaced. "Hamish never cared as much about them as I did."

An'gel — like the others, she had no doubt — burned to ask Hadley why he had left so abruptly all those years ago. There had been various rumors at the time. The one that had the most support was that Hamish had caught his brother in bed with his wife, Callie, and had thrown Hadley out of the house and told him never to come back. Another story held that Hadley embezzled money from his brother and skipped town to avoid prosecution, though many doubted Hamish would have suffered the indignity of putting his brother in jail. Hamish Partridge had been far too proud of his family name to allow that to happen.

"But now they're mine," Hadley said in a somber tone. "Poor old Hamish finally

24

passed on, and to my great surprise he left everything to me."

"I wasn't surprised in the least." Arliss fluttered her eyelashes at Hadley. "There was no one else, at least as far we know, and Hamish would never have left Ashton Hall to strangers."

"No, he certainly wouldn't." Lottie shook her head. "The last time I saw him, about three days before he died, he told me everything would be yours, Hadley." She paused to glance up at Barbie, then looked at Hadley again. "Especially since he had no idea where his wife was."

An'gel felt an immediate change of atmosphere in the room, and she could see that Hadley had tensed up. She had wondered how long it would take one of the women to mention Callie Partridge.

Calpurnia Partridge, actually, An'gel knew, but Callie had always hated her full name. Callie left Athena a couple of days after Hadley, so the story went, and everyone assumed she'd run after him.

"Poor Callie." Hadley sighed, his shoulders now relaxed. "Hamish never treated her the way he should have, so it's no wonder she bolted when she did." He paused to glance around the room. "I wonder what happened to her? Did any of you ever hear from her after she left Athena? Until I heard that Hamish left everything to me, I really thought I would find her still living at Ashton Hall."

No one responded right away to Hadley, and the silence lengthened. An'gel knew the others were no doubt as stunned as she was, because they had all assumed that Hadley and Callie had been together all these years. If Callie *hadn't* followed Hadley from Athena, what on earth had happened to her?

An'gel decided she might as well voice what everyone was thinking. "No one ever heard from her again, to our knowledge. Everyone thought, you see, that she had run away to join you because she didn't want to stay with Hamish."

Hadley didn't appear startled at An'gel's statement. He shrugged. "I'm not surprised by that. I know everyone thought Callie and I were having a passionate affair behind Hamish's back, but that simply was not the case. I never touched her, and she certainly didn't run off to be with me."

"Then where could she have gone?" Arliss threw up her hands. "She had no family left, as far as I know."

"She was a registered nurse, remember, even though she quit working after she married Hamish," Barbie said. "She could have found a job anywhere. Taken on a new name, even gotten married again for all we know."

"Hamish never said anything to *me* about divorcing her." Reba sniffed. "If she did marry again, she was committing bigamy."

"Hamish didn't tell *you* everything, Reba." Lottie simpered. "I was his closest confidante the last few years. If he had told anyone, he would have told *me*."

"Well, did he tell you whether he divorced her?" An'gel asked. Really, she could shake Lottie sometimes for her coyness.

Lottie shrugged. "The subject never came up. Hamish and I had other things to talk about when I visited with him."

When you were trying to get him interested in marrying you, *you mean.* An'gel resisted the temptation to say the words aloud.

Arliss saved her the trouble. She hooted with laughter, then said, "Hamish was too smart for you, Lottie. He knew better than to tell you any such thing. Otherwise you'd have dragged him to the altar before he could put on a fresh pair of socks and clean underwear."

"That's what *you* would have done, you mean-spirited woman," Lottie said. "I thought of Hamish as a friend, nothing more."

Hamish might well have divorced Callie, An'gel thought, but he was too canny to let any of the women in this group know. They all had men and marriage in their sights.

Everyone except her and Dickce, that is. An'gel had never cared much for Hamish, nor had Dickce. Neither of them understood why Callie married him. He was dour and cheap, the opposite of his brother. Hamish had been almost as handsome as Hadley in his younger years, and Callie had met Hamish first. He could be charming, An'gel admitted to herself, but whenever Hadley was present, Hamish got eclipsed.

"There's one possibility no one has mentioned." Sarinda crossed her arms as she surveyed the room. She let the silence lengthen before she spoke again. "What if Callie never left Athena at all?"

CHAPTER 3

An'gel felt a chill at those words as the implications sank in. Then she felt foolish and annoyed for letting Sarinda's love of drama affect her in such a way.

Reba guffawed. "That's about the silliest thing I ever heard, Sarinda. Tell me, do you think Callie's been living in the woods around Ashton Hall all this time? Or maybe she has taken on a secret identity." She continued to laugh.

"I have a confession to make." Barbie rose from her perch on the arm of the sofa and hung her head for a moment. "I've had Callie locked away in my cellar all these years. I suppose I should let her out now." She glanced around the room.

Lottie giggled. "She can't be in *your* cellar, Barbie honey, because I've got her in *my* attic."

An'gel checked Hadley's expression and found it guarded. What was his true reaction to these juvenile attempts at humor? she wondered. She herself found them distasteful.

"You can make light of it all you want," Sarinda said. "But can one of you tell me — tell all of us — where Callie is? And whether she is even still alive?"

"But *you* said, what if she never left Athena?" Arliss frowned. "That's quite a different question. If she never left, then something must have happened to her. Something *fatal.* That's what you really meant, isn't it?"

"Perhaps." Sarinda looked down at her lap.

An'gel had to suppress the urge to go grab hold of her shoulders and give her a good shake. What was Sarinda trying to do? Could she possibly know something about Callie's disappearance? An'gel felt that chill again.

"Callie kept in touch with several friends from nursing school," Hadley said. "Like Barbie suggested, Callie probably went to one of them, and they helped her find a job. She wanted to go back to work after she and Hamish got married, but he wouldn't hear of it."

"That seems likely to me." Reba nodded. "Yes, very likely. Sarinda, all you've ever wanted to be is the center of attention, and you'll say anything to get your way." She turned to Hadley. "What have you been doing all these years? You know we're all curious."

Hadley gave a brief smile. "I know y'all are. It's not really an exciting story, but basically I went to New York and got a job with a company that has offices around the world. I worked in various places over the years — Vienna, Sydney, Madrid, Paris, Los Angeles, and a few others. I became a corporate troubleshooter and did pretty well at it. I retired about three years ago in London, and that's where I was when I got word from Hamish's lawyers about his death."

"What part of London?" Lottie asked. "London is my favorite city in the world, and I've been oodles of times."

"Mayfair," Hadley said.

Mayfair, An'gel knew, was a pricey place to live, so Hadley wasn't short of a bob or two, as the Brits would say. He had apparently done well for himself as a corporate troubleshooter. His clothes were expensive, and An'gel could see he wore an expensive watch, one that cost at least fifteen thousand dollars.

"I just love Mayfair," Lottie said. "So exclusive."

Barbie spoke at the same time. "So glamorous, all those great cities. What an interesting life you have had."

Hadley shrugged. "Nothing particularly glamorous about it. I never had time to settle down long in one place because as soon as I finished one assignment they sent me off on another one. Eighty-plus-hour weeks and too much travel, if you want to know the truth."

To judge by the glum expressions of her fellow board members, An'gel reckoned they were disappointed with Hadley's prosaic explanation. The dashing playboy of four decades past had become a hardworking corporate type, and they evidently didn't see much glamor in that.

An'gel, while more than a bit surprised at Hadley's choice of profession, was nevertheless pleased to hear that he had buckled down and worked hard. He hadn't shown many signs of dedication to work before he left Athena, relying instead on charm, good looks, and his brother's checkbook in lieu of gainful employment.

"We're all happy to welcome you back home." An'gel nodded at Hadley. "We also hope you're truly here to stay. You're not planning to renovate Ashton Hall and the gardens so you can sell and then move back to London, are you?"

Hadley cocked his head to the side and regarded her with one of his patented slow smiles, designed to warm even the coldest heart. "I am here to stay, dear An'gel. Athena holds an attraction that, oddly enough, London doesn't."

He's pouring it on a bit too thick. An'gel wanted to box his ears. *Why is he singling me out like this?*

Once again she felt hostile glances. She gazed coolly around the room with a silent challenge. The other women's gazes dropped, and An'gel relaxed.

"We're all delighted to hear that you're staying," Dickce said. "Though if I had to pick between London and Athena, well, there are plenty of days I'd rather be in London."

Bless Sister for helping to break the tension. An'gel laughed. "Especially in August and September when it's unbearably hot here."

Barbie cleared her throat. "Time to get the meeting started. We really need to focus on the spring tour of homes. Now that we can include Ashton Hall I believe we can up the ticket prices by a few dollars. What do y'all think?"

"We've been charging twelve dollars for

the past ten years for a single house tour," Arliss said. "I don't see any reason why we shouldn't raise that to fifteen now. Three dollars isn't that much."

"I agree." Reba nodded. "And ten for children under sixteen. That seems reasonable."

"I agree," An'gel said, and Dickce echoed her. An'gel went on. "What about the package prices? Fifty dollars for four houses?"

"Sounds fine to me," Lottie said. "We need to increase our revenue. Preservation isn't cheap, and some of us don't have large bank accounts to pay for repairs to these old houses." She cut a sly glance at An'gel and Dickce.

An'gel ignored Lottie's remark. Lottie always liked to pretend she was the poorest member of the board, but An'gel knew Lottie was tight with money. Lottie's home, The Oaks, stayed in excellent condition.

"We can use the same schedule we have for the past few years," Barbie said. "What group should Ashton Hall be in? People will be excited since it hasn't been shown for over thirty years."

"Put it in the group with Riverhill," Hadley said. "That's the closest, and Fairleigh is the next closest in town."

Sarinda brightened at the mention of her

home. "Yes, I agree. It makes sense to group us together." She smiled at Hadley. "I can't wait to see Ashton Hall restored to its former glory."

"The tour generally starts the first weekend in March." An'gel looked at Hadley. "That gives you about four months to get the gardens and the house ready. Will you be able to do that?"

Hadley nodded. "I already have a team there inspecting the house and the gardens. The house mostly needs a good cleaning." He grimaced. "I'm afraid Hamish was none too particular about housekeeping recently."

"We're going to need a few pictures for the website," Barbie said. "How soon do you think we can get those?"

"I think I can find some suitable shots in the next few days," Hadley said.

"I'll be delighted to come over and help you look," Reba said. "My son Martin — do you remember him, Hadley? He was about five when you left — anyway, he takes all the pictures for the website, and we can come over and scout around."

Hadley shook his head. "Only vague memories, I'm afraid. I never paid much attention to children. I'm a more than decent photographer, if I do say so myself. I can take the pictures and send them. Who maintains the website?"

"Martin does," Reba said. "It really wouldn't be any trouble at all for us to take the pictures and save you the bother."

"I appreciate your offer," Hadley said. "But there are going to be so many workmen around the place that everything's going to be chaos for a while. I think it's better if I take the pictures myself."

Reba shrugged. "Well, if you insist. I'll give you Martin's email address."

Hadley had made it clear that he didn't particularly want visitors, at least for now, An'gel decided. She wondered whether the others would take the hint, or whether there would soon be a steady stream of casserole dishes and congealed salads making their way to Ashton Hall. She and Dickce would invite him to dinner soon, though, because it was the proper thing to do.

All the other women in the room would issue invitations as well, she knew. She wondered how many of those invitations Hadley would accept. Perhaps he had reformed his ways and was no longer a playboy. She realized suddenly that no one had bothered to ask Hadley whether he was married, or had been.

At the moment she couldn't think of a polite way to ask. She had noticed that

36

Hadley's left ring finger was bare, but that didn't necessarily mean Hadley was single. Still, surely Hadley would have mentioned a wife or a girlfriend if he had brought a woman home with him.

"If you take a look at the website, Hadley," Reba said, "you can see the kind of pictures we use. There is also a schedule up for this year, based on last year's, but we can revise it if we need to. Have a look, and let us know if you foresee any problems."

"Thank you, I will," Hadley said. "I do have a question for you, however. You're talking about raising ticket prices. Haven't they already been on sale for a while?"

"No, the tickets go on sale usually the first of December, so we've got time to get this all arranged," Dickce said. "We need to get the new prices on the website, though, right away. Will you tell Martin, Reba?"

"Yes," Reba said. "I'll have him take care of it today, as long as we're agreed on the new prices."

"Time for a vote," Barbie said. "All in favor of raising the prices as discussed, say *aye*."

A chorus of *ayes* sounded.

"Any *nays*?" Barbie asked. After a moment of silence, she continued, "The *ayes* have it, so the prices are approved."

"Don't the rest of the club members get a say in this?" Hadley asked. "Or does the royal council have complete power?"

An'gel saw Barbie, Lottie, and Sarinda bridle at that second question. The board could be high-handed, but the club charter gave the board the power to act in such matters. She explained this to Hadley. "The membership at large approved this as a change to the bylaws a good fifteen years ago. Most of them seem happy to leave financial matters to the board."

"Then that's good enough for me." Hadley grinned. "Is there any other business to discuss, ladies? Because if there isn't, I really need to get back home and check in with the workers. I have to talk to the contractor about repairs."

"Are you sure you can't stay a while longer and have a drink with us?" Sarinda pouted.

Hadley rose. "I would truly love to, Sarinda, but there's so much to do at Ashton Hall. Especially now that I have a firm deadline, and I don't want to let the club down. I'm sure you all understand."

"Certainly," Barbie said. "Let me show you out. I'll be back in a minute, girls. Feel free to head to the kitchen. The iced tea is ready." She laid her arm on Hadley's and led him out of the room.

"I'm ready for tea." Dickce stood. "How about the rest of you?"

"Might as well." Reba rose, and so did Arliss and Lottie. Sarinda remained seated.

"I'll join you in a moment," An'gel said. "I want to powder my nose first." She followed the others into the hall in time to see Barbie close the front door behind the departing Hadley. She ducked down the hall toward the washroom under the stairs ahead of the others on their way to the kitchen at the back of the house.

An'gel emerged from the washroom a couple of minutes later and walked into the kitchen. She was not surprised to hear her fellow members discussing Hadley and his appearance. She helped herself to a glass of tea. There was one full glass left on the tray, and then she realized that one member of the board was missing.

"Where is Sarinda?" An'gel asked during a brief lull in the rhapsodies over how handsome and distinguished Hadley was. She sipped her tea. Barbie brewed it dark and strong, exactly the way An'gel preferred it.

"Probably still sulking in the living room," Barbie said. "I'm sure she thought Hadley didn't pay her enough attention. Let her pout if she wants to."

"Yes, leave her alone," Lottie said. "You'd think she was a teenager sometimes, the way she has these little fits of hers."

"I'll go get her," Arliss said. "Leaving her alone just encourages her to be a martyr." She left the room, glass in hand.

Arliss returned moments later. "She's gone. I guess she's having a bigger snit than we realized. I'll call her later and make sure she's okay."

"This is odd, even for Sarinda." Dickce frowned.

"Yes, it is," An'gel said. "She doesn't usually disappear like this, even when she's having a good sulk."

"She was pretty fey about the whole Callie thing," Reba said. "Do you think she knows more than she's letting on about what happened to Callie forty years ago?"

CHAPTER 4

An'gel felt another frisson at Reba's words. Had Sarinda been hinting that she actually knew what happened to Callie? If she did know, why hadn't she spoken up before now?

An'gel decided that it might be a good idea for her and Dickce to pay Sarinda a visit soon. With coaxing, Sarinda might tell them what lay behind these cryptic questions. It might be nothing other than a bid for attention, but An'gel thought it would be better to know for sure. Perhaps they might go tomorrow.

"I thought Hadley seemed eager to leave." Barbie frowned. "After all these years you'd think he'd at least stay and visit with us a few minutes."

"Maybe Sarinda spooked him," Lottie said.

Arliss snorted. "Don't be ridiculous, Lottie. Hadley probably wanted to avoid more questions about what he's been doing the past forty years."

"And whether he has been married and might still be." Dickce grinned. "You notice he never mentioned anything about a wife or a girlfriend."

"He'd hardly pop that into the conversation without some sort of prompting," An'gel said. "Frankly, I don't think he's married. I never have thought he was the marrying kind. Variety is his stock-in-trade when it comes to women." She glanced around at her fellow board members, all of whom except her own sister seemed suddenly fascinated by the contents of their glasses. "You can set your caps at him all you want, but Hadley will outrun you all."

"Fine words coming from *you,* An'gel." Reba plunked her glass on the counter none too gently. "He sure did seem interested in you, or didn't you notice?"

"Yes, he gave you pretty marked attention." Arliss stared hard at her.

An'gel kept a tight rein on her temper, although she had halfway been expecting such a scene. "That was simply Hadley showing off. He has always liked to tease, and he knew it would annoy me."

"Call it what you like," Barbie said. "He paid more attention to you than he did to

42

anyone else."

An'gel spoke sharply. "I wasn't aware it was a competition." She regretted the tone immediately. Barbie and Arliss smirked at her while Reba glared. Lottie and Dickce giggled.

An'gel would have a few words for her sister as soon as they were on the way home. She was furious that Dickce had shared in their mirth.

"Thank you for hosting the meeting, Barbie," An'gel said. "We must be going now, so many things to do at home."

Dickce set her glass in the sink after a quick look at An'gel. "Yes, lots to do, always. See you later, ladies."

As An'gel and Dickce let themselves out the front door, An'gel could hear loud laughter coming from the kitchen. She resisted the urge to slam the door. When they reached the car, she held out her hand for the keys. Dickce handed them over right away.

An'gel focused her attention on driving. Unlike her sister, she preferred a more sedate pace, although to her that simply meant driving only a few miles over the speed limit, rather than ten or fifteen.

She spent the first five minutes of the drive with a critique of Dickce's behavior, during which Dickce remained silent. When An'gel finished, Dickce said, "I don't care what you say, Sister, it was funny. If only you could have seen your face when Hadley paid such attention to you. You looked like you didn't know whether to crawl under the rug or grab Hadley and kiss him."

An'gel did not find that amusing. "I suppose you would have kissed him, then? I wanted to slap his face."

"Then you should have." Dickce appeared unperturbed by An'gel's fit of pique. "Hadley knew, of course, that you would respond exactly as you did. That's why he singled you out. With any of the others, well, they would have taken it as a sign that Hadley was madly in love with them. He knew you wouldn't believe any such thing."

An'gel considered that for a moment and felt her irritation begin to fade. "It pains me to admit it, but I think you're right. They're all man-hungry, and there aren't that many good-looking, well-off men in our age group in Athena for them to choose from."

"It's going to be interesting having Hadley back," Dickce said. "No telling what some of them will get up to trying to entice him into either an affair or marriage."

"Let's hope it doesn't destroy the garden club," An'gel said as she turned into the driveway at Riverhill. "If they're all spitting and scratching at one another over Hadley all the time, we'll have nothing but trouble."

Benjy stared at the disarray in the flower bed, aghast, then turned to Peanut and Endora, sitting on the lawn nearby. He eyed the dirty paws of both animals and shook his head.

"Miss An'gel is going to be furious with you. You'll be lucky if she doesn't send you both back to the shelter, and me along with you."

He knelt on the ground in front of the two miscreants, who stared at him as if they had no idea what he meant. Benjy pointed to the flower bed and the five azaleas the two had dug up. "Miss An'gel planted those today, and I can't figure out what the heck possessed you to do this." He shook his head. "I guess I should have kept you inside with me and not let you run loose. You've both been really bad."

Peanut hung his head and whimpered. Endora looked at Benjy and meowed, as if she were apologizing. She moved closer to Peanut and rubbed her head against his. The Labradoodle whimpered again.

Benjy had to suppress a laugh at these examples of contrite behavior. He couldn't be angry for long with Peanut and Endora. They were behaving the way animals do, and animals got into mischief. But he also knew Peanut was smart, and that if he scolded the dog, Peanut would remember and not dig in the flower bed again.

"Listen, here, Peanut." Benjy waited until the dog raised his head to look at him. Benjy pointed to the azaleas and the holes in the bed. "This is a bad thing. Don't do this again. Bad, bad, bad."

Peanut whined, and Benjy scratched the dog's head. "I know you're sorry, and now you know better." Peanut barked.

Benjy turned his attention to the Abyssinian. "Now, Miss Endora, I figure you were the ringleader in this little escapade. I'm not sure it does any good telling you not to get Peanut in trouble again, but at least don't get him in trouble digging up the flower beds, okay?"

Endora gazed up at him a moment, uttered one quick meow, and rubbed against the dog again.

"Okay, you two." Benjy stood. "I'm going to try to get these back in the ground before Miss An'gel and Miss Dickce get home. I don't want them to get upset seeing the mess you made. But I am going to have to tell them what you did. Understand?" He waited a moment while the two animals stared at him, then he patted each one on the head. "You can sit and watch me undo your bad work."

He turned to the flower bed and examined it for a moment. There were distinct holes where each azalea had stood, and if he worked quickly enough he ought to be able to get them replanted before the sisters returned from the garden club board meeting. They had been gone only about an hour, he reckoned. He knelt in the bed and set to work while the two responsible for the mess watched quietly.

The soil was still soft from the watering Miss An'gel gave it when she finished planting the bushes earlier. He wasn't sure at first that he would like the feel of the damp dirt on his hands, but after a few minutes he began to enjoy the process of restoring the plants to the earth. Growing up in Los Angeles, he'd never had the chance to do any kind of gardening, and he began to understand the attraction it held for his two benefactors.

When he finished with the last azalea, he got to his feet and stepped back to examine his work. He hoped Miss An'gel would be pleased. He felt a momentary doubt. Perhaps he should have waited until the sisters returned and let them supervise him. No, he decided, he had done okay, and if Miss An'gel wanted them moved at all, he would do it for her.

Peanut barked suddenly and stared toward the driveway. He trotted several feet away from Benjy and stopped, still focused on the driveway. Benjy knew that meant the dog had heard a car, and moments later the sisters' Lexus came into view.

Benjy stared down at his filthy hands and his dirt-encrusted jeans and sighed. He had hoped to get cleaned up before he had to face the sisters but that wasn't going to happen. He trudged forward with Endora beside him. When they reached Peanut, the dog accompanied them to meet the sisters at the garage in back of the mansion. "Time to face the music, kids," he informed the animals.

After dinner in the kitchen that evening, Benjy excused himself when the sisters declined his offer to clear the table. He went off to his apartment over what had once been the stables with An'gel's reassurance that he had replanted the azaleas perfectly. When he was gone, the subject turned to Peanut and Endora and their misbehavior earlier in the day.

48

"They're mischievous children," Dickce said tartly. "Honestly, Sister, one would think you'd never been around house pets in your life."

An'gel glowered. "Dogs, yes. Cats, no. I wouldn't be surprised if Endora *was* the ringleader. She's so sly, and she loves to irritate me."

Dickce snickered. "You're getting paranoid over a cat that weighs less than five pounds. It's because Endora likes me better, isn't it? That's why you're always claiming she's got it in for you."

"If Endora were more like Diesel, I wouldn't have a problem with her. He's a much nicer cat, with better manners." An'gel thought with fondness of the Maine Coon that belonged to their friend Charlie Harris.

"Diesel is a wonderful cat," Dickce said, "but Endora is a sweet girl. You need to pay more attention to her instead of making a fuss over Peanut all the time."

"Perhaps you're right," An'gel said. "I guess I take after Mother when it comes to felines. You know she wasn't all that fond of them."

Dickce smiled at the thought of their beautiful mother who had always had at least two or three dogs in the house. "No, she wasn't. She was definitely a dog person, but she let me have cats, as long as it was one at a time."

An'gel nodded. "Yes, she did, and you wouldn't let me have much to do with them either." She shrugged. "Back to the present. Benjy said he gave them both a stern talking-to about digging in the flower beds. Peanut is smart, and I don't think we'll have a problem with him bothering the beds again. Unless Endora takes it into her head to dig."

"Of course she's going to dig." Dickce spoke tartly. "She's not always going to use the litter box indoors."

An'gel decided it was time to change the subject before they got deeper into a discussion of Endora's sanitary habits. "Enough of that. I'm curious about Sarinda and the way she behaved at the meeting today. Didn't you think she was odd?"

"Odder than usual, certainly," Dickce said. "Probably her same old pattern of trying to get more attention." She drained the last of the red from her wineglass and looked about for the bottle.

"Maybe," An'gel said, "but I'm uneasy. There was an undercurrent in that room today, once Hadley claimed he has no idea where Callie is."

"Don't tell me you're starting to think foul play was involved." Dickce shook her head before reaching for the wine.

"No, I wouldn't go that far," An'gel said, "but I'd certainly give a lot to know where Callie is right now. Aren't you curious about her?"

"Yes," Dickce said after a sip of wine. "I always liked her, and I was sorry when she disappeared like that. It would be good to know that she's alive and well and happy somewhere."

"I'm going to call Sarinda," An'gel said. "If she won't answer my questions over the phone, I'll insist that she allow us to come talk to her tomorrow."

"Fine with me." Dickce stood and began to clear the table. "You do that, and then you can help me here."

An'gel went to the phone on the nearby counter and punched in Sarinda's number. She waited for Sarinda to pick up, but instead the call went to voice mail. She left a brief message, then ended the call.

The phone rang a few minutes later as An'gel placed the last utensil in the dishwasher. She glanced at the display and saw that it was Lottie MacLeod calling. She grimaced. Lottie loved chatting on the phone, and An'gel wasn't in the mood for an hour-long conversation. She was tempted not to answer, but good manners prevailed.

"Hello, Lottie, how are you?"

"Oh, An'gel, it's terrible, I'm in total shock. I had no idea Sarinda was such a heavy drinker in private. It goes to show how little we really know each other, doesn't it? Poor thing. She must have been lonely. She reeked of bourbon when I found her." Lottie sobbed into the phone.

"What on earth are you talking about?" An'gel asked, bewildered from the gush of words. "Has something happened to Sarinda?"

Lottie sobbed again, then said, "She's dead. I found her ten minutes ago at the bottom of the stairs."

CHAPTER 5

An'gel went numb with horror. Lottie's words began to sink in. *Sarinda Hetherington was dead.* She didn't want to believe it. Surely Lottie, who got hysterical over the least little thing, was mistaken. An'gel felt her common sense return. Lottie had got it wrong.

She spoke sharply into the phone. "Listen to me, Lottie. Have you called 911 yet? Sarinda may need help."

"She's dead, I tell you. Dead, dead, dead." Lottie chanted the last three words, and An'gel would have given anything to be able to shake the woman back to reality at that moment.

"Did you call 911?" An'gel noticed that Dickce looked alarmed. "Sarinda fell down the stairs," she said in an aside. Dickce sank into a chair and stared at her sister.

An'gel repeated her question again, and finally Lottie answered in the affirmative.

"The ambulance is on the way. I checked her pulse, and she's dead. I swear she is."

"Hang on. Sister and I will be on our way there as soon as we can." An'gel mimed cranking the car, and Dickce stood and hurried out of the room in search of her purse. "Lottie, did you hear me?" She waited, but no response came.

"Drat the woman," An'gel muttered when she realized Lottie had ended the call. She debated calling back but figured it would be a waste of time.

Dickce hurried in with her purse and brandished the car keys. "Let's go. Fill me in on the way."

Two minutes later the Lexus headed down the driveway, Dickce at the wheel. An'gel shared the gist of Lottie's call with Dickce.

"I never realized Sarinda had a drinking problem," Dickce said when An'gel finished. "Had you?"

An'gel stared intently through the windshield into the dark night. "Don't forget to be on the lookout for deer."

"I won't," Dickce said. "Did you hear what I said about Sarinda?"

"I heard." An'gel scowled. "It's the first I've heard of it. Either Sarinda was incredibly adept at hiding it, or Lottie has things mixed up. Wouldn't be the first time she's gotten carried away on little evidence. I hardly believe Sarinda was *reeking* of bourbon."

"Doesn't sound like her," Dickce said as she guided the car at top speed down the highway into Athena.

"We'll find out," An'gel said as she braced her feet against the floorboards. "If we get there alive ourselves, that is. That was a stop sign back there, or didn't you notice?"

"I noticed," Dickce replied. "I could see there was no other traffic, so I didn't think there was any reason to stop."

An'gel uttered a prayer under her breath. If they didn't get killed, they ought to arrive at Sarinda's house in record time.

Sure enough, five minutes later Dickce screeched into a spot by the curb a couple of houses down from Sarinda's lot. An'gel caught her breath while she surveyed the scene.

The rotating lights of the ambulance and two police cruisers flashed against the white facade of Sarinda's large three-story Greek Revival–style house. The house, known as Fairleigh, stood well back from the street in one of the oldest residential areas in Athena. The large lawn, though not as generous in proportion as the one at Riverhill, was nevertheless spacious at an acre and a half.

The houses on either side had been built within a few years of Fairleigh, but those across the street dated from the late nineteenth century. Sarinda had inherited the house upon her parents' deaths in an accident when she was in her twenties and had lived there alone ever since.

A group of people milled about in the street. Neighbors come out to gawk, An'gel thought grimly. She opened the door and stepped outside. She shivered. The night was chilly, and neither she nor Dickce had thought to bring a coat with her.

An'gel strode down the sidewalk, aware that Dickce walked barely two paces behind her. They approached a police officer, Pete Peterson, a grizzled veteran they had known since he was born. They had funded the scholarships that put his younger brother through college and medical school after their father died when they were teenagers. He smiled when he recognized the two new spectators.

"Good evening, Miss An'gel, Miss Dickce." Peterson nodded. "What are y'all doing out tonight? This lady here a friend of yours?"

An'gel and Dickce returned the officer's greeting. Then An'gel said, "Yes, Pete, she is a good friend of ours. Another friend, Lottie

MacLeod, called us. She said she'd found Miss Hetherington and that she was dead. Can you tell us, is that true? Is Miss Hetherington really dead?"

Peterson looked uncomfortable. He glanced around and, evidently satisfied that no one would overhear, he said, "Yes, ma'am, I'm afraid so. EMTs tried to revive her, but she was gone. I sure am sorry."

An'gel felt Dickce's arm slip around her waist, and the sisters leaned against each other for comfort. After a moment An'gel pulled away and said, "Thank you for telling us, Pete. This is terrible. We were truly hoping that Lottie was wrong."

Peterson shook his head, his expression one of sympathy. "I sure am sorry," he said again. "I think it's best if you ladies go on back home. It's getting chilly out here, and you need to be somewhere warm. There's nothing you can do here."

An'gel appreciated the officer's concern and said so. "We'll go in a moment. First, though, did you go inside the house? Did you see?" She couldn't quite say the words *the body* aloud.

Peterson glanced around again before he replied. "Yes, ma'am, I did. You sure you want me to tell you what I saw?"

"Yes, Pete, I'm sure," An'gel said. "I know

57

this could get you in trouble, but I promise we won't tell anyone."

"I know, Miss An'gel, I know," Peterson said. "Well, the lady was lying at the bottom of the stairs. Looked like she fell headfirst and landed on her front." He hesitated. "There was a broken bottle of bourbon on the floor by her."

An'gel swallowed. She hated the picture of Sarinda that now lodged in her mind. "Thank you, Pete. I think you're right. Sister and I had better go home now."

Dickce thanked the officer also before they turned to walk back to their car. Peterson offered to accompany them, but they declined.

Before they had taken more than a few steps, however, a voice hailed them. An'gel tensed. She recognized the voice. She and Dickce halted and turned. They looked at each other and grimaced.

"Martin, what are you doing here?" An'gel eyed Reba Dalrymple's forty-five-year-old son warily.

Martin, who always made An'gel think of Ichabod Crane, wasn't quite the goofy old scarecrow described by Washington Irving, but he came close. He shambled to a stop about two feet from the sisters and stared at them, his eyes large with excitement.

"Mother sent me." Martin shoved his hands in the pockets of his suit jacket, a habit with him. All of his jackets sagged on the sides. An'gel had never seen him in one that didn't.

"How did Reba know anything had happened?" An'gel asked. Martin might be a wiz with computers, she thought, but he had no more social skills than a sock monkey. Talking to him always wore her patience thin.

"Miz Gross called her." Martin blinked at her.

Because Lottie called Barbie first, as she always did. Lottie made few moves without Barbie's knowledge and approval. The two were as close as she and Dickce, but Lottie did not have nearly as forceful a personality as her best friend.

"Did your mother send you for any particular reason?" Dickce asked after a sideways glance at An'gel.

"She wanted to know what's going on." Martin giggled. "You know how she is. Nosy Rosy." He giggled again. "Looks like Mother isn't the only Nosy Rosy."

An'gel ignored that. "Did you find out anything?" She doubted he had, but she might as well ask.

Martin shrugged. "Not really." He stepped

59

back. "Better get home. Mother is waiting."
With that he turned and loped off.

"He is so aggravating," Dickce said.
"Sometimes you just want to jerk that knot
in his tail."

"Dickce, why do you have to use that awful expression?" An'gel shook her head. "I
agree, though. He can be mighty exasperat-
ing. I think he did find out something but
he's going home to tell Reba first. Come
now, let's go home."

An'gel didn't feel like talking during the
drive back to Riverhill, and apparently
neither did Dickce. An'gel pondered Sarinda's sudden and rather odd death. How
could they have all missed the fact that Sarinda had a drinking problem?

An'gel knew that many alcoholics were
adept at disguising their addiction, and
perhaps Sarinda had been among their
number. An'gel found it sad. Sarinda had
never married, though An'gel was never
certain why. She wondered whether Sarinda
had been carrying a torch all these years for
Hadley Partridge. Seeing him today might
have been a shock, although An'gel would
have supposed it to be a pleasant one.

But for Sarinda, it might have been a bit-
ter reminder of forty lonely years. Could
Hadley's sudden return — and show of

pointed interest in her, rather than in Sarinda or any of the other women — have had anything to do with Sarinda's getting so drunk she fell down the stairs?

Another, more sinister interpretation of Sarinda's death occurred to her. Sarinda had asked the odd question, "What if Callie never left Athena?"

They had all thought it was merely a bid for attention this afternoon. In light of Sarinda's sudden demise, however, An'gel found herself reconsidering the idea that Sarinda had had another purpose in mind when she posed the question. If she *had* known more than she let on about what happened to Callie all those years ago, and if what happened to Callie was the result of foul play, could someone in that room today have been responsible? Not only for Sarinda's death, but also for Callie's disappearance?

Had both women been murdered?

CHAPTER 6

You've been watching too many reruns of old detective shows. Turning everything into a mystery.

An'gel scolded herself mentally for the wild ideas she was entertaining over Sarinda's death. The timing of it was simply coincidence. If Sarinda truly had been a secret drinker, then it was only a matter of time before she had an accident. In this case, it sadly turned out to be a fatal accident.

An'gel's thoughts had seesawed back and forth between a verdict of sad accident and deliberate murder since the previous evening. As she sat finishing her third cup of coffee at the dining room table this morning, she was glad she hadn't shared any of this with her sister.

Dickce broke into her thoughts. "You've hardly said a word since we got in the car last night to drive home from Sarinda's. I've been waiting for you to tell me what's on your mind. You're stewing over Sarinda's death, obviously."

Her sister knew her only too well, An'gel reflected. "Yes." She hoped the terse response would be enough to quell her sister for the moment, but Dickce didn't snub that easily.

"You think someone pushed Sarinda down the stairs, don't you?" Dickce toyed with a small bit of scrambled egg on her plate.

"I think it's a possibility," An'gel said.

"I do, too." Dickce set her fork down and leaned back in her chair. "Maybe we're simply all off balance, thanks to Hadley, but the more I think about the meeting yesterday, the more I believe there was something going on underneath it all that we don't understand."

"That's what I've been feeling," An'gel said. "But I wonder whether I'm trying to make too much out of Sarinda's behavior yesterday."

"It's possible," Dickce said. "After what we've been through the past few months, we're bound to be oversensitive, I suppose. Murder here at Riverhill, and then more murder at Willowbank, when we went to St. Ignatiusville for the wedding."

An'gel grimaced. "The last thing we need

is to be involved in another murder, and I'm hoping that this turns out to be an accident." She pushed away from the table and stood. "All right. I've had enough of this. The sun is shining, the morning is warm, and I have gardening to do."

"You'd better get it done this morning," Dickce said. "I was listening to the weather report before I came down to breakfast, and we've got a storm system coming our way by mid-afternoon. Sounds like we could be in for nasty weather. Heavy rain, thunderstorms, and high winds."

An'gel pushed her chair in to the table and stood with her hands along the back. "I didn't check the forecast this morning." She paused. "If we've got that kind of weather coming, I shouldn't bother putting in new plants, then. The wind is liable to wreak havoc with whatever I do today. Not to mention the azaleas I planted yesterday."

"In that case," Dickce said, "why don't you come with Benjy and me this morning? I'm taking him shopping for clothes and shoes. He's going to need new things for when he starts at Athena College in the spring."

"Thanks for the offer, but I think I'll stay here." An'gel didn't care much for shopping, though her sister did. "I need to catch up on correspondence and a few other business issues."

Dickce stood and began to gather the breakfast dishes. "Suit yourself. If you get bored and want to join us in town later, we're going to be lunching at the Farrington Hotel."

"You're taking Benjy's car, then?" An'gel referred to the small sedan they had bought their ward two weeks ago so he would be able to drive back and forth to classes and also run errands when needed.

"Yes, Benjy insists on driving, so we'll leave the car for you." Dickce, plates and utensils neatly stacked in her hands, walked out of the dining room.

An'gel realized suddenly that she would no doubt be left in charge of Peanut and Endora, because Dickce and Benjy certainly wouldn't take them shopping. The animals could spend part of the time in the kitchen with Clementine, the housekeeper, An'gel decided. Clementine was fond of both pets and didn't mind keeping an eye on them. An'gel's office was on the small side for one woman, a dog, and a cat — particularly a dog and a cat that liked to play while the woman tried to concentrate on business.

After a heavy sigh, An'gel picked up her coffee cup and saucer and bore them off to the kitchen. After a brief chat with Clementine about Peanut and Endora, An'gel went to her office to work.

Her first chore was to check e-mail and deal with any messages that needed an immediate response. As she worked, she found her mind drifting to the death of her friend. After reading one message three times and failing to comprehend it, she gave up and picked up the phone handset on the desk beside her computer.

She hesitated a moment, then punched in the number for the Athena Police Department. She identified herself and asked to speak to the chief of police, Drew Carson. After a delay of about thirty seconds, Carson came on the line.

"Good morning, Miss An'gel, how are you and Miss Dickce these days?"

"We're doing fine, Drew, and I hope you and Adele are doing well."

"Tolerable, Miss An'gel, tolerable." The police chief chuckled. "Adele's busy playing with the new grandbaby."

"That's right," An'gel said. "Your son and his wife have a new baby. Another boy, I believe."

"Yes, ma'am," Carson said. "He's doing fine. Growing like a little weed."

The pleasantries continued for a moment,

then Carson said, "What can I do for you, Miss An'gel? You wouldn't be calling about the death of Miss Sarinda Hetherington, would you?"

An'gel chuckled. "I'm afraid you know me too well. Yes, I'm calling about Sarinda. Dickce and I were stunned to hear about her death, naturally, but even more stunned to hear the cause of it."

"What exactly did you hear, if you don't mind my asking?"

An'gel registered the note of caution in the chief's question. She couldn't blame him for being wary, because he wasn't a man who appreciated outside interference in the work of his department.

"We heard that she had been drinking heavily and fell down the stairs and died. Broke her neck, presumably," An'gel said. "And that surprised us both, because we had no idea Sarinda was a heavy drinker."

"I have to tell you, in my experience, alcoholics can be real clever in concealing the fact that they drink. Especially when they drink in secret. Miss Hetherington lived alone, far as I know, and didn't go out a lot. Not an unusual pattern."

"I suppose not," An'gel said. "But Sarinda was active in her church and with different clubs, including the garden club. We saw her yesterday at a garden club board meeting, in fact." She debated whether to confide in the police chief her misgivings over Sarinda's behavior at the meeting and her sudden disappearance. She made a quick decision to keep it to herself for the moment. Thus far Carson hadn't said anything to indicate he considered the death anything other than accidental.

"We'll be looking at the whole picture," Carson said. "I know you're upset about your friend, but I promise you we'll investigate thoroughly. We'll be talking to her neighbors and her doctor. I have to say, though, I think this one's going to be pretty quickly wrapped up."

"I appreciate your time, Drew. If you wouldn't mind letting me know the outcome of the investigation, I'd be grateful." Struck with a sudden idea, An'gel was eager to conclude the call. She, Dickce, and Sarinda all went to the same doctor and had done so for the past thirty years. The minute she got Drew Carson off the phone she planned to call Dr. Gandy. She had a few questions to put to him, and she hoped he would be willing to answer under the circumstances.

After she bade Carson good-bye, An'gel ended the call and reached for the phone book to double-check the doctor's number.

Once she found it, she punched in the number and waited for an answer.

"I made a list of the things I think you'll need." Dickce pulled a small notepad from her purse and opened it to the page where she had jotted her notes.

"It's awesome of you and Miss An'gel to buy me new clothes and stuff," Benjy said, his gaze focused on the road ahead. "But I really don't need that much, honestly."

Dickce smiled and shook her head. He was a dear boy and always seemed to be worried about any money she and An'gel spent on him. He had fussed about the car, too, but Dickce knew how thrilled he was to have his own transportation. At nineteen, he needed to be able to come and go on his own, and he was a responsible driver.

"I swear you've grown an inch in the past three months," Dickce said. "Your ankles are sticking out of your jeans, and surely your shoes must be giving you blisters by now." She glanced down at the ragged sneakers he was wearing. They definitely had to go, plus the boy needed dress shoes and a couple of suits for formal occasions.

Benjy laughed. "That's thanks to Clementine's cooking. I have to admit my jeans have been getting a little tight around the waist. I've never eaten so much good food in my life."

Dickce felt a momentary pang. She recalled how Benjy looked and acted when they first met him, back in August. Thin, defensive, shy, and neglected. What a difference good food and affection had made in him.

"You're still growing," Dickce said around the small lump in her throat. "So you eat and enjoy. Clementine has perked up considerably, I can tell you, now that she has a healthy appetite to cook for."

When they reached town, Dickce directed Benjy to the square. Their first stop was the best men's store in town, where Dickce intended to find the suits, dress shirts, shoes, and ties on her list. After that they would visit another store for casual wear.

By the time Dickce and Benjy finished shopping, nearly three hours later, boxes and bags filled the trunk of Benjy's car and most of the backseat. Benjy appeared dazed at the amount of clothing and accessories he had suddenly acquired, but Dickce was determined that her ward was going to have a proper wardrobe for the first time in his life.

"Don't forget about the fitting next week," Dickce said as she watched Benjy load the final bag into the car. "After they do the alterations we agreed on today, you'll need to try everything on again to make sure the fit is right. You won't need me for that."

"I won't forget," Benjy said. He brandished his cell phone. "I've already put the appointment in here."

"Excellent." Dickce smiled. "Now, I don't know about you, but shopping always gives me an appetite. I'm ready for lunch."

Benjy laughed. "I guess it gave me one, too, because I'm starving."

"The Farrington Hotel is two blocks away. Let's walk, but be sure the car is locked." Dickce waited for Benjy to check the locks, then led the way down the sidewalk toward the hotel.

In the entrance to the dining room, Dickce greeted the hostess with a smile and inquired after the woman's family. Once the pleasantries were finished, the hostess took them to a table in a corner that overlooked the square and left them with menus.

"Doesn't look like An'gel is going to join us," Dickce said as she gazed around the room. Her eyes lit on a couple seated at a table in the far corner, partially obscured by a large ficus.

"Now, isn't that interesting," she murmured, mostly to herself, while she stared

71

at the man and woman. "*She* certainly isn't wasting any time making a play for Hadley."

CHAPTER 7

While she waited to be connected to Dr. Gandy, An'gel considered her best plan of attack. Would it be better for her to talk to the doctor in person, or would he find it easier to tell her what she wanted to know over the phone? She decided he would have a harder time ducking her questions if they were face-to-face. By the time he came on the line, she was prepared.

After the doctor greeted her by name, An'gel said, "Sorry to bother you, Elmo, but I was wondering if you could work me in today. It won't take long, I promise, but I need to discuss something with you."

Gandy's voice boomed in her ear when he replied, "I can always find time for you. It's not your back again, is it?"

An'gel wondered if Elmo realized how loud he was talking these days. To her it was a sure sign of a hearing problem, but whether the doctor would ever admit it, she didn't know. She replied, "No, not my back. What time should I come by?"

"How about a quarter of twelve?" the doctor said. "Should be done with the morning's patients by then. I've been cutting back, not seeing as many patients the last few months. Thinking about retiring finally."

Considering that Elmo Gandy was only two years younger than she, An'gel knew he could have retired years ago had he wanted to. "I don't know what Dickce and I will do when you do retire," An'gel said. "But if anybody deserves a chance to relax and not work, it's you, Elmo. I'll see you at quarter to twelve."

An'gel replaced the handset and sat for a moment, lost in thought about Elmo Gandy. He had been a widower for the past fifteen years, and after about seven years of widowerhood he began proposing to her and Dickce in turn. Fond as they both were of Elmo, neither sister fancied getting married after decades of happy spinsterhood. Elmo never seemed to take umbrage at the refusals, but he also never seemed to be squelched by them. The proposals came at regular intervals.

"Well, I'll deal with that when, and if, he proposes again," An'gel said to the computer screen. She checked the clock and saw that

74

she had about two hours before she needed to dress and head into town for her appointment. Once she was done with Elmo she could drop by the Farrington Hotel and have lunch with Dickce and Benjy if they hadn't finished by then.

Peanut and Endora dropped by for a visit about an hour later. An'gel stopped what she was doing and gave the animals her complete attention. Though she fussed a bit about Endora and her aloofness, An'gel was actually fond of both animals. Peanut, however, was her favorite, because he was a clever dog and learned everything quickly.

Peanut gazed at her intently while she talked to him. "I hope you listened to what Benjy said about not digging in the flower beds. I really can't have you making a mess of the yard." She wagged a finger at the dog, and he barked as if to tell her he understood.

"Good boy." An'gel patted him on the head before she turned to look at Endora, perched on the arm of a nearby club chair. "As for you, missy, I expect you to behave, too. You're smart enough when you want to be, so I'd better not catch you digging things up."

Endora yawned and then began to wash her right front paw. An'gel was not surprised at the cat's response.

"Okay, you two, y'all go on back to Clementine, and let me finish up."

Peanut barked and approached the cat. He nudged Endora with his nose, then turned and loped out of the room. The cat rose, stretched, then hopped down and ambled out of the room. An'gel smiled and went back to work.

By the time she was ready to leave for her appointment with the doctor, An'gel had managed to get caught up with e-mail and business matters. She had to tell Peanut and Endora that they couldn't come with her, and she apologized to Clementine for leaving them in her care. The housekeeper laughed and assured her it was no problem.

"They're good company when everybody else is out of the house," Clementine said, her voice husky from decades of smoking. "You don't be worrying about us. We get along fine."

Thus reassured, An'gel headed out. Twenty minutes later she pulled the car into a parking space near the building where Dr. Gandy had his office. The building stood on a side street about three blocks from the square, and once An'gel had finished with the doctor, she had only a short trip to the hotel.

The waiting room was empty when An'gel

76

entered. She went straight to the frosted glass window and rapped gently. The receptionist opened the window right away and smiled at her. "You can go right on back, Miss Ducote. The doctor's ready for you."

An'gel thanked the young woman and went through a nearby door into a hallway. The doctor's office lay at the end. She paused at the open door and cleared her throat.

Elmo Gandy turned his chair to face the doorway, and his homely hound-dog face split into a huge grin at the sight of her. He rose and came around the desk to usher her to a chair. "Lovely as ever, An'gel. Now, tell me. What's bothering you?" He perched on a corner of the desk and straightened his tie.

Though she had rehearsed what she planned to say during the drive into town, An'gel nevertheless hesitated. She had never before asked the doctor to violate the confidence of another patient, even a deceased one, and she wasn't sure how he was going to react. She took a deep breath. She had to know.

"I'm personally fine, Elmo," she said. "Except that I'm really upset over Sarinda Hetherington's death."

At the mention of his late patient's name,

Dr. Gandy frowned. He got up from the desk and went around to resume his seat behind it. Arms on the desk, he leaned forward and regarded An'gel. "Sarinda's death came as quite a shock to me, too, I have to say." He shook his head. "Poor soul."

"Have the police spoken to you yet about it?" An'gel asked.

Dr. Gandy nodded. "First thing this morning."

"I was shocked to hear," An'gel said, "that she had been drinking heavily and fell down the stairs to her death. I had no idea she drank like that." She watched the doctor to register his reaction to her words.

Dr. Gandy frowned again and leaned back in his chair. He stared at her for a long moment. "Why are you so interested in this?"

An'gel knew she had to be completely honest with him. "I'm worried that there was something odd about Sarinda's death. I wonder if she really *did* have a drinking problem."

"The police asked me the same thing," the doctor said. "I will tell you what I told them. Ordinarily I wouldn't tell even you this, An'gel, even though I know you have Sarinda's best interests at heart." He paused.

An'gel nodded. "I understand that you

wouldn't want to violate a patient's confidentiality, even once that patient was dead."

"Yes," the doctor said. "Normally I wouldn't share this, but I don't want to see Sarinda's name blackened, have her labeled an alcoholic when I know damn well she wasn't one."

Dickce couldn't tear her eyes away from the table in the corner. "Just look at them," she muttered.

Benjy looked up from the menu he had been perusing with great interest. "Who are you talking about?" He glanced around.

"That table in the far corner," Dickce said in an undertone. She picked up her own menu and stared at it. "The silver-haired man and the redheaded woman. See them?"

"Yes," Benjy said. "Who are they? I don't think I've seen either of them before."

"Hadley Partridge," Dickce said. "And Arliss McGonigal. Hadley has come back to Athena after being gone for forty years. Arliss is a friend of mine and An'gel's. She's a member of the garden club board."

"Is there anything strange about the two of them being together?" Benjy asked, obviously puzzled. "I guess they know each other, right?"

Dickce grimaced. "They do, and I wonder

79

just how well they know each other." Every time she glanced over at their table, Dickce saw Arliss touching Hadley, and Hadley didn't appear to be bothered by it. There was an air of intimacy between the two, and Dickce found it unsettling.

Exactly why she found it unsettling, she refused to consider. She thought Arliss was behaving in a slightly brazen manner.

"Why don't you go over and say hi to them?" Benjy asked.

Dickce stared with suspicion at his bland expression. Then she laughed as the humor of the situation struck her. Here she was, dining with an attractive young man sixty years her junior, and she thought Arliss brazen for dining with Hadley, a man roughly her own age.

She decided she had better come clean with Benjy about Hadley Partridge. "All the women in town were in love with him forty years ago," she said. "Even An'gel and I were both a little smitten with him. He was always the handsomest and the most charming man we all knew. He dated lots of women but he never would settle down with any one woman. We all thought he was carrying a torch for his brother's wife, and that's why he wouldn't commit to anyone else."

"Sounds like an old movie," Benjy said. "You said he was back in town after forty years. Why did he leave? Didn't he ever come back for a visit?"

"The story was that he left because his brother threatened to kill him if he didn't leave his wife alone. Hadley never did get along well with Hamish," Dickce said. "Hamish wasn't easy to live with, and they all lived together at Ashton Hall."

"That's the old house down the road from Riverhill," Benjy said. "Didn't you tell me the guy that owned it died recently?"

Dickce nodded. "Yes, Hamish Partridge. That's why Hadley came back, apparently. Hamish left everything to him."

"What about Mrs. Partridge?" Benjy asked. "Is she still living?"

"That's what's so mysterious," Dickce said. "Callie left town right after Hadley did. Most of us thought she ran away to be with Hadley, but at the garden club board meeting yesterday Hadley swore to us he never saw Callie again once he left Athena."

"Now it really *does* sound like an old movie," Benjy said.

The waitress arrived to take their order, and they both decided on the day's special, chicken and dumplings. The waitress noted their orders, removed the menus, and left them.

"They won't be as good as Clementine's," Dickce said. "But they're still pretty good."

"Nothing's as good as Clementine's cooking." Benjy leaned back and patted his stomach. "I'm proof of that." He grinned.

"Look," Dickce said in a low tone. "They're getting ready to leave. I wonder if they've seen us."

Benjy turned his head, and Dickce watched as Hadley, courtly as ever, pulled back Arliss's chair for her and extended his arm when she stood. Arliss leaned against him and looked up into his face with what she no doubt thought — Dickce guessed — was a seductive glance. Dickce was pleased to note that Hadley appeared unaffected by the lingering gaze. The couple left the dining room without a glance in Dickce's direction.

Dickce would have given a lot to have heard the conversation between the two. She couldn't wait to tell An'gel about seeing Arliss and Hadley together.

"Do you think Miss An'gel is going to join us?" Benjy asked.

"Doesn't look like it," Dickce replied. Then she glanced over Benjy's shoulder to see her sister advancing toward them. "No,

I was wrong, because here she is."

An'gel reached them, and Benjy jumped up to pull out a chair for her. An'gel smiled her thanks, and Benjy reseated himself.

"I saw Hadley and Arliss leaving the hotel when I pulled in," An'gel said. "They were down the street before I could get out of the car and say hello to them. Were they dining in here?"

Dickce snickered. "Yes, they were dining. Did you think they'd spent the night here and were strolling out for fresh air?"

An'gel frowned and glanced sideways at Benjy. "Sister, I'm surprised at you. You shouldn't say things like that."

"It's okay, Miss An'gel," Benjy said. "You don't have to worry on my account."

An'gel looked slightly flustered at that, and Dickce snickered again. "We didn't have a chance to speak to them either. I don't think Arliss, at least, would have welcomed any interruption, especially from either of us."

"No, I doubt she would have." An'gel shook her head.

The waitress approached the table with a menu and a glass of water. An'gel inquired about the daily special and when told it was chicken and dumplings, decided she would have that and a glass of iced tea. The

83

waitress nodded, took back the menu, and walked away.

"Let's leave the subject of Arliss and Hadley for the moment," An'gel said. "I have something to tell you."

"What have you been up to?" Dickce asked. "I thought you had a lot of work to do."

"I did, and it's taken care of," An'gel said. "I found the time to talk to Drew Carson." She turned to Benjy. "He's the chief of police here."

"Did you call him about Sarinda?" Dickce asked.

An'gel nodded. "He didn't tell me much, really, but I decided I would talk to Elmo Gandy and see what he would tell me about Sarinda."

"Dr. Gandy is our family physician," Dickce explained to a bewildered-looking Benjy. "An'gel and I have been going to him practically forever, since he first got out of medical school and came back to Athena to set up a practice." She looked at An'gel. "What did Elmo tell you?"

An'gel glanced around before she answered. "He told me that Sarinda was definitely not an alcoholic. He thinks it was extremely unlikely that she would have been drinking bourbon, at least enough to get

84

drunk and lose her balance coming down the stairs."

Dickce's eyes narrowed. "Does this mean he thinks her death wasn't an accident?"

An'gel nodded. "He's pretty sure it wasn't, and he told the police that. He thinks she was most likely knocked down the stairs."

CHAPTER 8

After lunch, Benjy headed home to unload his car while Dickce remained in town with An'gel. During the meal the sisters discussed the ramifications of the doctor's thoughts on the death of their friend, and when they were ready to leave the hotel restaurant, An'gel had a suggestion.

"Let's pay a call on Lottie," she said. "I want to find out what she was doing at Sarinda's house in the first place, and what she saw while she was there."

Dickce glanced at the sky before she opened the passenger door and climbed into the car. "That's a good idea," she said, "but I don't think we should linger in town too long. Clouds are moving in, and I don't want to be on the road when those storms get here."

"Agreed." An'gel cranked the car and backed it out of the parking space. "If we catch Lottie at home, it shouldn't take too long to find out what we want to know."

"If she's not at home, she'll probably be at Barbie's house," Dickce said. "We can try there if we need to."

"Yes, we can, but I'd rather talk to Lottie on her own," An'gel replied. "Barbie has a tendency to speak for Lottie when they're together, and I'm not in the mood for it today."

Ten minutes later An'gel pulled into the driveway of Lottie's two-story brick house. Though not of antebellum vintage, the MacLeod home was over a hundred years old and occupied a spacious lot with a beautifully kept yard.

An'gel and Dickce made their way up the hedge-bordered walk to the front door, and An'gel rang the bell. After a brief wait, the door opened, and Lottie's housekeeper, Sarah, admitted them. "Miz Lottie's upstairs. Y'all come on in, and I'll let her know you're here."

"Thank you, Sarah," An'gel said as she and Dickce followed the housekeeper into the front parlor. They seated themselves while they waited for Lottie to come down.

An'gel heard Lottie giving instructions to the housekeeper to bring in iced tea before she joined them in the parlor. Then she breezed into the room.

"Good afternoon, girls. I thought y'all might drop by sometime today." Lottie chose a chair opposite the sofa the sisters occupied. "Isn't it terrible about Sarinda?" She frowned.

"Yes, it is," An'gel said. "We apologize for not calling first."

Lottie waved away the apology. "It's fine."

"Finding poor Sarinda like that must have been an awful shock," Dickce said.

"Oh, it was, it surely was," Lottie said, her eyes closed for a moment. Then she blinked at the sisters. "At first I couldn't believe what I saw seeing. Sarinda lying on the floor like that. It seemed like a nightmare."

"Yes, I'm sure it must have," An'gel said. "If you don't mind my asking, would you tell us exactly what you saw?"

Lottie stared at her for a moment. "Well, I guess I don't mind. It's not like I'm going to forget it anytime soon." She paused for a moment. "I walked in the front door, and at first I didn't see her. I had to find the light switch because the front hall was a bit dark. Then, when the light came on, I turned, and there she was, sprawled facedown on the floor at the bottom of the staircase." She shuddered.

"What did you do then?" An'gel asked.

"I think I screamed," Lottie said. "Then I

88

tried to gather my poor wits about me and do something. I went over to her and knelt by her head." She shuddered again. "Her eyes were wide-open, and I could tell already she was dead. I did feel for a pulse on the side of her neck, but there wasn't one."

Sarah came into the room with a silver tray and set it on a table next to Lottie. Lottie thanked her. "We'll serve ourselves."

Once Sarah left the room and her guests had glasses of tea, Lottie continued. "That's when I noticed the bottle of bourbon on the floor near her. And the smell." She wrinkled her nose at the memory. "I don't know why I hadn't noticed it before. I suppose it was the shock of seeing poor Sarinda on the floor like that."

"No doubt," An'gel said. "Was there much bourbon in the bottle? Did you notice?"

Lottie considered that for a moment. "I think there might have been a little. There was some on the floor, and I noticed Sarinda's blouse was a bit damp when I pushed it aside so I could check her pulse at the neck."

An'gel exchanged a glance with Dickce. Was Sarinda drinking from the bottle when she fell — or was shoved — down the stairs? That could account for the liquor on her blouse. Or, An'gel thought, the person who knocked her down could have poured the bourbon on Sarinda after she hit the floor. An'gel felt sick to her stomach at the thought.

"What did you do after you checked for a pulse?" Dickce asked. "Was that when you called 911?"

"I think so." Lottie wrinkled her nose. "Things are a bit fuzzy. I think I probably called 911 first. But I might have called either you or Barbie first. I can't remember." She took a sip of tea.

"Did you call anyone besides Barbie and us?" An'gel asked. Lottie shook her head. "No, just you two and Barbie."

"What about today?" An'gel asked. "Have you talked to any of the other board members this morning?"

"Barbie said she would let people know," Lottie said. "I didn't feel up to it last night or this morning."

"Why did you call us last night, as opposed to other board members?" Dickce asked.

"I'm not sure," Lottie said, appearing slightly confused. "It just seemed like the right thing to do at the time. You've known Sarinda longer than the rest of us, and I thought you should know."

90

"We appreciate you thinking of us like that," An'gel said. "Yes, I suppose we've known Sarinda most of our lives, but we had no idea about the drinking." She shot a warning glance at her sister and hoped that Lottie didn't notice.

"She spent an awful lot of time alone in that big house," Lottie said. "Well, except for her housekeeper, of course. That's not the same as spending time with friends, but she did spend time with the garden club and a couple of other clubs."

"Don't you think it's strange that none of us picked up on the drinking before now?" Dickce asked.

"Barbie said she thought Sarinda was drinking in secret for years after I told her last night what I found." Lottie smiled. "Barbie likes to knock back the gin herself, you know, and I suppose she saw the signs in Sarinda."

An'gel wanted to offer a tart reply to that, because they all knew about Barbie and her gin. They all also knew Lottie was every bit as fond of gin as Barbie. Sarinda, on the other hand, never had more than one cocktail whenever she was with the other garden club members.

"Why did you go to Sarinda's last night?" An'gel asked.

"She called and asked me to come over," Lottie replied. "She said she wanted to talk to me, but she wouldn't say exactly why."

"You didn't press her for an explanation?" An'gel set her empty glass on a coaster on the table in front of the sofa.

Lottie shrugged. "I tried, but she wouldn't really tell me anything. Only that it was important. I thought her voice sounded strange, come to think of it. Hoarse, kind of like when someone's been crying a lot, if you know what I mean."

An'gel was about to reply in the affirmative when a loud crash of thunder startled them all. "Heavens," she said. "That storm is moving in."

Dickce stood. "We'd better get home right away, Sister. Thanks for the tea, Lottie."

An'gel rose as well. "Before we go, however, one more question for you. Two questions, actually. What time did Sarinda call? And when did you arrive at her house?"

Lottie thought for a moment. "I went right over as soon as I hung up the phone. It takes about ten minutes to walk over there, and it was a nice night so I walked. I guess I got there around seven, or maybe seven fifteen?"

The thunder boomed again, and An'gel hastily thanked Lottie. Then she and Dickce headed for the car, thankful to discover that though the sky had darkened considerably, the rain hadn't yet moved in.

"I hate weather like this," An'gel muttered as she slid behind the steering wheel and pulled her door shut.

"I don't mind the rain." Dickce buckled her seat belt. "I hate the wind and how destructive it can be. We've been lucky not to have extensive damage to the house over the years."

"Yes, we have." An'gel backed out of Lottie's driveway and headed the car toward home. "We've had a few close calls, though. Remember the tornado three years ago that touched down about three miles from us?"

Dickce shuddered. "I certainly do. That was a terrifying night. Thank the Lord, though, it touched down in an area where there were no houses. Can you imagine if it had hit Athena?"

"Let's just pray that whatever this storm brings, it's not tornadoes," An'gel said.

An'gel drove the rest of the way in silence under a rapidly darkening sky. The wind was picking up, and An'gel felt the car buffeted by the occasional gust.

The rain started moments after An'gel and Dickce gained the safety of the house. They were relieved to find Benjy and the animals in the kitchen with Clementine.

"We've been listening to Clementine's weather radio," Benjy said. "I think we're in for some really bad weather."

"Then you, Peanut, and Endora are definitely staying here with us," An'gel said. "Clementine, I think you'd better stay here, too, but if you want to go home, I think you should go right away before the worst weather moves in."

Clementine nodded. "I'd best be getting home, then, Miss An'gel." She grabbed her purse and an umbrella and left by the back door.

"Lord, I hope she makes it home okay," Dickce said. "I don't blame her for wanting to be home with family, but they don't have a basement like we do."

"Basement?" Benjy asked. "I didn't know there was a basement."

"There is," An'gel said. "We don't use it that often, except in threatening weather. The door is in the pantry, so that's probably why you haven't noticed it."

"I think we'd better check down there right now," Dickce said. "If we have to spend the night down there, we'd better make sure the ventilation is working properly."

"I'll go with you," Benjy said. "I'm curious to see it."

94

"You two check it out," An'gel said. "I'm going to see what the weather people are saying." She went to her office and checked the forecast on the Internet. From the radar loops she watched online, she gathered that the brunt of the storm wasn't due in their area for about three hours. Wind gusts in the system topped out around sixty miles an hour. Not quite tornado speed, she was relieved to note. Still capable of damage, however, because the storm was moving slowly. It could last for several hours in their area.

Time to close the outside shutters, An'gel decided, to protect against window breakage. She found the controller in the desk drawer where it resided, and clicked the switch to start the process. She and Dickce had the system installed several years before, and the motorized system had saved their windows from storms ever since.

If only we could protect the flower beds and the trees as easily. An'gel sighed. Tomorrow they would probably have a lot of work to do, setting the grounds to rights.

Dickce and Benjy came back to report that the basement was dry, though the air was a bit stale. They spent half an hour taking provisions down in case they ended up spending the night there. Benjy made sure there was enough food for Peanut and Endora, and he took down a litter box for the cat.

About half an hour before the heaviest winds reached the area, An'gel made the decision for them to move into the basement. They had enough to eat and drink for the evening, a small bathroom for their needs, and comfortable seating along with several twin beds. An'gel listened to the weather radio while Dickce and Benjy played cards and the animals napped.

An'gel was too preoccupied by the weather and thoughts of Sarinda Hetherington's death to be able to focus on the card game. She thought back over her conversation with Elmo Gandy. His certainty that Sarinda was not a heavy drinker had convinced An'gel. They'd talked about the manner of her death, and Gandy was convinced foul play was involved. He'd told the police that, and the next step was an autopsy to look for evidence to confirm his assertion.

The thought of an autopsy upset An'gel, but she knew it was necessary if the truth were to be discovered. If this turned into a murder investigation, she figured Kanesha Berry, chief deputy with the sheriff's department, would investigate. The police usually turned over homicide investigations to the sheriff's department, and Kanesha had established a reputation for thorough investigations that brought results.

Eventually, exhausted by the events of the day and her worries over the weather and Sarinda's death, An'gel fell asleep in her chair, even as the storm began to subside.

CHAPTER 9

The next morning after breakfast, Dickce and Benjy made an inspection of the outside of the house and the grounds to assess the damage from the storm. The storm brought with it cooler temperatures, and the damp, cold air felt like a return to fall after a short warm spell. There didn't appear to be any damage to the house, Dickce was relieved to see. Oak and pine branches of varying sizes lay scattered around the extensive yard, and the wind had flattened flowers in several places. Overall, though, the problems that needed addressing were minor.

Peanut and Endora accompanied Dickce and Benjy on the tour, and Benjy made sure there was no digging in flower beds. Peanut twice grabbed limbs in his mouth and tried to drag them to Benjy, but his selections proved too heavy for him to shift more than a few inches. Benjy thanked the dog for being helpful, and Peanut barked and wiggled his tail in response. Endora regarded the dog's antics with her usual calm, though she did sniff around a few of the limbs.

"I can clear the debris away," Benjy said. "Where should I put it all?"

Dickce shook her head. "Most of the branches are a little too large and will need to be cut up. You haven't ever used a chainsaw, and I'm not strong enough these days. We can get Clementine's nephew, Ron, and his son to come take care of them, and they can have it all for firewood."

Benjy appeared crestfallen, and Dickce patted his shoulder. "I appreciate how much you want to help. Whenever Ron and his son get here, you can help them. Chainsaws are dangerous if you don't know what you're doing." She paused. "Frankly, they're dangerous even when you do know what you're doing, as far as I'm concerned. It's better to have someone experienced deal with this."

"You're right." Benjy grinned. "I don't like the idea of losing a finger or a hand because I don't know what I'm doing."

Peanut barked as if he agreed, and Benjy and Dickce laughed.

"There you have it," Dickce said. "Peanut has spoken. I think we're done here. I don't know about you, but I could use another cup of coffee. I'm chilled to the bone."

"Me, too," Benjy said. "Coffee sounds good. Come on, guys." He urged the animals to follow them to the back door and into the kitchen.

Clementine poured coffee for Dickce and Benjy while they shed their jackets and rubber boots in the small mud room off the kitchen. Benjy toweled off paws as well. He knew Clementine wouldn't appreciate wet or muddy prints on the floors she kept generally spotless.

"Thank you, Clementine." Dickce accepted her mug gratefully. "This will warm me right up." She had a sip. "Do you think Ron and his son might have time today or tomorrow to come clear away the storm debris? There are some large branches down that will need to be cut up."

Clementine nodded. "I'm sure he can. I'll give him a call. What do you want done with the wood?"

"If Ron can use it for firewood, he's welcome to it," Dickce said. "I think it's no more than two hours' work."

"He'll appreciate that," Clementine said.

"Has An'gel come down yet?" Dickce asked.

Clementine shook her head. "No, I took coffee up to her about thirty minutes ago.

She said she had a crick in her neck, and she was planning to take a long, hot shower."

"Poor thing fell asleep in a chair in the basement," Dickce said. "Had her head lying back when I woke her up about four this morning when we all came upstairs. I don't know why she didn't lie down on one of the beds."

"Because I fell asleep in the chair and didn't stir until you woke me." An'gel spoke as she walked into the kitchen. She set her coffee cup in the sink and approached Dickce. "The shower helped the sore neck. Tell me, what's the damage outside?" She patted Peanut's head after he ran to her and whined.

"Nothing major." Dickce gave her sister a quick summary of what she and Benjy had found in the yard.

"That's a relief," An'gel said. "I was worried the damage would be worse. I wonder how the people in town fared."

"I didn't hear any reports of serious trouble on the news this morning," Clementine said.

"I'm glad to hear that," Dickce said. "It could have been a disaster with all that wind."

The phone rang, and An'gel stepped over

101

to the counter to pick up the handset. After identifying herself, she listened for a moment. "We'd be more than happy to, Hadley. We'll be over in about ten minutes." She ended the call.

"What does he want?" Dickce asked.

"He wants to consult us about some of his plans for the gardens at Ashton Hall," An'gel said. "Sounds like he's had more wind damage there than we've had here. He's got a couple of trees down, and he's considering his options."

Dickce clapped her hands together. "Wonderful." She grinned. "Not that he's had a lot of damage. Wonderful that he wants to consult us. I've been dying to see Ashton Hall for the past few years."

An'gel nodded. "Yes, I'm afraid Hamish neglected the house and the grounds terribly. He became so odd over the years, wouldn't have much to do with anybody."

"Except Mrs. Danvers, of course." Dickce grimaced.

"Who are you talking about?" An'gel asked. "I thought the housekeeper's name was Turnipseed."

"It is," Dickce replied. "I was referring to the spooky housekeeper in *Rebecca*. Mrs. Turnipseed has always reminded me of her."

"Who's Rebecca?" Benjy asked, obviously

102

confused.

"*Rebecca* is a novel by Daphne du Maurier," Dickce explained. "A wonderful book, and the housekeeper in it, Mrs. Danvers, is truly menacing." She shivered. "In the movie she's really scary."

"Played by a wonderful actress named Judith Anderson," An'gel added. "We have it on DVD if you're interested."

Benjy nodded. "I like old movies, but I probably should read the book first."

"I'll lend it to you," Dickce said. "It's one of my favorites."

"Hadley is expecting us," An'gel said. "We'd better get going. Why don't you come with us, Benjy, and bring Peanut and Endora. They can explore the grounds with us."

"Are you sure it would be okay with the owner?" Benjy asked. "He might not want these two running around."

"Nonsense." Dickce stood. "Hadley always loved animals, and I'm sure he'll love these two rascals."

"Awesome," Benjy said. "I'd really like to see his house."

"It's gorgeous," Dickce said as she, Benjy, and the two animals followed An'gel out the back door to the garage. "At least, it used to be. There's no telling what kind of

103

condition Hadley's brother let it get into."

"We'll soon see," An'gel said as she backed the car out of the garage.

Eight minutes later the car topped a rise in the driveway to Ashton Hall, and An'gel stopped the car to allow them all to look down toward the house.

Dickce pointed to the side of the redbrick, three-story structure. "There's one of the trees that went down. Oh, I hate that, it's one of the old oaks. Must have been as old as the house, if not older."

"Hamish abandoned the gardens," An'gel said. "Look at the overgrown mess. Hadley has made some progress, but it's going to take months to get the grounds back in shape for the pilgrimage." She put the car in gear and drove them down the rise to the front of the house.

Hadley came out of the front door before they were all out of the car. Peanut bounded up to Hadley and woofed at him, tail wagging.

"Hello there, handsome." Hadley smiled and rubbed the dog's head. "You're a pleasant surprise." He greeted the humans, with kisses on the cheek for the sisters and a handshake for Benjy. He held up his fingers to allow Endora, perched on Benjy's shoulder, to have a sniff. To his obvious pleasure, she rubbed her head against his hand.

"You have quite a job on your hands," Dickce said.

Hadley offered them a wry grin. "Yes, my brother really let things go, as you can see. My plan is to restore the gardens to basically what they were in my mother's time. Do you remember what they looked like then?"

An'gel nodded. "Yes, your mother had the most incredible green thumb. She could get anything to grow."

"Our mother was always jealous of her." Dickce giggled. "She loved to garden but she didn't have the knack Mrs. Partridge did."

"Mother loved her garden, I think, even more than she loved her family." Hadley smiled. "I've found pictures from that period, but I confess I don't know the names of all the plants. I'm sure you can help me identify them."

"We'd be glad to," Dickce said. "An'gel is the real expert, though. I mostly do what she tells me when she needs help with weeding or planting."

Benjy startled them all by yelling, "Peanut, you come back here!" Benjy turned to their host. "If you'll excuse me sir, I'd better go after him. He might try to dig up something."

"By all means." Hadley laughed. "Though I doubt he can do much damage."

Benjy nodded, then took off after the dog who had headed toward the side of the house where the massive oak had fallen. Endora clung to his shoulder.

"Come on in." Hadley turned and gestured toward the front door. "It's a bit damp and chilly out here. After we've looked at the pictures, perhaps we can come out and have a look at the grounds."

"Sounds good to me." Dickce climbed the few steps to the small porch and walked through the open door, followed by An'gel and Hadley.

When their host had shut the door behind him, Dickce asked, "Is Mrs. Turnipseed still the housekeeper?"

Hadley shook his head. "No, she retired when Hamish died. He left her a nice pension." He grinned. "She never liked me, and the feeling was mutual. She always reminded me of that ghoulish woman in *Rebecca*."

Dickce and An'gel laughed, then Dickce explained, "That's what I said before we came over."

Hadley chuckled. "Well, great minds and all that. Come, let's go into the parlor. I've

106

got a fire going in there. The new house-keeper I hired will bring us hot coffee in a few minutes. I hope that's fine, or I could ask her to make hot tea."

The sisters assured him that they were happy with coffee and followed him into the parlor.

Dickce noticed that the room appeared clean, though the furnishings were shabby from years of neglect. *Such a shame. This was such a beautiful house.* The drapes appeared threadbare, as did the furniture, and there were holes and dark spots in the antique carpet. Fire burned brightly in the fireplace, however, and Dickce approached it, grateful for its warmth. The room felt a bit damp away from the fire.

Hadley had set three chairs near the fireplace, and he seated the sisters in turn, An'gel first as befit her status as the elder sister, before retrieving an album of photographs and seating himself beside her. He opened the album and turned a few pages.

"Here," he said as he handed the album to An'gel. "There are four pages of photographs of mother's gardens taken not long before she died forty-two years ago."

An'gel accepted the album and set it in her lap. Dickce inched her chair closer in order to view the album along with her sister. Dickce pointed to one photo. "Here are roses. I'm not sure what the varieties are, though."

"Hybrid tea," An'gel said. "The inner ring are grandiflora."

Before An'gel could continue identifying more plants in the photos, Benjy burst into the room with an excited Peanut alternately barking and whining.

"Benjy, what on earth is going on?" Dickce said, alarmed by the young man's strange expression.

"I think you'd better come outside." Benjy paused for a couple of deep breaths. "Peanut started digging around that tree that came down, and he found bones."

CHAPTER 10

As the first shock of Benjy's announcement began to pass, An'gel said, "They're probably quite old. If they were under the tree, they'd have to be. That oak is at least a hundred and fifty years old."

Hadley nodded. "I think it was planted by the ancestor who built the house, and that was in 1827."

Benjy looked confused for a moment. "I don't think the bones were actually *under* the tree. Not under the roots, anyway. More like beside them. Come look." He turned and led Peanut out of the room.

"That's odd." Hadley rose from his chair. "I'd better go have a look. Why don't y'all stay here where it's warm."

"No, I think we'd better come with you." An'gel lay the album aside on a nearby table and stood. She was concerned by Benjy's assertion that the bones were in the ground beside the tree. That brought an unsettling

109

thought to mind. "Come on, Sister."

Hadley shrugged before he turned and strode out of the room. An'gel and Dickce followed right behind.

"Who do you think it could be?" Dickce whispered her question near to An'gel's ear.

An'gel shook her head. "Not now."

Hadley quickly outdistanced them, and when they caught up with him and Benjy, the two men and the dog stood staring at the ground near where the magnificent oak had once stood.

"The wind must have been really strong to bring it down like that," Benjy said.

"Had it been healthy, it might not have fallen," Hadley replied. "But it was dying, and it had evidently been hit by lightning at some point in the past few years."

An'gel saw the massive trunk had snapped about four feet from the ground, and the fall had shifted the stump at a thirty-degree angle. The ground near the stump was disturbed, and An'gel understood what Benjy meant.

"Here are the bones." Benjy, his hand firmly on Peanut's collar, stepped closer and pointed down at a spot twelve inches or so from the exposed root.

An'gel and Dickce came nearer, while Hadley squatted for a closer look. "That's a

110

hand," Hadley said, his tone subdued. "A human hand."

An'gel saw the delicate bones of the fingers jutting out of the soil and felt a wave of sadness. She thought immediately of Callie Partridge. Then a flash of movement caught her eye, and she turned to see Endora on the ground nearby playing with an object of some kind. She hoped fervently that it wasn't a bone.

"Dickce, look at Endora," she said. "See if you can get whatever that is away from her."

Dickce turned to see what her sister was talking about. Endora was slapping at something in the grass a couple of feet away from them on the other side of the tree stump. She made her way around while the others watched, talking to Endora the whole time.

"You clever kitty," she said in a soothing tone. "You found something, didn't you? You're such a smart girl. Will you let me see what it is?"

When Dickce, still talking, reached the cat, Endora stopped playing with the object and meowed. Dickce bent down to retrieve the cat's erstwhile toy. She stood, her palm extended toward the others. On it lay a ring.

"Let me see that." Hadley's harsh tone startled An'gel. He reached for the ring and almost snatched it away from Dickce. An'gel watched while he examined it and would have sworn he paled under his tan.

The ring was a small band of what looked like gold, and there were stones mounted on it. They were encrusted with dirt, however, and An'gel couldn't tell what they might be. Hadley pulled out a handkerchief and rubbed some of the dirt away. An'gel caught her breath as the sun hit the now exposed stones.

An emerald, surrounded by diamonds. She recognized the ring.

Hadley closed his eyes and clutched the ring to his chest. His words came out with a sob. "It's Callie's."

An'gel's gaze shifted to the finger bones sticking out of the earth, and her eyes filled with tears. Sarinda Hetherington might have been right after all, she realized.

Callie Partridge perhaps never left Ashton Hall alive.

An'gel stared dully into the fire in the front parlor at Ashton Hall. Her back ached, and she wanted to be at home. She'd had to feed the flames several times in the nearly two hours they'd been waiting in the parlor. Dickce sat nearby with Endora curled up in her lap. Benjy occupied one end of the sofa, and Peanut lay at his feet. Their host was in the library across the hall, talking to Kanesha Berry, chief deputy from the Athena County Sheriff's Department. They had each already had a turn with the deputy, but she had asked them to wait for a while longer.

"Just because her ring was found there doesn't necessarily mean those bones are Callie's." Dickce stroked the cat's head. "She could have lost it there. Maybe those bones are two hundred years old. The grave might have been there when Hadley's ancestor planted the tree, and he never knew it."

"I would give a lot if that were indeed the case," An'gel said. "It would be a whopping coincidence, though, don't you think?"

"Yes, I suppose so," Dickce replied. "But I'm certainly going to hope and pray that's the truth of it, and it's not poor Callie lying there in the ground."

An'gel cast a quick glance at the sheriff's deputy who stood right outside the open door of the parlor. She got up from her chair and sat next to Benjy on the sofa. In an undertone she said, "Could you see Hadley's face when he first looked at the bones?"

Benjy nodded. "He looked shocked to me."

113

"Shocked as if he was upset the bones were found, or shocked as if he had no idea they were there?"

Benjy considered that a moment. "Shocked like I don't think he knew the bones were there, but I don't know him at all."

"We don't really know him ourselves, not anymore," Dickce said. "Forty years ago he was a carefree, irresponsible playboy. The man who came back could have changed a lot."

"He did seem stunned when he realized he was holding Callie's ring," An'gel said. "I would swear that was a complete surprise to him."

"Do you remember when Hamish gave Callie that ring?" Dickce asked. "I do."

"Yes," An'gel said. "It was for their tenth anniversary." For Benjy's benefit, she added, "Hamish threw a lavish party here at Ashton Hall, and he gave her the ring in front of everyone."

"Three years before Hadley disappeared from Athena," Dickce said.

"Hamish sounds like a romantic kind of guy," Benjy said.

"He was, where Callie was concerned," An'gel said. "He loved her deeply, so deeply that at times I think it frightened her."

"She was the center of his life." Dickce picked Endora up and cradled the cat in her arms. Endora yawned and stretched before settling down contentedly against Dickce's chest.

"He must have been pretty devastated when she disappeared," Benjy said.

"He never got over it," An'gel said.

"If that's really her out there by the tree," Benjy said after a brief silence, "do you think he could have killed her?"

An'gel shuddered. "I'd hate to think so, but he was so obsessed with her. If he thought she was in love with someone else, well, I suppose he could have killed her in a fit of jealous rage."

"What about Hadley?" Dickce asked in a low voice. "If he killed her, that might be why he disappeared and stayed gone so long."

"But then why would he come back?" Benjy said. "If he did kill her, wouldn't it be safer for him to stay away?"

"Yes, it would be safer," An'gel said. "But there's the matter of Ashton Hall and whatever money Hamish had. Hadley probably inherited a fair-sized fortune on top of the house and the land. That might have been a powerful enough lure to bring him back even if he murdered his own sister-in-law."

The sound of a voice coming from the hallway ended their conversation. An'gel turned her head to observe Kanesha Berry advance into the room. Since her earlier conversation with the deputy she had debated whether to bring up the death of Sarinda Hetherington. She decided that she ought to share her ideas and suspicions with Kanesha.

Kanesha regarded them with her habitual calm expression. "Ladies, and Mr. Stephens, I'm sorry to keep you waiting this long, but it was helpful to have you here in case I needed to talk to you again. But you can go now. I'll follow up with you soon, once we know more about the identity of the remains."

Peanut walked over to the deputy and stared up at her, waiting to be noticed. She had been friendly before, and he now expected some attention from her. Kanesha frowned at him for a moment, then patted his head. "Nice to see you, too, Peanut."

The dog barked and wagged his tail. Happy now, he returned to Benjy's side. Endora paid the deputy no attention whatsoever.

An'gel rose. "We'll be happy to get home.

But there is a matter I'd like to discuss with you. Do you think you might have time to come by Riverhill for a few minutes?"

"We could talk here," Kanesha said. "Mr. Partridge is allowing us to continue to use his library for as long as we need."

An'gel shook her head. "I'd really rather discuss this away from Ashton Hall. I would consider it a great favor if you could come by Riverhill sometime today."

"Very well, Miss An'gel," Kanesha said. "I'll come by right after I leave here. It may be another hour."

"That's fine," An'gel said. "Now we'd better take our leave of Hadley."

Kanesha said, "He went upstairs a couple of minutes ago. I don't think he'll be back down for a while."

"Poor man," Dickce said. "I can't blame him. This has been a terrible shock to all of us."

"I'm sure it has," Kanesha said. "I will be working hard to find out exactly what happened here."

An'gel nodded. "I know you will figure it out." She turned to Dickce and Benjy. "Come now, let's go home." She headed for the door, her heart heavy and her mind troubled.

Back at Riverhill ten minutes later, they

117

shared the shocking news with Clementine while Benjy took Peanut and Endora outside for a walk. The housekeeper shook her head. "Lord, to think Miss Callie might've been lying there all these years, and nobody knew."

"We can't be completely certain that the remains are Callie's," An'gel said. "My heart tells me they are, though."

"If they are Callie's, then the person who put her there certainly knew," Dickce said. "It makes me angry to think that someone might have gotten away with murder all these years."

"Kanesha will see to that," An'gel said. "I'm expecting her to come by to talk to me in the next hour or so, Clementine."

"Yes, ma'am," the housekeeper said. "What would you like to do about lunch?"

An'gel glanced at the kitchen clock. Ten minutes to eleven, she read. "Let's say twelve thirty. Is that okay with you, Sister?"

Dickce nodded. "Yes. I hate to say it, after the upsetting morning we've had, but I know I'll probably be really hungry by then."

"It'll be ready," Clementine said. "In the meantime, would you like coffee or some hot tea?"

"Tea would be nice," Dickce said.

"Yes, it would. We'll be in the front parlor," An'gel said. "Thank you, Clementine." She headed out of the kitchen, followed by her sister.

When they were seated comfortably in the parlor, Dickce asked, "What is it you want to talk to Kanesha about?"

"Sarinda," An'gel said. "If those remains are Callie's, then I think it's likely Sarinda might have known who put Callie in that grave."

"And that person killed Sarinda because they thought Sarinda was going to expose them."

"I think it's possible," An'gel replied. "Maybe I'm indulging in a wild flight of fancy, but I think there has to be a connection."

Clementine came in with a serving tray and set it on the coffee table. Along with the teapot and cups, there was a plate of her homemade shortbread.

An'gel thanked her, and Clementine nodded. Dickce poured the tea for them both. She picked up a piece of the shortbread and began to eat.

They had finished the tea and the plate of shortbread by the time Kanesha arrived forty minutes later. An'gel answered the door and ushered the deputy into the parlor.

"Would you care for anything to drink?" An'gel asked.

"No, ma'am, I'm fine." Kanesha perched on the edge of the chair her hostess had indicated. "What is it you wanted to discuss with me?"

"Sarinda Hetherington's death," An'gel said. "I don't think it was an accident."

"And if those bones turn out to belong to Callie Partridge," Dickce said, "we think there's a connection."

"I'm sure you've talked to Chief Carson," An'gel said. "Did he tell you about our conversation?"

Kanesha nodded. "He did. I've also spoken with Dr. Gandy, and he is adamant that Miss Hetherington wouldn't have drunk enough bourbon to incapacitate herself enough to fall down the stairs."

"I believe him," An'gel said. "So what's being done about it?"

"We are treating it as a suspicious death," Kanesha said. "There is some evidence to indicate that it wasn't an accident."

"What evidence?" An'gel asked.

Kanesha frowned. "I can't go into detail, and I wouldn't tell anyone else outside the force this, Miss An'gel. But I'll tell you and Miss Dickce. I know it won't go any further."

"No, it certainly won't," Dickce said.

"There are marks on the body that indicate Miss Hetherington might have been shoved down the stairs," Kanesha said. "I emphasize *might*. We won't know for sure until the examination is complete, and that could take several weeks."

"The important point to me, at the moment, is that you're investigating and not dismissing it as what it looked like," An'gel said.

"I never accept anything at face value." Kanesha pulled out her notebook and pen. "Now, ladies, if you don't mind, tell me again who was at the garden club meeting and what Miss Hetherington said and did." She slipped open the notebook and prepared to write.

Dickce gave her the names, then turned to An'gel to let her sister relay the rest of the information.

An'gel ran through the conversation leading up to Sarinda's startling question. "Maybe I'm imagining it now," she said. "At the time, however, there seemed to be an undercurrent of tension in the room after Sarinda said what she did."

"No, I felt it too," Dickce said. "Though to be fair, it could be that everyone was tense because they thought Sarinda had finally gone completely around the bend."

Kanesha appeared a little puzzled.

"Sarinda was inclined to be dramatic when she wanted attention," An'gel said.

"I see. What happened after she asked her question?" Kanesha said.

"No one appeared to take her seriously at the time." An'gel continued with her summary of the meeting and concluded with, "I thought it strange, even for Sarinda, to take off like that. But she could be so moody when she didn't get the attention she wanted."

"Neither of you spoke to her at any point after the meeting?" Kanesha asked.

"No," An'gel said. "I wish now, of course, that I had called her, or that we had gone by her house to check on her. But we had other things on our minds."

"We'll always regret it," Dickce said. "The only thing we can do for her now is to help find out who pushed her down the stairs."

"Now that this grave has been found at Ashton Hall," An'gel said, "and Callie's ring with it, I have to think Sarinda did know something about Callie's disappearance. Perhaps she even knew that Callie was dead."

"Those are questions I will be trying to answer." Kanesha tapped her pen against the notebook. "I might be wrong, but I don't think Mr. Hamish Partridge ever filed a missing persons report on his wife. I'll have to check that out."

"He would be the most likely suspect, wouldn't he?" Dickce asked.

"We always look first at the spouse." Kanesha rose. "You've given me a lot to think about, and I promise you I will consider all the possibilities. It would help me if the two of you could write down everything you remember that happened around the time Hadley Partridge left town and Mrs. Callie Partridge was rumored to have run away after him."

An'gel stood. "We will do that. Let me show you out." She accompanied Kanesha to the front door and moments later returned to the parlor.

"That's going to be quite a job," Dickce said. "I'm not sure how much I can remember from forty years ago. That's a long time."

"Yes, it is," An'gel said as she resumed her seat. "I'm not sure either, but we'll have to do our best." She thought for a moment. "I imagine it won't take long for the news to get around about the remains found at Ashton Hall. That will be the only subject anybody's talking about."

"So it won't hurt if we talk about it to the garden club board and see what we can find out about what they were all up to at the time." Dickce nodded. "I like that. We can be snoopy, and it ought to seem natural."

"Natural enough, perhaps," An'gel said. "We'll have to be careful, though, because there'll be at least one person who'll be anxious to hide what she was doing at the time."

"It's hard to think of one of those women as a murderer," Dickce said.

"One of them very well could be, because I doubt Hamish came back from the dead to push Sarinda down the stairs."

"No, of course not." Dickce shook her

head. "But we can't forget Hadley. It could just as easily be him as one of the board."

"Yes, you're right." An'gel thought for a moment. "I think we need to spend some time getting reacquainted with Hadley, don't you?"

"What do you have in mind?" Dickce asked.

"First, let's invite him here for dinner tonight. If, that is, he hasn't already accepted another invitation." An'gel grimaced. "I have a feeling he's getting all kinds of invitations from the other board members."

"Then you'd better call him right now," Dickce said. "Let's not waste any time."

"As soon as I look up the number for Ashton Hall." An'gel rose to search for the local telephone book. "I hope the phone is still connected there, because I don't want to have to drive back over there to invite Hadley to dinner."

"I believe it's in the drawer in the hall table," Dickce said. "The one right outside the parlor door."

An'gel found the book where Dickce said it would be and came back into the room, riffling the pages in search of the number. "Here it is." She went over to the desk by the front windows, picked up the handset there, and punched in the number. Dickce

125

came over to stand near while she called.

"Good afternoon," she said. "This is An'gel Ducote. I would like to speak to Mr. Partridge if he's available." She put her hand over the mouthpiece to speak to her sister. "She's gone to get him."

Nearly a minute passed before An'gel heard Hadley's voice on the other end. "An'gel, my dear, how are you and Dickce? I must apologize for disappearing on you like I did. I have to tell you, I was pretty unsettled by what we found this morning. I guess my manners went completely by the wayside as a result."

"No need to apologize," An'gel said. "We completely understand. It was quite a shock."

"Yes, it was," Hadley said. "I'm praying that who we found isn't Callie."

"We are, too," An'gel replied. "I know things are still unsettled there, and Dickce and I would love to see you. Why don't you come to dinner here tonight? Around seven?"

"Thank you, I'd like that very much," Hadley said with what sounded like true gratitude. "I think it will do me good to be out of this house for a few hours."

"I'm sure it will," An'gel said. "We'll see you at seven, then." She ended the call and replaced the handset.

"I heard most of it," Dickce said. "His voice came through clearly. I'm glad he's coming. I hope we can get him to open up about why he really left Athena."

"We can but try." An'gel shrugged. "Lunch should be about ready. I'd better tell Clementine that we'll be four for dinner tonight."

Hadley rang the bell at seven that evening, and An'gel, who had been waiting nearby, admitted him. Hadley gave her a swift kiss on the cheek, and An'gel greeted him and took his jacket.

"Would you like something to drink before we go in to dinner?" An'gel laid the jacket across the back of the sofa in the parlor where Dickce greeted him and received her own brief kiss.

Hadley grinned. "I wouldn't say no to a whisky and soda."

"Coming right up." An'gel moved to the liquor cabinet in the corner and prepared his drink. "Dickce, what would you like?"

"The same," Dickce said.

"I'll make it three." An'gel smiled. Moments later the drinks were ready, and she handed her sister and Hadley theirs and then took up her own.

127

"May I propose a toast?" Hadley asked. "I know it's usually the hostess's prerogative."

"Go right ahead," An'gel said.

Hadley raised his glass. "To homecomings and good friends."

An'gel and Dickce raised their glasses to his. "To homecomings and good friends," they said in unison.

All three sipped their whisky. Hadley smiled appreciatively. "Let me guess," he said. "Laphroaig."

An'gel nodded. "Our favorite."

"Mine, too." Hadley drained his glass. "Thank you. That went down a treat, as my friends in England would say."

"It always does." Dickce giggled before she too drained hers.

"How about another one?" An'gel asked.

Hadley refused with a smile. "I have too great a fondness for it, so I try to limit myself."

An'gel nodded. "That's smart." She set her glass on the tray on the liquor cabinet and did the same with the other two. "Let's go in to dinner then."

Hadley escorted An'gel into the dining room and pulled out her chair for her. Then he pulled out Dickce's chair before he took his own seat at An'gel's right hand.

"What a beautiful table," Hadley said. "I

feel honored."

Clementine had set the table with exquisite taste, as always, An'gel thought. The housekeeper had used linens belonging to the sisters' grandmother Ducote, and the silver was the wedding set their parents received. The table sported the best Wedgwood china and Waterford crystal they had. Clementine had obviously been determined to impress Hadley Partridge, and it seemed she had succeeded.

Benjy hurried into the dining room with a smiled apology and took his seat next to Dickce. "Good evening, Mr. Partridge. How are you?" he said after greeting the sisters. He exchanged pleasantries with Hadley, and then An'gel said grace.

When she finished the brief prayer, An'gel stood. "Everything is here on the sideboard. Hadley, please go first. Clementine has prepared a traditional Southern meal for us. Fried chicken, rice, homemade biscuits, cream gravy, sweet tea, and green beans."

Hadley grinned. "I'll enjoy every bite of it, I'm sure, although I'll have to jog to Memphis and back tomorrow to make up for it." He rose from the table with his plate and began to load it from the sideboard.

Soon all four diners returned to the table with full plates, and eating commenced.

An'gel kept the conversation general, though she had plans a little later to hone in on Hadley's life during his forty-year absence from Athena. She waited until Hadley was nearly finished with his second helping of biscuits and gravy before she introduced the subject.

"I'm glad to see that forty years away hasn't affected your appetite for Southern food. I thought perhaps you had become too sophisticated for plain, down-home cooking." She smiled to remove any sting from the words.

"I'll admit that I did develop tastes for a wide range of different cuisines," Hadley said after a sip of tea. He set down the glass and smiled at his hostess. "The South is in my blood, in my DNA, as it is in yours and Dickce's. No matter how far I strayed or how long I was gone, I never forgot my roots." He paused, and his expression turned serious. "I never lost the desire to return home. It simply wasn't possible as long as Hamish was alive."

"Why ever not?" Dickce asked.

"He swore he'd kill me if I ever came home," Hadley said.

CHAPTER 12

An'gel nearly choked on her tea. She set the glass down on the table. "He left you Ashton Hall. Surely that meant he was no longer angry with you."

Hadley shrugged. "I'm the last male in the direct line. Hamish probably hated the thought of anyone other than a Partridge laying claim to Ashton Hall more than he hated me. The irony is that I have no son to inherit it after me. Hamish had no idea, of course, but the end result is that the direct line will go kaput after all when I'm gone."

"What will you do about the property?" Dickce asked, then blushed when she caught the irritated glance An'gel shot her. "Sorry, that isn't any of our business."

"I don't mind," Hadley said. "It's a good question, and although I've thought about it, I haven't come to any decision yet. I'm open to suggestions."

An'gel didn't want to discuss this particular subject at the moment, interesting as it was. She and Dickce faced a similar situation, but with Benjy now in their lives, they did have more options. Right now she wanted to steer the conversation back to Hadley's long absence and the reason for it.

"I'm going to be blunt, Hadley." An'gel regarded him with a determined expression. "You can refuse to answer, but frankly, I think you owe us all an explanation for why you disappeared from Athena. We were all your friends — good friends, we thought — and you walked away from all of us. That was painful. We are glad you're back, but we can't help but wonder why you left."

"Ah, yes." Hadley picked up his tea glass and stared into it. He drained the contents and set the glass down again. "Yes, I suppose I do."

"Well, aren't you going to tell us?" Dickce said, her tone sharp, after Hadley failed to continue right away.

Hadley took a deep breath and looked at each of them in turn. "I loved Callie. She was my very dear friend, and I loved her. I wasn't *in love* with her, however. She was more like a sister to me. She was in an unhappy marriage. Hamish became more and more jealous of any attention she paid me, and he took it out on her. He threatened

132

me, as I've already said, and I was afraid that if I didn't go, he *would* kill me, and possibly Callie, too. I tried arguing with him, but he had lost his reasonableness, if you understand what I mean. So I left." He shrugged. "I thought that if I were out of the picture, Hamish would no longer have a reason to be jealous. That he might treat Callie better, and she could find some kind of happiness with him."

An'gel felt a sudden rage toward Hamish Partridge. She had little doubt now that he had killed his wife, even though Hadley left in order to protect her.

"That's horrible." Dickce pulled a handkerchief from her sleeve and dabbed at her eyes.

"And you had no contact with Callie after you left?" Benjy asked. He also, An'gel noticed, appeared moved by Hadley's story.

"I never saw her again," Hadley said.

That struck An'gel as an evasion after she thought about it a moment. She challenged him. "You never saw her again, but did you *speak* to her after you left? Or perhaps exchange letters?"

"You should have been a lawyer, An'gel," Hadley said with a wry smile. "Yes, I did talk to her. When I left I went to Memphis. I had a good friend there, and I knew he'd put me up for a few nights. Callie knew him, too, and she figured that's where I'd go. So she called me there. She had to go into town to do it."

"How long had you been gone when she called you?" An'gel asked.

"Let me think." Hadley got up from the table and went to the sideboard to refill his tea. That accomplished, he returned to his seat. "I left the first Saturday in June, three days before my birthday. Callie called me on Monday, sometime around noon, I think it was."

"How was she?" Dickce asked.

"Upset that I had left, although she understood why, naturally." Hadley sipped from his glass. "She said Hamish was calm, almost pleasant, once he knew I was gone. She told me he had invited guests to dinner that evening, something he hadn't done in months. I remember thinking, 'Well, she'll be okay now.' But evidently she wasn't. She disappeared, too, and I had no idea until I came back here."

"Weren't you surprised when you never heard from her again?" An'gel asked.

"Not really, no," Hamish said. "I told her it was best if we had no contact. She didn't like it, but I finally persuaded her it was the only way to keep her safe. I left Memphis a few days later for New York, and then on to London about a week after that."

"You could have called one of us," An'gel said, now suddenly angry at him. "You should have. We could have done something to help her."

"I know that now." Hamish gazed at her, and she could see the anguish he felt. "At the time, though, I thought the best thing was to disappear. Make a complete break with the past. Obviously I was wrong."

An'gel wanted to say, *And Callie paid the price for it,* but his obvious distress prevented her. She couldn't be that cruel. "When you had that last conversation with Callie, did she give you any indication that she was afraid of Hamish?"

"No." Hadley frowned. "That's why I find it so strange that she apparently disappeared so soon after I left. When was the last time either of you saw or spoke to her?"

"We've been racking our brains trying to remember," Dickce said. "I think the last time we saw her was a few days before you left."

"There was a party that Friday, June seventh," An'gel said. "Wedding reception at the country club. Hamish and Callie were invited, but they didn't show. None of us thought much about it at the time, because

135

Hamish had done that before. The following week they didn't turn up for another function — a Chamber of Commerce dinner — and I called to check on them at that point. The housekeeper merely said that Mr. and Mrs. Partridge had suddenly left on an extended vacation and weren't expected back for at least six weeks."

"We didn't realize until later that Callie had actually disappeared not long after you left," Dickce said. "That story about an extended vacation was a lie, of course, but by then people thought they knew what happened and left Hamish alone."

"What about the housekeeper? The one you called Mrs. Danvers." Benjy looked at Dickce. "She has a weird name that I can't remember. If she's still around, couldn't you talk to her?"

"Excellent point." Dickce smiled fondly at Benjy.

"She retired when my brother died," Hadley said. "She was local, so I suppose she might still be in the area. I will see if I can locate her."

"Perhaps you had better leave that to us," An'gel said. "If she didn't like you, as you told us this morning, I think Dickce and I would have better luck getting her to talk."

"You're right." Hadley grimaced. "She

would probably slam the door in my face if she saw me standing there. Even after all these years."

"We'll start asking around tomorrow," Dickce said. "I'm sure we can track her down pretty quickly."

"And if we can't," An'gel said, "I'm sure Kanesha can."

Hadley frowned. "That's the deputy, right?"

"Yes," An'gel said.

"How well do you know her?" Hadley asked. "She seemed competent, but I found her intimidating."

"We've known her all her life," Dickce said. "She *is* competent, and she *can* be intimidating. She has to be, in her position. I don't know if there's another woman in the whole state who is a chief deputy, let alone an African American woman."

"I see what you mean," Hadley said. "I didn't think about that. After living abroad for so long, I'm having to readjust to some of the attitudes here."

"Backward attitudes, you mean," An'gel said. "Unfortunately there are still many people here whose minds are stuck in the 1950s when it comes to race and gender."

"If you think Kanesha is intimidating, wait until you meet her mother." Dickce chuckled. "Azalea Berry is the most formidable woman I've ever known."

"She's housekeeper for a friend of ours," An'gel said. "Charlie Harris. We'll have to introduce you to both of them, and to Charlie's cat, Diesel." She smiled fondly. "He is the dearest thing on four legs."

"He's a Maine Coon," Dickce said. "And he's the biggest house cat you'll ever see. But he's sweet and really smart."

"I really have to meet this paragon." Hadley smiled. "But what about your two four-legged friends? Where are they tonight?"

"They're in my apartment," Benjy said. "Over what used to be the stables."

"I'd love to see them again," Hadley said. "I owe the cat — Endora, isn't that her name? — a treat of some kind for finding Callie's ring."

"Yes, Endora," Benjy said. "And Peanut is the dog. He's a Labradoodle."

"How about coffee?" An'gel asked. "We have one of Clementine's carrot cakes for dessert, if anyone's interested."

Benjy's face lit up. "I am. I love carrot cake."

Hadley groaned. "After all I've eaten already, I shouldn't. But I could never pass up carrot cake."

An'gel smiled as she stood. "Then Dickce

and I will clear the plates away, and we'll be back in a few minutes with the coffee and carrot cake."

Both Benjy and Hadley offered to assist with the clearing away, but the sisters declined. They quickly gathered the plates and took them to the kitchen. Clementine had set the timer on the coffeemaker, and the coffee was ready. Dickce prepared the beverage while An'gel sliced the cake and placed the servings on a tray. They were soon back in the dining room, where they found the men discussing the adoption of shelter animals.

"Mr. Partridge is thinking about adopting a dog," Benjy told them.

"I really wish you would call me Hadley," Hadley said. "I don't feel like Mr. Partridge."

Benjy laughed. "All right then. Hadley."

"That's better," Hadley said as he accepted his coffee and cake. "This looks wonderful."

They chatted about what kind of dog Hadley wanted, but after a few minutes, An'gel steered the conversation back to the topic uppermost in her mind. "I think that we are all making the assumption that if the remains we found are truly Callie's, then it must have been Hamish who put her there.

Correct?"

Hadley appeared startled at the abrupt shift in subject. He laid down his fork and gazed at An'gel. "Though I hate to think of my brother as a murderer," he said, "I think you're right. I am hoping against hope that those remains aren't Callie, though."

"I think we have to work under the assumption that they are," An'gel said. "I would love to believe that Callie is alive somewhere, happy and flourishing, but it simply isn't realistic."

Hadley sighed. "I know you're right. Finding the ring is evidence enough, I suppose."

"Did you have to turn it over to Kanesha?" Dickce asked.

"Yes," Hadley said. "I will get it back eventually, but I hated to let go of it." Suddenly he pushed back his chair and stood. "This was a wonderful meal, but it's been rather a long day."

An'gel rose. "Yes, it has, and the conversation hasn't been particularly cheerful. We've enjoyed having you here. Let me show you out." Dickce and Benjy stood also.

"Thank you for being so understanding." Hadley came to her and gave her a quick kiss on the cheek. Then he went around her to do the same for Dickce. He extended his hand to Benjy, and they shook.

An'gel escorted Hadley to the front door. Hadley turned to her and said, "Thank you again," before he walked through the door and into the night.

An'gel closed the door behind him and stood there for a moment, thinking about the evening. She looked up to see Dickce and Benjy walking toward her.

"I'm sorry if we upset him," Dickce said.

"Yes, but it couldn't be helped," An'gel replied. "We have to talk about these things. We can't simply ignore Callie's death."

"No, of course not," Dickce said. "Poor Hadley. I feel so bad for him."

"He seems like a nice guy," Benjy said. "There's one thing I've been thinking about, though." He paused.

"Go ahead," An'gel said. "Say what's on your mind."

"Okay." Benjy frowned. "I was thinking about that phone call. The one he told us about. What if he was making that up?"

CHAPTER 13

An'gel nodded. "You're right, Benjy. I've been thinking about that myself. We also have only his word that he was not in love with Callie, that he thought of her only as a friend, and not a lover."

"If he's not telling the truth in either case, I'm wondering why he would be lying," Benjy said.

"To shift the blame completely to his brother, for one thing." Dickce frowned. "It's a little drafty here by the door. Let's go back to the dining room and finish clearing the table. We can discuss Hadley while we do that."

An'gel and Benjy followed her. When they reached the dining room, An'gel said, "We need to track down Mrs. Turnipseed. Even though she'll be biased against Hadley, according to him, she still might be able to tell us something."

"Especially about the last few days before

Callie disappeared." Dickce paused in stacking dessert plates on the tray. "I just thought of something. Wasn't there another woman who worked for them? A housemaid, I seem to remember. Now, what was her name?"

"You're right, there was a woman," An'gel said. "I can't remember her name at the moment, but I do remember that Callie was fond of her and thought she was a good worker. We'll have to ask Clementine tomorrow if she can think of the woman's name if it doesn't come to one of us before then."

"My memory simply isn't what it was." Dickce sighed. "I used to be able to remember people's names and their faces."

"We both did," An'gel said. "No use complaining about it now. Let's get all this to the kitchen and be done with it."

They carried everything to the kitchen and set the dishes and cutlery in the sink. Benjy bade them good night.

"I need to let Peanut out for one last run before bedtime," he said. "See you in the morning." He gave them each a quick peck on the cheek before he left through the back door.

"He's such a sweet boy," Dickce said as she filled the sink with hot water to soak the dishes. "I worry about him, though. He needs friends his own age. Right now all he has is the two of us, Clementine, Peanut, and Endora."

"I think he's doing fine," An'gel said. "He needs time to adjust after everything that's happened to him in recent months. Once he starts classes at Athena in the spring, he'll start to make friends."

"Yes, I suppose so." Dickce turned off the tap and wiped her hands on a dish towel. "That's done. I'm ready to call it a night and get ready for bed. I hope I don't have nightmares about what we found today."

"That was gruesome," An'gel said as she followed Dickce out of the kitchen. She left one light burning in the hall before they climbed the stairs to their respective bedrooms on the second floor. "Try to think about other, more pleasant, things before you go to sleep. That usually works for me. Good night."

"I'll try, but I don't know whether it will work. Good night." Dickce stepped into her room and shut the door.

An'gel forced her thoughts away from the subject of Callie Partridge while she prepared for bed. Once she was done, instead of climbing into bed, she went to the armchair by the window where she liked to read and turned on the lamp. She didn't feel ready for sleep, and reading often calmed her thoughts and helped her drift off more easily.

Charlie Harris had recommended that she try a series that featured a Scottish noblewoman in post–World War I Scotland. She was halfway through *After the Armistice Ball*, the first book by Catriona McPherson, and enjoying it thoroughly. Within moments of picking it up she found herself once more immersed in the story.

By the time An'gel turned the last page, the clock read 11:14. An'gel yawned and set the book aside. She would have to thank Charlie for his recommendation and find more books by the author. Right now, though, she was ready to climb into bed. She soon fell asleep and slept soundly until her alarm went off at seven.

At breakfast forty-five minutes later she eyed Dickce with concern. "You obviously didn't rest well, Sister. Did you get any sleep at all?"

Dickce yawned before she answered. "I tossed and turned a good bit of the night. I couldn't go to sleep for the longest time, and when I did I had nightmares about bodies rising out of graves and coming after me."

"I'm sorry you didn't sleep well." Benjy

145

frowned. "Maybe you should go back to bed."

"Heavens, do I look that bad?" Dickce smiled. "I may take a nap sometime today, but for now, I'm awake. This coffee ought to perk me up."

"Clementine's coffee is strong enough to do the trick," Benjy said. "One cup is enough to do me for the rest of the day." He nodded at his empty cup before he picked up his glass of orange juice.

"We've been drinking it for years," Dickce said. "Takes me at least three cups to get completely awake on days like this."

"If you drink three cups of that coffee, you'll be running around the house like a hamster on its wheel," An'gel said. "I'd advise you to have one at the most and in a little while, go back upstairs and lie down for an hour or two."

"Thank you, Sister," Dickce said. "But I'll follow my own prescription if you don't mind." She picked up her cup and drained it, then got up to go to the sideboard to refill it from the carafe there.

An'gel frowned but didn't otherwise respond. She knew how Dickce was when she got in one of these moods. She decided to concentrate instead on finishing her meal. She was eager to start the search for

Hamish Partridge's faithful housekeeper, Mrs. Turnipseed, and the housemaid whose name she had finally remembered this morning while she was in the shower.

The housemaid had such a distinctive name, An'gel was surprised she hadn't remembered it last night. *Coriander Simpson.* Surely a woman with a name like that wouldn't be hard to trace. An'gel hoped she was still living. She thought the woman was in her late twenties — early thirties at most — during the time she worked at Ashton Hall.

Mrs. Turnipseed had to be around somewhere, she reasoned, if Hamish Partridge had left her a pension in his will. If all else failed, she could contact Hamish's lawyer to find out whether the firm had any contact information for the housekeeper. That would mean asking Hadley the name of the firm. She was pretty sure it hadn't been Pendergrast and Harris, the firm now run by Alexandra Pendergrast and Sean Harris, Charlie's son. Hamish had detested Alexandra's father, Q. C. Pendergrast, founder of the firm. The loathing had been mutual.

But first, she realized, she needed to talk to Kanesha Berry. She wanted to propose her scheme to meet with the women to the deputy before she went ahead with it. An'gel didn't want to compromise Kanesha's investigation, but from what she remembered of Mrs. Turnipseed and certain of her attitudes, she thought she stood a better chance of getting information from her than the deputy did. The housemaid might be a different matter, but An'gel still thought it couldn't hurt for her to talk to Coriander Simpson first.

An'gel shared her plan with Dickce and Benjy. When she finished, she asked, "What do you two think?"

"I think you definitely should talk to Deputy Berry first," Benjy said when Dickce didn't respond right away. "She doesn't seem like the type of person who would like other people doing her job for her."

Dickce chuckled. "No, she surely is not that type."

"What will you do if she tells you she doesn't want you to talk to these women?" Benjy asked.

An'gel frowned. "I would comply with her wishes in that case. I'm not going to rush in like one of those snoopy old ladies in a mystery novel and have Kanesha angry with me. I do believe, though, she will welcome my — our — help in this instance."

"Especially with that Turnipseed woman." Dickce sniffed. "I've recalled a few things about her, and I don't think she would respond well to Kanesha. I remember Callie telling us one time she had to speak to Mrs. Turnipseed about how badly she treated the housemaid."

"What do you mean?" Benjy asked. "I think I can guess."

"Mrs. Turnipseed had pretty outdated ideas about race and the way other people should be treated." An'gel grimaced. "I have no time for those attitudes, and if I do talk to her, I imagine it will be difficult not to tell her exactly what I think about that."

"Knowing you, you'll go all Julia Sugarbaker on her." Dickce giggled.

Benjy laughed, too. "I know what *that* means."

An'gel did not share their amusement. "If I do talk to Mrs. Turnipseed, I had obviously better do it on my own."

"Oh, come on, Sister, don't get huffy." Dickce grimaced at An'gel. "You know how you can be when you get angry over stuff like that."

"I suppose you're right," An'gel said after a moment's reflection. "I do sometimes get caught up in the moment."

The doorbell rang. An'gel frowned. "It's pretty early for anyone to come calling. Is either of you expecting someone?"

"Not I," Dickce said.

"Me either." Benjy pushed his chair back. "I'll go see who it is, and then I probably need to rescue Clementine from looking after Peanut and Endora."

"Thank you, Benjy," the sisters said in near unison.

"It might be Kanesha," Dickce said. "Or do you suppose it could be Hadley?" She brightened.

"Kanesha, perhaps," An'gel said. "But I can't see Hadley ringing our doorbell at eight fifteen in the morning."

An'gel heard two feminine voices in the hallway as their unexpected guests approached. She and Dickce rose from their chairs.

Benjy ushered in Barbie Gross and Lottie MacLeod. Both women appeared excited.

"Morning, girls," Barbie said. "Sorry to burst in on you like this." She glanced at the table. "But I see you've been having breakfast, so you can handle the news."

"What news?" An'gel said, trying not to sound annoyed or impatient.

"We had to tell you in person." Lottie's voice dropped to a hoarse whisper as she continued. "Sarinda's ghost is haunting her house."

150

CHAPTER 14

"*That* is about the most ridiculous thing I've ever heard."

An'gel frowned and shook her head. "Even coming from the two of you, and I've heard plenty of ridiculous things from you before."

Lottie stepped back as if An'gel had offered to slap her.

"Well, who wee-weed in *your* grits this morning, Miss An'gel Ducote?" Barbie snorted. "If you would stop and listen, instead of popping off at the mouth the minute somebody pauses, you'd hear the whole story." She pulled Lottie forward again. "Why don't you offer us coffee, and we'll tell you all about it."

An'gel, though annoyed with herself for her outburst, still felt irritated with Barbie and Lottie. "Dickce, would you mind asking Clementine to make us a fresh pot of coffee? In the meantime, ladies, why don't we move to the parlor?"

"Fine with us," Barbie said.

Dickce headed for the kitchen, trailed by Benjy, and An'gel led the two unexpected guests to the front parlor. She bade Barbie and Lottie be seated, indicating the sofa. She chose a chair facing them across the coffee table. She eyed their morning attire. Both women wore silk tracksuits and sneakers. Not exactly what she would choose to make an impromptu call on friends.

Dickce walked into the room and announced, "Coffee will be ready in a few minutes." She took the chair near her sister's.

"So what is all this about a ghost in Sarinda's house?" An'gel hoped her tone didn't sound surly to their guests. She could almost hear Dickce telling her to chill.

"Let's get one thing straight," Barbie said. "I didn't say I believed in the ghost, and neither did Lottie. We came here to tell you about it. I think we all need to put our heads together to figure out what's going on at Sarinda's house."

"I see," An'gel said. *Why didn't you tell us that in the first place?* She kept her expression bland.

"How did you find out about the so-called

ghost?" Dickce asked. "Did you see it yourself?"

Lottie's eyes grew round, and she shivered. "No, thank heavens. I don't know what I'd do if I came face-to-face with a real live spirit."

"It wasn't a ghost, I keep telling you that." Barbie rolled her eyes. "You'd pass out and wee all over yourself if you ever did see one. Neither of us saw the light in Sarinda's house. One of Sarinda's neighbors told us about it this morning in swim class."

"You really ought to come join us," Lottie said. "It does wonders for your joints."

"Thank you for the invitation," An'gel said. "I'll keep that in mind if my joints start acting up."

"Which neighbor of Sarinda's told you about the ghost?" Dickce asked in a more diplomatic tone.

"The one who lives directly across the street, Mrs. Harrington," Barbie replied. "She apparently stays up late at night writing in one of the front rooms of her house, and her desk looks straight out the window at Sarinda's place."

"She was working last night," Lottie said. "I believe she's writing a cookbook. It was about midnight." She turned to Barbie. "Wasn't that what she said? Midnight?"

"Yes," Barbie replied. "Anyway, she was working, and she stopped for a few minutes to rest her shoulders. She was staring out the window, and she suddenly noticed a small light moving around in Sarinda's house. From what she said, I think it was her parlor."

"Couldn't it have been the reflection of a headlight from a car passing by?" An'gel asked.

"We thought of that." Barbie glared at her hostess. "You're not the only two who read murder mysteries, you know. Barbie and I both read them. Anyway, I asked Mrs. Harrington that same question, and she said the street was quiet. They hardly ever have traffic that late at night."

"Besides," Lottie added on a triumphant note, "she could see the light going up the stairs after a few minutes. You know how Sarinda has that huge glass front door, and the staircase is straight ahead of it when you walk into the house."

"And she just happened to have a pair of opera glasses nearby," Barbie added. "I think she snoops on her neighbors, frankly, because who keeps opera glasses in their front room? Anyway, she snatched up her glasses when she saw the light start going up the stairs, and she looked, and all she could see was the light. No outline of a body, nothing. Only the light."

"Are there any lights on inside Sarinda's house?" An'gel asked.

Barbie and Lottie looked at each other and shrugged.

"Any outside light?" Dickce asked.

"There's a streetlight by the sidewalk right between her house and the one to the north," Barbie said after a moment's thought. "We drove by the house before we came here, and there weren't any outside lights on that we could see from the street."

"We didn't notice any lights on inside, either," Lottie said. "But it would have been hard to tell without getting out of the car and walking around the house. It was daylight outside."

"If you're trying to make out that the light Mrs. Harrington saw was a reflection from an outside light or one from inside, I think you're wrong," Barbie said. "She saw what she saw."

"All right." An'gel put up her hands in a gesture of surrender. "Mrs. Harrington saw the light, and it went up the stairs. Did she see it upstairs?"

"I don't think so," Lottie replied. "If the person with the light stayed toward the back of the upper floors, Mrs. Harrington couldn't have seen anything."

"Sarinda's bedroom is at the back of the house, you know," Lottie said.

"Yes, we remember that," Dickce said.

"Somebody was snooping," Barbie said. "I'm wondering what it is they were looking for."

"Yes, me, too," Lottie added. "Sarinda kept all her jewelry in a safe deposit box at the bank. If the ghost was looking for diamonds, he was bound to be disappointed."

"If you really believe there was an intruder in Sarinda's house last night," An'gel said, "then you should inform the police."

"We did that." Barbie shot An'gel a smug look. "They said they would go talk to Mrs. Harrington. I'm sure they'll check with Sarinda's other neighbors to find out if they saw anything."

An'gel found her patience wearing thin. Most of the time she didn't find Barbie and Lottie so annoying, but today they were.

Clementine entered the room, pushing a rolling cart. She brought it to a stop by the coffee table and commenced to unload its contents onto the table. In addition to the large carafe of coffee and the necessary accoutrements, An'gel saw a plate of cookies. Clementine knew their guests well, because

Barbie and Lottie could never resist Clementine's cookies.

"Thank you so much, Clementine." Barbie's eyes shone when she saw the treats.

"Yes, thank you," Lottie said. "You make the best cookies in Athena."

"You're welcome, ladies," Clementine said with a wink at An'gel. "I'm glad you enjoy them." She left the room.

While An'gel poured and served the coffee, the guests picked up their plates and loaded them with cookies.

"If there's anything to find," An'gel said in a return to the previous subject, "I'm sure the police will find it. I'd like to talk about another matter with you. I was going to call you this morning."

"What matter?" Barbie bit a chunk out of an oatmeal raisin cookie.

"Dickce and I have been thinking lately about getting someone to assist Clementine." An'gel smiled before she went on mendaciously, "Actually, Clementine is hinting about retiring, and we thought we'd get someone in that she could train to take her place when she finally does leave." She shot a warning glance at her sister and hoped that their guests didn't notice.

"You certainly can't have my housekeeper," Barbie said. "I'd claw both your

157

eyes out if you tried to hire her away from me."

"You can't have mine either." Lottie sounded alarmed. She dropped a piece of cookie on the sofa and then snatched it up. "I wouldn't know what to do without her."

"You don't need to get all upset," Dickce said. "An'gel and I wouldn't think of trying to hire your housekeepers away from you. We know how you depend on them."

"We already have a couple of candidates in mind," An'gel said, "but we don't know if they're still in the area. We wanted to see if you knew anything."

"Who are they?" Barbie sipped from her coffee.

"They both used to work at Ashton Hall," Dickce said.

"Good heavens," Barbie said. "You're not talking about that awful woman, Mrs. Turnipseed, are you? You wouldn't want her." She shook her head. "Besides, she'd have to be close to eighty by now."

"Isn't she still working at Ashton Hall?" Lottie asked. "She was there for nearly forever."

"No, she left when Hamish died, apparently," An'gel said. "I couldn't remember how old she is, and if she's that age, she probably wouldn't want to work any longer."

"Still, if we could talk to her, she might know what happened to that wonderful housemaid Callie had," Dickce said. "Callie always seemed happy with her work, and if she's around and in need of a job, she might fit the bill nicely."

Barbie stared at her, then fixed her gaze on An'gel. "What's going on here? First you want to talk to an eighty-year-old woman, then you want to talk to a woman who worked for Callie Partridge *forty* years ago? Come on, what's the real story?"

An'gel shrugged. Barbie was shrewder than she'd thought, although Lottie looked slightly bewildered. An'gel decided to tell at least part of the truth. They hadn't brought up the remains found at Ashton Hall, so they probably hadn't heard about them yet.

"Now that Hadley's back, and he says he has no idea what happened to Callie," An'gel said, "we got to wondering what *did* happen to her. Dickce and I discussed it, and we decided that Mrs. Turnipseed and the housemaid — Coriander Simpson is her name, I'm pretty sure — might tell us what happened at Ashton Hall right after Hadley left."

"They might be able to shed some light on why Callie ran away," Dickce said.

"I for one am having a hard time believing Hadley when he says he wasn't in love with Callie." Barbie's eyes narrowed. "They were close. I caught them with their heads together more than once at the country club and at parties. They always looked guilty, too. Something was going on between them."

"You're right," Lottie said. "They spent an awful lot of time together, and Callie a married woman." She sniffed.

"As I recall it, Hadley also spent a fair amount of time chasing after a number of different women." An'gel stared hard at Barbie. "Word at the country club was that he caught more than a few of them. Some of them were even married at the time."

"If you're talking about me, An'gel Ducote, why don't you come out and say it?" Barbie reached for another cookie.

"All right, I will, Barbara Gross," An'gel replied. "There were plenty of rumors going around that you were one of Hadley's conquests, and your husband was still in the picture back then."

"I'll admit I flirted with Hadley for all I was worth," Barbie said. "But *all* I did was flirt. I loved my husband, but he was on the dull side and got duller every day he aged. Hadley was never dull. He also never got me into bed, although he tried."

"What about you, Lottie?" Dickce asked. "There were stories about you and Hadley as well."

Lottie blushed. "My husband and I hadn't been married long back then, and he was gone half the time on business. I got a bit lonely, and when Hadley paid me attention, I couldn't help but respond."

"You never told me that," Barbie said.

"We weren't good friends then like we are now," Lottie said. "Now I tell you *every* thing. But don't start thinking Hadley got me into bed, either, but it wasn't for lack of trying. My husband would have killed both of us if he'd thought I cheated on him."

An'gel said wryly, "Hadley flirted with every woman in a two-hundred-mile radius."

"Including the two of you," Barbie said with a hint of rancor.

"Yes, including us." Dickce smiled. "Hadley is mighty good at it. But flirting was as far he got with either of us."

An'gel heard the front door open. Then Benjy's voice saying, "Please come in. I'm sure they'll be happy to see you."

Peanut loped into the room with Endora riding on his back. He came immediately up to An'gel and woofed. Endora hopped down, walked over to Dickce, and climbed into her lap.

Barbie and Lottie appeared bemused by the sudden intrusion. Before An'gel could apologize for the animals, Benjy walked into the room, trailed by Reba Dalrymple and her son, Martin.

Reba made a beeline for An'gel without acknowledging the presence of anyone else.

"Have you heard what they found at Ashton Hall?" Reba asked, her eyes alight with excitement. She gave An'gel no time to respond. "They dug up Callie Partridge."

CHAPTER 15

Peanut and Endora were both evidently startled by Reba's loud voice and abrupt approach to An'gel. Endora dug her claws into Dickce's lap before she launched herself onto the floor and ran away. Peanut chased after the cat, barking, and Benjy went after the animals.

Grateful for the thick weave of her skirt that protected her legs from the cat's claws, Dickce thought for a minute that Lottie MacLeod's eyeballs were going to pop right out of her face when she heard what Reba said about Callie. She knew there was nothing funny about finding remains at Ashton Hall, but she had to suppress a snort of laughter at the sight of Lottie's face.

Barbie's expression was almost as comical, she thought. Both women were speechless, and that was something that rarely ever happened.

"As a matter of fact, Reba," An'gel said,

"we were there when the remains were found yesterday morning. Why don't you and Martin have a seat, and I'll go see about more coffee, if you'd like some."

After staring hard for a moment at her hostess, Reba accepted the offer of coffee and seated herself between Barbie and Lottie on the sofa. Martin wandered over to the desk and sat there. From what Dickce could see, he was simply staring out the front window.

An'gel had barely left the room before Reba demanded, "What were you two doing at Ashton Hall yesterday morning?"

Dickce thought Reba sounded resentful, or perhaps she was jealous. Dickce wondered why Reba would be jealous. She said, "We went over because Hadley asked us to. He wanted to talk to us about his plans to restore the gardens. He wants to bring them back to how they were when his mother was alive."

"Mrs. Partridge did have the greenest thumb around," Reba said. She glanced at Barbie, then at Lottie. "You two didn't get to know her, because she died around the time you moved here. My mother was one of her dearest friends, so we naturally spent a fair amount of time at Ashton Hall."

"Is that right?" Barbie said. "I seem to

have heard that somewhere before." She grimaced at the back of Reba's head as Reba turned to smile at Lottie. "Many times."

Dickce noted that Reba didn't acknowledge the dig, although she would have sworn that Reba's nostrils flared briefly.

Instead, Reba said in the same airy tone she'd used before, "Yes, Mother and Mrs. Partridge were the best of friends. They were at Sweet Briar together in its early days, you know."

"Really?" Barbie said. "I didn't think it opened until *after* the Civil War."

Dickce had to work hard not to snigger this time. Reba talked about her mother going to Sweet Briar all the time, and they had all tired of it long ago. Barbie, however, was the only one who tried to break Reba of the habit by being rude about it.

Thus far, rudeness appeared to have had little effect.

Dickce figured she'd better intervene before the claws came out any further. "We were all upset at the sight of bones," she said. "But you shouldn't jump to conclusions. We don't know that the remains are Callie's. They could be far older."

"Where were these remains?" Barbie asked.

"Near a really old tree on the side of the house," Dickce said.

"Do you think they could be Native American?" Lottie shivered. "What if Ashton Hall is built over a Native American burial ground? That's scary."

"What on earth are you talking about now?" An'gel asked.

Dicke glanced up at her sister and was not surprised to see her frowning.

"We were discussing the remains," Dickce said, "and I warned everybody not to jump to conclusions. Lottie simply asked whether they could be Native American."

"I see." An'gel resumed her seat. "The coffee will be ready in a few minutes."

"But what if they really are what's left of Callie?" Reba asked. "How did they get there? That's what I want to know."

"Do you think Callie was murdered?" Barbie asked. "Who on earth would want to murder her? I didn't know her that long, but she seemed like a sweet person. Not the kind of woman who gets murdered, for heaven's sake."

"Hamish was terribly possessive of her," Reba said. "When Hadley disappeared, she might have decided to go after him. But then Hamish found out and killed her in a fit of jealous rage."

Dickce didn't like the note of smug self-satisfaction in Reba's voice. She looked sharply at the other woman.

"That's horrible," Lottie said, obviously distressed.

"I agree," Dickce said. "You have to presume a lot to come up with those conclusions."

"What do you mean?" Reba asked.

Dickce ticked them off on her fingers. "First, you have to presume that Hadley was in love with Callie, and second, that Hamish told his brother to leave Ashton Hall because of it. Third, that Callie was so in love with Hadley that she was willing to run away from her husband. Fourth, that Hamish was in such a tremendous rage that he killed his own wife when she said she was leaving him, and, fifth, buried her practically in his own front yard without anybody noticing." She paused and looked at her fingers. "I think that's it. Five things you have to presume."

"Did anyone ever ask Hamish Partridge what happened to his wife?" Barbie asked. "I don't remember seeing him around much, once word got out that both Hadley and Callie were gone."

"I talked to him a couple of weeks after everyone realized Hadley was gone, and by

167

that time, we realized no one had seen Callie around during that period," Reba said. "Poor man. I asked about Callie, and all he would say was that she was gone. No other explanation, and I didn't feel that I could question him further." She shrugged. "I took it to mean she'd run away with Hadley, and that was the end of it."

"Except now we know that maybe it wasn't," Barbie said.

Dickce waggled her fingers in Barbie's direction.

"Yes, that's presuming a lot," Barbie said in response. "But surely if Ashton Hall were built on a Native American site, they would have found evidence of it when they were building it."

"But that was nearly two hundred years ago," An'gel said. "At the time, if they had discovered anything, they might not have thought too much about it. They didn't have a lot of respect for Native American culture in the early nineteenth century."

"That's true," Dickce said.

Clementine brought in the fresh pot of coffee then, along with extra cups. She accepted their thanks and withdrew.

An'gel poured coffee for Reba and Martin first. Martin had been so quiet that Dickce had forgotten he was in the room. She noticed now that he had his phone out, and his gaze seemed focused on it, even as he accepted his coffee.

An'gel offered refills to Barbie and Lottie, but they declined. An'gel set down the carafe and leaned back in her chair.

"How long is it going to take before they decide who was buried there?" Barbie asked.

"Several weeks at least, if not two or three months," Dickce said.

"Can't they match up dental records?" Lottie asked. "I've heard of that, and surely it can't be that hard."

"If they have access to the records," Barbie said, "it probably *isn't* all that hard. But that was forty years ago. Who knows what could have happened to any dental records Callie might have had?"

"I hope it does turn out to be a Native American burial from centuries ago," Reba said. "That would mean poor Callie might still be alive somewhere."

"There ought to be one way to tell," Lottie said. "Grave goods."

Dickce stared blankly at Lottie for a moment. The she realized Lottie was right. Native Americans, from what she knew, did bury their dead with objects of different kinds.

"Did you see any grave goods?" Barbie asked.

An'gel answered. "No, all we saw were a few bones."

Dickce had not mentioned the ring Endora found, and An'gel apparently wasn't going to mention it either. Had the ring, however, been the grave goods buried with Callie? She shivered at the thought.

"They might have been looted by the Partridge that built Ashton Hall. So all they could have found was the bones."

Dickce glanced toward the front window in surprise. Martin evidently was paying attention to the conversation, though she had assumed he was focused solely on his phone. After those two sentences, though, he turned back to the device.

"That's an excellent point, darling," Reba called out. "Thank you." Martin did not appear to hear his mother, Dickce noted. *Perhaps he's used to tuning her out.* They had an odd relationship, or so it seemed to Dickce. Martin acted more like a henpecked husband than he did a son, but he appeared content to let his mother run his life.

"We can speculate all we want among ourselves about those remains," An'gel said. "But I think we should all be careful around

170

Hadley and not bring them up unless he does."

"Yes, it must be terribly upsetting to him," Lottie said. "To think that your own brother might have killed his wife and buried her in the garden."

"We'll have to rally around him and give him all the support he needs." Barbie assumed a doleful expression. "Poor Hadley."

Dickce could picture it now. A steady stream of casseroles and various delicacies making their way to Ashton Hall, all borne there by women eager to offer solace to the master of the house. She permitted herself a brief smile. Hadley might actually enjoy the attention, unless he had changed dramatically in the past forty years.

"How did they find the bones in the first place?"

Once again Martin Dalrymple startled them all by speaking from his seat at the desk.

"An excellent question, darling," Reba said. "Yes, just how *did* they find the remains? You never told us that part."

"And how you came to be there when it happened," Barbie added.

"I told you that already," Dickce said. "Hadley asked us over to consult on the garden."

"Hadley had pictures of the gardens from when his mother was still living, and he wanted us — well, me, actually — to help him identify plants. We were discussing roses, I believe, when Benjy came in with Peanut to tell us there was something Hadley needed to see right away." An'gel glanced at Dickce.

"Yes, that's right," Dickce said. "We went out with Benjy to the side of the house where an old tree had come down. Hadley said the tree was dying, and the storm uprooted it. There, in the disturbed ground near it, was where we saw the remains."

"They weren't actually under the tree?" Barbie asked.

"No, I don't believe so. They were in the ground near the trunk, however," An'gel replied.

"Did Native Americans place burials beside trees? Do any of you know?" Barbie asked. "I think I'll go to the library and look that up." She stood. "Come on, Lottie, we don't want to outstay our welcome."

"Goodness, no," Lottie said as she popped up from the sofa. "Thank you for the coffee and those delicious cookies, An'gel, Dickce."

Nice words considering you showed up at the door without letting us know you were coming. Dickce smiled as she and An'gel

172

rose to see their guests out. She saw An'gel look pointedly at Reba.

"Come along, Martin," Reba said. "We'd better be going, too. I'm sure An'gel and Dickce have things to do." She waited until Martin approached her and held out a hand to assist her before she rose from the sofa. "I'm sure we'll all be talking more about this in the days to come."

"No doubt," Dickce murmured as she trailed behind the group headed for the front door, preceded by An'gel.

The moment the door closed behind the visitors, An'gel turned to Dickce. "Thank the Lord they're gone. I couldn't believe they all showed up on our doorstep like that without even calling first."

"Curiosity is more powerful than good manners, I reckon." Dickce shrugged. "They probably realized that if they had called first, we would have told them we were too busy."

"We certainly would have," An'gel said. "Now that they're gone, I am moving ahead with my plan. I need to talk to Kanesha."

Dickce was struck by a sudden thought. "I wonder why Arliss didn't show up. Since the others did, I'm surprised she didn't pop in, too."

"Perhaps she hasn't heard about the

discovery at Ashton Hall," An'gel said. "Nor the ghost at Sarinda's place. Interesting that Barbie and Lottie didn't bring that up after Reba arrived."

"Reba didn't exactly give them much chance," Dickce said. "By then they were probably more interested in hearing about the remains and speculating on whose they are."

"True," An'gel said. "I wonder if the police have checked Sarinda's house yet. Perhaps Kanesha will know. I'm going to call her right now." She walked back into the parlor to use the phone.

Dickce stood where she was, lost in thought. An idea had occurred to her, and she wondered for a moment why neither she nor An'gel had thought of it before. While An'gel talked to Kanesha, Dickce went to look for Benjy. He was just the person to carry out her idea.

CHAPTER 16

An'gel debated whether to call Kanesha's cell phone. She preferred not to unless there was an emergency, and she couldn't justify wanting to poke her nose into the investigation as an emergency.

Instead she punched in the number for the sheriff's department. "Good morning, this is An'gel Ducote. Could I speak to Chief Deputy Berry if she's available?" She was put on hold for a moment, and then the receptionist came back on the line to inform her that the chief deputy was not available at the moment. An'gel declined to leave a message and ended the call.

Now what to do? She could get her own cell phone and send Kanesha a text message, although she rarely used that feature and felt awkward when she did. After debating with herself for a moment longer, she decided she might as well send a text. Where was her cell phone?

After several minutes of an increasingly annoying search, An'gel found the phone on the dressing table in her bedroom. She picked it up and hunted for the icon for messaging, and after a couple of false starts, she got to the right place and managed to send Kanesha a brief request to give her a call when she could.

She took the phone downstairs with her, hoping to hear from the deputy soon. In the meantime, she wanted to discuss strategy with Dickce. An'gel didn't find her sister in the parlor or in any of the nearby rooms. She headed to the kitchen where she found Clementine busy with preparations for lunch.

"Smells wonderful," An'gel said as she caught a whiff from the pot of meat sauce the housekeeper was stirring on the stove. "Pasta for lunch, then."

"Yes, ma'am." Clementine smiled. "By special request. Benjy said he sure would love some of my spaghetti and meat sauce for lunch today."

"You're spoiling that boy," An'gel said in a mock-complaining tone. "He's got you and my sister wrapped around his fingers."

Clementine knew her employer well enough to know that An'gel wasn't really bothered by the choice of meal. "There's just something about that boy makes you want to mother him. I'm glad you and Miss Dickce took him in. Livens up the place, that's for sure."

"He definitely needs mothering," An'gel said. "When I think of that horror of a mother he had, well, it's a wonder he turned out to be such a smart, sensible young man."

"He's going to be a credit to you and Miss Dickce," Clementine said.

"Speaking of my sister," An'gel said as she remembered why she came into the kitchen, "do you know where she is?"

"With Benjy," Clementine said. "Came in here and said she wanted him to look up something on his computer."

"I think I'd better go find out what those two are up to," An'gel said. "The last time they were plotting behind my back we ended up with a dog and a cat." She headed for the back door, cell phone in hand.

"Lunch is going to be ready in about an hour," Clementine called after her.

"I'll tell them," An'gel said before she stepped outside.

Though the sun shone brightly, the air was cool. An'gel hurried across the area between the back of the house and the garage. Benjy lived in an apartment over the garage and appeared to be happy with it. An'gel had thought he would be fine in the house with her and her sister, but Dickce insisted that a young man Benjy's age would prefer to have his own separate space.

She and Dickce had the apartment renovated, however, before Benjy moved in. After a six-week project, the space had a more modern look, with every thought given to comfort and the needs of a young man. An'gel opened the door to the stairs and stepped inside.

When she arrived at the top, An'gel paused on the small landing to catch her breath. She glanced around the space and noted with approval that Benjy continued to keep things neat and tidy. Benjy and Dickce were seated at the table in the small kitchen, and they were staring at the screen of Benjy's laptop.

Peanut came loping out of the bedroom at the far end, and he made a beeline for An'gel. He greeted her with several gentle woofs, and she patted him on the head and told him what a good boy he was. His tail thumped against the floor. An'gel wondered where Endora was. She spotted her in Dickce's lap.

"Your timing is perfect, Sister," Dickce said. "I was about to call you so you could see what Benjy found. Come look."

Intrigued, An'gel walked over to the table and stood behind Benjy and Dickce. She bent down between the two to peer more closely at the screen and the small print she saw there. "What am I looking at?"

"An address in Athena for Mrs. Thomasina Turnipseed," Benjy said. "Miss Dickce asked me to help her find this lady, and we did."

Benjy started to explain how he had found the information she and Dickce wanted, but An'gel forestalled him. When Benjy got to talking about the Internet, he quickly lost her most of the time. Benjy took no offense when An'gel stopped him, she was thankful to see. He simply grinned at her and winked.

"The short version is that I found her through property tax records," Benjy said.

"We checked the phone book first," Dickce said, "but she isn't listed."

"How recent is the property tax record?" An'gel said.

"It's for the most recent tax year," Benjy replied. "So the information isn't quite a year old."

"Once you've got permission from Kanesha," Dickce said, "we can drive over to her house and see if she'll talk to us."

"I haven't been able to talk to Kanesha

yet," An'gel said. "I sent her a text message asking her to call me when she can."

Her cell phone rang, startling her so much that she almost dropped it. She steadied it and glanced at the screen. "Not Kanesha," she said. "Barbie Gross. What on earth can she want now?"

An'gel greeted her caller and waited for Barbie to explain.

"I'm calling a special meeting of the garden club board for this afternoon," Barbie said. "We need to put our heads together about some kind of memorial service for Sarinda. She didn't have any family, and we're the next closest thing."

"That's a kind thought," An'gel said, "but we don't even know when Sarinda's body will be released. Plus she may have left instructions with her lawyer."

"I'm not talking about her funeral," Barbie said, her tone sharp. "What I think we should do is a memorial service for her, and we don't need her body for that. And we don't need instructions from her lawyer, either."

"I see. What time is this meeting?" An'gel asked.

"Three o'clock at my house," Barbie said. "Can I count on you and Dickce to be there?"

180

"Yes, we'll be there." She ended the call and set her phone on the table.

"Where are we going?" Dickce asked. "And when?"

After An'gel explained, Dickce frowned but otherwise offered no objection to the meeting.

"Do you want to make a call on Mrs. Turnipseed before we go to the meeting?" Dickce asked.

"If I hear back from Kanesha in time and she has no objection," An'gel replied. "I'm eager to talk to Mrs. Turnipseed."

"I hope she'll talk to you," Benjy said. "From what Hadley said, though, she could be difficult."

"We'll have to try." An'gel rose and picked up her phone. "Lunch should be ready soon. I'll see you at the table."

Peanut accompanied her down the stairs and would have followed her to the house, but Benjy called him back. He hesitated a moment, then trotted up the stairs. An'gel smiled as she closed the door behind her. Benjy had done a good job training the dog. An'gel wasn't sure whether he had tried to train Endora. Somehow she didn't think Endora would go along with any such attempts.

Her phone rang, and this time, An'gel was

happy to see, the caller was Kanesha Berry. "Hello," she said. "Thanks for returning my call."

"My pleasure, Miss An'gel," Kanesha said. "What can I do for you?" She listened without interruption while An'gel explained her plan.

"What do you think?" An'gel asked once she finished.

Kanesha didn't respond for a moment. "Normally, I would ask you to leave this to me, but I am familiar with Mrs. Turnipseed. You're right about her attitudes. I could send Bates, I suppose, but he can be pretty gruff with witnesses. I think under the circumstances it might be okay for you and Miss Dickce to try talking to her first."

"Thank you," An'gel said. "We will do our best not to make you regret your confidence in us."

Kanesha chuckled, a rare sound. "I'm sure you will. Y'all take care now."

An'gel thanked her and wished her a good day before she ended the call. She entered the house with her mind focused on the best approach to take with Mrs. Turnipseed when they found her.

When they left the house at twelve forty, An'gel declared that she would drive. In the car, she waited for Dickce to fasten her seat belt, and then she backed out of the garage.

When they reached the end of the driveway and An'gel prepared to turn onto the highway, Dickce spoke. "I looked up the address on a city map, and it's not far from the square. Would you mind stopping at the bookstore for a minute so I can run in and pick up a book they're holding for me?"

An'gel sighed. "I suppose not." She preferred not to stop, but Dickce would get annoyed with her if they didn't.

The bookstore occupied a space down the street from the point at which they entered the square. Traffic was heavy, and An'gel had to drive slowly.

Dickce clutched at her arm suddenly. "Look over there."

"Where?" An'gel said.

"There, going into Helen Louise's bistro." Dickce pointed.

An'gel glanced over in time to see Hadley Partridge open the door and usher Arliss McGonigal inside. Then the car in front of them started moving, and An'gel had to switch her attention back to the street ahead of them.

Dickce giggled suddenly. "Oh, my, this is going to be interesting."

"What?" An'gel said. With traffic moving

she wasn't going to look and risk running into the car in front of her. "What did you see now?"

"Barbie Gross just came out, carrying a box, and she looks peeved at something. Or someone."

"You're imagining things." An'gel was happy to find an open parking spot right in front of the bookstore. She pulled into it.

"I'm not going to waste time arguing with you." Dickce unbuckled her seat belt. "I'll be back in a minute or two." She slipped out of the car and shut the door.

An'gel watched as her sister entered the store. She thought about what Dickce said. An'gel knew what her sister was thinking, that Barbie was annoyed over the fact that Hadley and Arliss were going around together. Unless Hadley took turns squiring all of the garden club board members around, most of them were bound to be peeved at not getting attention from him.

For Pete's sake, An'gel thought, *we're not in high school. We're all old enough not to fall into these traps.*

Dickce was as good as her word. She returned promptly to the car, book in hand. In a moment they were on their way to Mrs. Turnipseed's house.

Dickce directed her to the right street, and

not more than five minutes later they pulled up in front of the house. The neighborhood was an older one of smallish houses on large lots. The lawns all looked well-kept, except for that of Mrs. Turnipseed. The grass needed cutting, and the house could have used a fresh coat of paint, An'gel thought. The house looked unoccupied, and that worried her.

She and Dickce walked up to the front door, rang the bell, and waited.

CHAPTER 17

An'gel was about to ring the bell again when the door opened abruptly.

A tall, angular, gray-haired woman, around eighty years of age, dressed in a calf-length dressing gown and flat-soled shoes, stared at them. "What do you want?" Her tone sounded belligerent, An'gel thought.

She wasn't about to let that faze her, however. "Mrs. Turnipseed?" After the woman nodded, she said in a pleasant tone, "Perhaps you remember me? I'm An'gel Ducote. This is my sister Dickce Ducote."

Mrs. Turnipseed said, "I remember you, sure. What can I do for you?"

"I know this is an imposition, just showing up on your doorstep," An'gel said, "but if we could have a few minutes of your time, we'd like to talk to you."

Mrs. Turnipseed stared at them a moment. An'gel thought the woman was about to slam the door in their faces. Instead, she stepped back and waved them in.

An'gel entered, Dickce right behind her. Based on what she'd seen of the yard and the outside of the house, An'gel expected signs of similar neglect inside. Her jaw nearly dropped, however, when she walked into the small living room.

Opulently furnished with antique furniture, the room looked spotless. There was a scent of lemon furniture polish in the air, and every surface gleamed. An'gel suspected the large rug on the floor was Aubusson. It reminded her of their own carpets at River-hill. She wondered whether Hamish Partridge had given Mrs. Turnipseed these beautiful furnishings or whether they'd been in her family for several generations.

"What a beautiful room," Dickce said with an appreciative smile.

"Yes, it certainly is," An'gel said.

Mrs. Turnipseed nodded to acknowledge the compliment. She pointed to the sofa. "Why don't y'all have a seat, ladies?"

"Thank you," An'gel said. She and Dickce did as their hostess directed. Mrs. Turnipseed chose a chair that faced the sofa across an ornately carved coffee table. She stared at them, evidently waiting for them to speak.

"Again, we apologize for dropping by unannounced," An'gel said.

"You said that already. What is it you want?" Mrs. Turnipseed crossed her arms over her flat chest.

An'gel didn't appreciate her rude tone and, under different circumstances, wouldn't have tolerated it. Now, however, she and Dickce needed information from this woman, so she let it pass.

"You worked for many years for a friend of ours, Hamish Partridge," An'gel said. After Mrs. Turnipseed nodded, she continued. "I'm sure you're aware of the fact that Hamish left everything to his brother Hadley in his will."

Mrs. Turnipseed scowled at the mention of Hadley's name. She did not speak, though, so An'gel forged ahead.

"We've seen Hadley since he returned to town," An'gel said. "He seemed to be quite surprised that no one knew anything about the whereabouts of his late brother's wife, Callie." She paused to gauge Mrs. Turnipseed's reaction. There was none that she could discern.

"At the time Hadley went away," Dickce said, "no one seemed to know why he left so abruptly. Then, when it turned out Callie was gone, too, well, people just assumed she had gone with him."

"But Hadley says she didn't," An'gel

added. "And Hamish never would say anything about it either."

Mrs. Turnipseed shrugged. "Mr. Hamish didn't have to share his private business with anyone."

"We respected his privacy at the time," An'gel said, "but perhaps that was a mistake. Callie disappeared, and if she didn't run off to join Hadley, what happened to her? Can you tell us anything about it?"

"I don't see that it matters none now." Mrs. Turnipseed shrugged again. "That was forty years ago. What she did was her business, that Mrs. Partridge. All I know is, she was gone, and Mr. Partridge never mentioned her name to me the rest of his life."

"He didn't tell you *anything* about why she left or where she went?" Dickce said.

"Wasn't my business," Mrs. Turnipseed replied. "Look here, I wasn't even there when Mrs. Partridge up and left. I was gone to my sister's house to visit a few days, and when I come back, well, Mrs. Partridge and that no-good Hadley were gone. Mr. Partridge never offered to explain, and I didn't ask. Wasn't my business."

"I see." An'gel felt suddenly deflated. She had been so sure that Mrs. Turnipseed would know something about Callie's disappearance. She wondered whether the former housekeeper had heard about the discovery at Ashton Hall. If she hadn't, should she and Dickce be the ones to break the news?

She glanced at her sister, and Dickce raised her eyebrows. An'gel had no doubt Dickce knew exactly what she was thinking. After a moment, An'gel decided she might as well tell Mrs. Turnipseed. The news was probably all over town by now anyway.

"You may not have heard," An'gel said, "but there was a startling discovery at Ashton Hall a couple of days ago. Do you know about it?"

Mrs. Turnipseed tensed and shook her head. "No, I don't."

Noting the reaction, An'gel said, "They discovered the remains of a person on the grounds of the house." She kept her gaze riveted on their hostess.

"Don't see what that has to do with me," Mrs. Turnipseed said. "Not my business what they find." She stood. "Now, if you don't mind, ladies, I've got an appointment I have to get to."

An'gel was certain the woman knew something, but she obviously wasn't willing to tell them. The news of the discovery at Ashton Hall had shaken her, An'gel would have bet on it. They couldn't press the matter now, however. She and Dickce stood and followed their hostess to the front door.

"One more thing." An'gel paused on the threshold as she remembered that they had one other person to inquire about. "Do you have any idea where we could find the housemaid that was there at the time? Coriander Simpson, I believe her name was."

"How should I know?" Mrs. Turnipseed scowled. "Not my business to keep up with colored trash." She slammed the door in An'gel's face.

An'gel stood there a moment, furious with Mrs. Turnipseed. The woman was lying, she was certain. The housekeeper knew something about Coriander Simpson.

"Come on, Sister," Dickce said. "She's not going to talk to us anymore. At least for now." She headed down the walk toward the car.

An'gel knew Dickce was right, but she found it hard to let go of her anger.

In the car, Dickce said, "What did you think about that furniture?"

"I was completely surprised," An'gel replied. "It certainly wasn't anything like what I expected."

"I know," Dickce said. "I'd swear that sofa we were sitting on is exactly like the one Hadley's mother had in her bedroom. I used to covet it because it would have been perfect in my bedroom."

"I think you're right," An'gel said after a moment. "That carpet looked familiar, too."

"I wonder what the rest of her house looks like," Dickce said.

"What I'm wondering is, did Hamish *give* her all those furnishings? Surely she didn't just take them after he died?"

"I doubt she'd be that brazen, because Hadley would have the law on her in two seconds flat," Dickce said. "Hamish probably did give them to her. The real question is *why.*"

"A bribe?" An'gel said. "I think we may be onto something. What does that woman know?" She started the car.

"She's a tough nut," Dickce said. "I don't think she's going to tell anybody what she knows, not easily anyway."

"Did you notice her reaction when I told her about the remains that were found?" An'gel said.

"She didn't seem interested, and that was really odd," Dickce said. "She kept saying it wasn't her business. Anybody else would have been more curious about the remains. The fact that she didn't ask questions or really react to the news convinces me she lied to us."

"She was nasty when I asked her about Coriander Simpson." An'gel grimaced. "I could have slapped her right then and there."

"We could have predicted that," Dickce said. "We already knew what she was like in that regard."

"True, but it was still nasty," An'gel said. "What time is it?"

"A little after one thirty," Dickce said.

"It's too early to show up at Barbie's house for the meeting," An'gel said. "I don't feel like driving home and then back again. What shall we do in the meantime to kill ninety minutes?"

"Back to the bookstore," Dickce replied promptly. "We have to go that way, more or less, and I haven't been in to spend any time in . . . I don't know when. I wouldn't mind a chance to browse and chat with Jordan instead of just running in to pick up a book and running out again."

"We'll both end up with a sackful of books by the time we're ready to leave," An'gel said.

"And what's wrong with that?" Dickce grinned. "You know you love looking at books as much as I do."

An'gel didn't reply. She put the car in

gear, and they headed back to the town square.

They spent over an hour chatting with Jordan Thompson, the owner of the bookstore. Jordan had named it The Athenaeum, a play on the town's name, but also a nod to the ancient Greek and Roman places of learning. Jordan knew her customers and their tastes well and never failed to recommend books she knew they would enjoy. As An'gel predicted, they each left the store with a large bag of books.

They arrived at Barbie Gross's house a few minutes before three. Barbie met them at the door and waved them in.

"Come on in, girls, everyone else is here." She ushered them into the living room.

An'gel noticed that the *everyone else* didn't include Hadley Partridge. She wondered whether he'd been invited, but she decided he was probably too busy with the ongoing work at Ashton Hall.

Judging by the other board members' choice of attire for an afternoon meeting, however, An'gel suspected they thought Hadley would be among them. All four of the other women were dressed as if they were about to head out to dinner with a beau. Arliss, An'gel decided, appeared to be wearing the same dress they had seen her in earlier, coming out of Helen Louise Brady's place.

After exchanging greetings with Lottie, Arliss, and Reba, An'gel sat next to Dickce in the same seats they'd occupied a few days ago.

"Where is Hadley?" Reba frowned at their hostess. "I thought surely he'd be here since we invited him back on the board."

Before Barbie could respond, Arliss spoke. "I'm afraid Hadley is swamped at the moment." She laughed. "The poor man has so much to do at Ashton Hall."

"How do you know so much about it?" Reba asked.

"Arliss had lunch with Hadley today," Barbie said in an arch tone. "I ran into them at Helen Louise's when I went to pick up some pastries for our meeting."

Arliss smiled. "I have to admit it, Barbie caught us." She sighed. "I've shared several meals with Hadley. He is still the most charming companion a woman could ask for."

"That was fast work, even for you." Lottie sniffed. "I guess I shouldn't be surprised you're trying to line up husband number three. You've been chasing any man who'd give you a second look for years."

Arliss laughed. "Well, honey, at least I'm

getting second looks, and that's more than I can say for some of you."

Why do women do this? An'gel found it distasteful in the extreme. Women old enough to know better, yet here they were carrying on over a man like, well, the only words she could come up with were vulgar. She didn't even want to soil her thoughts with them.

"Ladies, I think it's time we focused on the reason Barbie called this meeting," An'gel said. "We need to be thinking about our friend and the proper way to pay tribute to her memory and to her contributions to the club."

"Hear, hear," Barbie said. "I checked with the pastor at Sarinda's church, and he says they will be happy to host a memorial. We need to come up with a date, though, and let him know."

"I volunteer to be in charge of the arrangements," Arliss said. "I'll draw up a budget for flowers and food, and we can split the cost among us. Agreed?"

"Sounds fine," An'gel said. "If you need help with anything, let me and Dickce know. We'll be happy to do what we can."

Arliss nodded. She picked up a pad and pen from the table by her chair and started jotting things down as the group discussed the service.

Thirty minutes later the board had a plan everyone agreed upon, and An'gel was relieved that there had been no further mention of Hadley Partridge. He seemed to bring out the worst among the members, and An'gel was weary of dealing with their behavior. She said as much to Dickce as they climbed into the car after the meeting ended.

"Some women think their lives aren't complete if they don't have a man on their arm," Dickce said. "You know that as well as I do, Sister."

"Yes, I do, but it still aggravates me to no end when otherwise intelligent women carry on like they were doing today over Hadley." An'gel sighed and cranked the car. "I'm beginning to wish Hadley had never come back."

CHAPTER 18

"I understand how you feel," Dickce said, "but they'll all settle down soon, especially when they see that Hadley is not going to rescue them from the loneliness of widowhood."

An'gel snorted. "What a ridiculous phrase. *Rescue them from the loneliness of widowhood.* Spare me the purple prose."

"My choice of words aside," Dickce said, slightly nettled by her sister's reaction, "the point is, Hadley's only been back a short while. They'll get over this silly competitiveness for his attention."

"I certainly hope so," An'gel said.

Dickce decided it was time to move on to a different subject. "When are you going to call Kanesha and tell her about our little talk with Mrs. Turnipseed?"

"Right now," An'gel said. "I'm heading to the sheriff's department since's it not all that much out of the way. We might as well talk to her in person if she's in the office."

"Good idea," Dickce said.

Moments later they pulled into the parking lot at the Athena County Sheriff's Department. Inside they inquired whether the chief deputy was available. She was, and soon an officer ushered them into Kanesha's office.

"Good afternoon, Miss An'gel, Miss Dickce." Kanesha rose as they entered and waited until they were seated before she resumed her own seat behind the desk. "Have you got information to share with me?"

"Yes, we do," Dickce said. "We went to talk to Mrs. Turnipseed this afternoon."

"That was fast," Kanesha said. "Did you find out anything useful?"

"Not directly, no," An'gel said. "The woman kept saying everything wasn't her business. According to her, she was out of town visiting her sister when Hadley and Callie left Ashton Hall."

"She claims all that Hamish said to her was that Callie was gone," Dickce added. "Then she said he never mentioned Callie's name again for the rest of his life."

"What did you think of her responses? Was she telling the truth?" Kanesha asked.

"She's holding something back," An'gel

said. "We both thought so."

"Yes, we did," Dickce said. "The other thing is, her living room is full of antique furniture and things that we think came from Ashton Hall."

Kanesha frowned. "Do you think she stole all this stuff?"

"No," Dickce said. "We don't think she'd be that stupid."

"We think Hamish gave it all to her," An'gel said. "But we're wondering exactly *why* he gave it to her."

"For years of faithful service?" Kanesha said, one eyebrow raised.

"One of the pieces — in fact, the very sofa that An'gel and I sat on during the visit — came from Hamish's mother's bedroom," Dickce replied. "Both Hamish and Hadley were devoted to their mother, and I can't see Hamish just handing over something of hers, even as a reward for faithful service."

"Hamish was never known for his generosity," An'gel said. "We approached him time after time to contribute to different charitable causes, and the most he ever gave at one time was fifty dollars." She shook her head. "Getting that much out of him was a major triumph, I can tell you."

"So if I understand where you're going with this, you think he gave Mrs. Turnipseed all these valuable antiques and furnishings in exchange for her silence?" Kanesha asked.

Dickce and An'gel shared a glance, then they said in unison, "We do."

"I agree that it could be a possibility," Kanesha said. "Especially with what you've told me about Mr. Partridge's stinginess and devotion to his late mother. I'll keep that in mind."

"I also asked Mrs. Turnipseed if she knew anything about the whereabouts of Callie Partridge's housemaid, Coriander Simpson," An'gel said. "Her answer to that was extremely nasty and rude."

A faint smile crossed Kanesha's lips. "I can certainly imagine. I've had experience with Mrs. Turnipseed before."

"We both think the housemaid might know something useful," Dickce said. "Do you know anything about her?"

"Only that she's no longer in the area, as far as we can determine," Kanesha said. "We haven't found any family of hers, either, and that's a bit odd."

"We'll check with Clementine," An'gel said. "If anyone knows anything about her, Clementine will. I meant to ask her this morning but I forgot."

"If you do get any leads, I know you'll pass

201

them on to me," Kanesha said. "In the meantime, I have a little news for you."

"What?" Dickce said eagerly.

"The police department investigated the ghost that was allegedly roaming around in Miss Hetherington's house," Kanesha said. "According to them, there was evidence of an intruder. The lock on the back door was forced, and several rooms were disturbed. They are checking with her lawyer for an inventory of property to determine whether the intruder took anything of value."

"Sarinda had some jewelry handed down through her family," An'gel said. "We believe she kept that in a safe deposit box at the bank, though."

"Do you think it was just someone who heard about her death who broke in to steal?" Dickce asked. "Or was there some other purpose behind it?"

"A little too early to tell, frankly," Kanesha said. "Until the police and the lawyer check everything and determine whether any valuables are missing, we don't really know."

"If it would help," An'gel said, "Dickce and I would be happy to go through the house with the lawyer. We knew Sarinda for many years and are familiar with much of the contents of her home."

"I will let the police department know,"

Kanesha said.

"Thank you," Dickce said. "Have you found out anything more about the remains from Ashton Hall?"

"Not yet," Kanesha said. "We're consulting with a faculty member from the college who is a physical anthropologist. He has extensive experience with Native American remains and funerary practices. He should be able to tell us pretty soon whether we're dealing with an old burial or a comparatively recent one."

"That's excellent," Dickce said. "We both hope it turns out to be a really old burial. Neither one of us wants it to be poor Callie."

"Either way, there will still be a mystery about what happened to her," An'gel said. "Someone knows the truth, and I frankly think it's Mrs. Turnipseed."

"Would you like for us to try talking to her again?" Dickce asked.

"At the moment, no," Kanesha said. "I will send one of my deputies over to talk to her. He's a good-ole-boy type, and he may have better luck with her. If he doesn't get anywhere, I might ask you to try one more time."

"We'll be glad to," An'gel said.

"Thank you, ladies." Kanesha rose. "I appreciate you coming by. Now, I'm afraid I have to show you out. I've got another case to work on."

The sisters rose. "Of course," An'gel said. "We understand how busy you are."

Back in the car, Dickce said, "I think we should put Benjy to work on finding Coriander Simpson."

"Why so?" An'gel said as she put the car in gear and backed out of the parking space.

"He's smart about computers, for one thing," Dickce said. "I bet he will be able to turn up something as fast as the sheriff's department can. Probably faster."

"Maybe so," An'gel said. "I suppose it can't hurt for him to try."

"As soon as we get home, I'm going to talk to him about it," Dickce said.

Twenty minutes later, Dickce was seated at the table in Benjy's apartment, and the two of them were talking about the search for Coriander Simpson.

"I'll search for her online," Benjy said. "It's an unusual name, and that helps." He thought for a moment. "Do you know whether she was a live-in maid?"

Dickce shook her head. "I don't recall. It's possible she was. I'll check with Hadley, because he will certainly know."

"Good," Benjy said. "If she wasn't live-in,

204

though, I might be able to trace her through old phone directories. Do you know whether the public library has kept any?"

"I'm not sure," Dickce said. "I'd be willing to bet, though, that they have. The Athena Historical Society has worked closely with the library for many years to document the town's history. They've collected all kinds of things, and much of it is housed at the library." She paused for a moment. "And if they don't have it, you might talk to Charlie Harris about the college archive. It could be that the college has some."

"I'll keep that in mind. I'll go to the public library first thing tomorrow and start there," Benjy said. "I can check their databases, too. See if I can find anything about her that way. In the meantime, I'll search tonight at home."

"Thank you, dear," Dickce said. "I have a feeling that if anyone can find Coriander Simpson, it will be you."

Peanut, who had been napping on the floor between Dickce and Benjy, suddenly gave a woof, as if he agreed. Dickce and Benjy laughed. Endora, as usual asleep in Dickce's lap when it was available, yawned and stretched. Dickce rubbed the cat's head for a moment, and Endora purred.

"I guess I'd better get back over to the house," Dickce said. "An'gel is going to ask Clementine if she knows anything about the woman, and I want to hear what she has to say." She gently picked up the cat and set her on the floor. Endora shot her a reproachful look before stalking off, tail straight up in the air, to the couch. She leapt up, found her favorite spot, and curled up.

Dickce shared another laugh with Benjy. She patted his shoulder before she rose. "Dinner should be ready in about an hour. I'll see you at the table."

"Yes, ma'am." Benjy stood to see her to the head of the stairs.

Dickce hurried across the back lawn to the kitchen door. She found her sister inside with their housekeeper. An'gel was talking while Clementine worked at the stove.

". . . such a nasty woman," An'gel was saying. "But I have to say she appears to keep a spotless house."

"Mrs. Turnipseed," Dickce said.

"Yes," An'gel replied. "I was just telling Clementine about our visit with her."

"Better you than me," Clementine said.

"Have you asked yet about Coriander Simpson?" Dickce said.

"I was about to," An'gel replied. She addressed the housekeeper. "Did you know

Mrs. Partridge's housemaid at all, Clementine?"

The housekeeper frowned as she checked a pot of boiling cabbage. "I can't say as rightly I did. I don't think she was from around here."

"What makes you think that?" Dickce asked.

"I'm trying to remember," Clementine said. "I didn't see her much, except every once in a while at church. She kinda kept to herself." She paused. "I believe somebody at church told me they thought she didn't have any people around here."

"I wonder how she came to be in Athena, then," An'gel said.

"Where was it Callie was from?" Dickce said. "I know Hamish met her in Memphis. Was that where she was from?"

"I believe so," An'gel said. "Do you think she might have known Coriander Simpson in Memphis?"

Dickce shrugged. "It's possible. Maybe she had worked for Callie's family, and Callie hired her after she married Hamish."

"I can't remember," An'gel said. "That's entirely possible."

"I think that may be right," Clementine said slowly. "I seem to remember something about Memphis and that Simpson girl." She shook her head. "Can't get it just now, but I'll keep thinking on it."

"Thank you," An'gel said. "I think we'd better get out of your way now and let you finish cooking dinner. Dickce and I will set the table."

"Yes, ma'am," Clementine said. "I hadn't gotten around to that yet."

"I told Benjy dinner would be ready in about an hour," Dickce said. "Was that all right?"

"That's fine," the housekeeper replied.

Dickce followed An'gel to the dining room, and they had the table set in a few minutes.

"Now that we're done with this," Dickce said, "why don't we call Hadley and ask him what he knows about Coriander Simpson?"

"I did that while you were talking with Benjy," An'gel said. "He was out, and the housekeeper didn't know when he'd be back. She said she'd ask him to call us back."

"That's frustrating." Dickce led the way out of the dining room and into the front parlor. "Let's have a drink before dinner."

"Yes," An'gel said. "Your usual?" She walked over to the liquor cabinet.

Dickce nodded. "I wonder if he's out with Arliss again."

"Possibly," An'gel said as she poured the Laphroaig. "He could also be out doing business related to Ashton Hall."

"Of course," Dickce said. "But do you think he's seriously interested in Arliss?"

An'gel shrugged and handed Dickce her whisky. "If he hasn't changed, then, no, I'd say he isn't. But we'll have to see. Surely after forty years he's matured and grown out of that idle playboy phase."

"I would certainly hope so." Dickce sipped at her whisky.

An'gel drained her glass and set it on the tray on the liquor cabinet. "I think I'll go up and read for a bit before dinner. I need to think about something else for a little while."

"Good idea." Dickce knocked back the contents of her glass. "I want to look through the books I bought today and decide which one to read first." She followed her sister out of the room and up the stairs.

Several hours later, after both had retired for the night, they were awakened by the ringing of the house phone. Dickce glanced with eyes barely open at the luminous dial of her bedside clock. Who was calling them at seven minutes past midnight?

She picked up the handset from the night-stand and hit the answer button. "Hello," she said, her throat dry. She identified herself. "Who is this?"

"It's Barbie," the caller replied.

"Who?" An'gel said from the extension in her bedroom.

"Barbie Gross," Dickce said. "What is it, Barbie. What's wrong?"

Dickce heard someone draw a long breath. Then Barbie said, "I just heard the news. Arliss is in intensive care at the hospital. They won't know if she's going to make it until morning."

CHAPTER 19

"Good heavens," An'gel said, stunned and still half-asleep. "What happened?"

"Car wreck," Barbie said. "Her car went into a ditch on the highway between where you live and town, evidently. Somebody came along and found her and called 911, thank the Lord."

"Gracious," Dickce said. "I wonder what caused her to go off the road?"

Barbie said, "Well, she has been known to drink more than she should and then get behind the wheel. I suspect that's what happened."

"Yes, I suppose so," An'gel said. "Where was she going? Has anybody been able to talk to her?"

"I don't think so," Barbie said. "She's in a coma. I thought y'all should know. She's going to need all the prayers she can get."

"Poor Arliss," Dickce said. "We certainly will pray for her."

211

"Thank you for letting us know, Barbie," An'gel said. "We'll get over to the hospital first thing in the morning to check on her and see if there's anything we can do."

"I'll see you there," Barbie replied. "Bye."

An'gel and Dickce hung up their phones, and An'gel walked out of her room into the hall. Dickce met her there.

"Sister, what on earth is going on?" Dickce said after a yawn. "First Sarinda, and now Arliss. Could they both be accidents?"

"Mighty coincidental if they are," An'gel said. "Come on, I don't know about you, but I could use a hot drink. Let's make hot chocolate."

Dickce nodded and followed An'gel downstairs to the kitchen. An'gel took charge of making the hot chocolate, and Dickce retrieved mugs from the cabinet. Neither spoke again until they had filled their mugs and were sitting at the kitchen table.

After a couple of sips, An'gel spoke. "Barbie said Arliss was found in a ditch along the highway between here and town. I think she was probably on her way home from Ashton Hall."

"Or going *to* Ashton Hall," Dickce said. "If she had a snootful, it's the kind of thing she would do. She's brazen enough when she's sober, but she gets reckless when she's had too much to drink."

"I suppose," An'gel said. "I think it's more likely she was on her way home." She had more hot chocolate. "There's one way to find out."

"Call Hadley, you mean?" Dickce asked.

An'gel nodded. "I imagine Barbie has already called him, so he's probably awake. Shall we?" She gestured toward the kitchen phone.

"Why not?" Dickce asked. "You do it."

"All right, I will." An'gel stared at her mug for a moment before she set it aside and went over to the phone. "Do you remember the number?"

"I think so." Dickce recited it, and An'gel punched it in.

After three rings, a sleepy voice answered.

An'gel put her hand over the mouthpiece. "Not Hadley. A woman. Maybe the house-keeper?" She took her hand away and said, "I'm so sorry to wake you. Is this Ashton Hall?"

"Yes, it is. Who are you, and why are you calling in the middle of the night?" the woman asked, obviously annoyed.

"This is An'gel Ducote. I'm trying to reach Hadley. A mutual friend of ours was badly injured in an accident on the highway

213

near there. I'm trying to get in touch with him to let him know."

"I see." An'gel heard the sounds of bedcovers rustling. "Let me see if I can find him for you. Does he have your number?"

"Yes, he should," An'gel said.

"Okay, then, I'll go find him and tell him to call you."

An'gel heard a dial tone. She came back to the table with the handset. "She's going to look for him and have him call us."

"I feel bad we woke her up." Dickce frowned. "Why didn't Hadley answer, I wonder?"

Nearly ten minutes passed before the phone rang. By then they had both finished their chocolate and Dickce was washing out the mugs and saucepan.

An'gel answered the call. She barely had time to say *hello* before Hadley launched into speech.

"An'gel, thanks for calling, but I'm about to head to the hospital," he said.

"Obviously you already know about Arliss," An'gel said. "I guess Barbie Gross called you."

"No," Hadley said. "The hospital called my cell phone. Evidently Arliss had me listed as an emergency contact. Look, I really need to get to the hospital."

"Be careful," An'gel said. "Call and let us know if there's anything we can do."

"Sure." Hadley ended the call.

An'gel replaced the handset. "That was peculiar."

"What are you talking about?" Dickce asked. "What did Hadley say?"

An'gel shared Hadley's part of the conversation with her sister. When An'gel finished, Dickce shook her head.

"Why would Arliss have *him* listed as her emergency contact? She has a cousin in town, and a sister in Jackson. That's strange. He hasn't been back in town that long."

"They must have struck up a relationship almost immediately," An'gel said. "Or else Arliss was jumping the gun. I wouldn't be surprised if that was the case."

"Maybe," Dickce said. "Did he sound really upset?"

An'gel nodded. "Maybe he's closer to her than we realized."

"You didn't get to ask him whether Arliss had been with him at Ashton Hall tonight," Dickce said. "I suppose we'll find that out tomorrow. In the meantime, I'm going back to bed."

"Me, too." An'gel followed her sister out of the kitchen and back up to the second floor.

"Good night again," Dickce said.

"Good night." An'gel closed her bedroom door behind her. She removed her robe and laid it across the foot of the bed. Then she climbed in and got comfortable before she reached over to turn out the light.

She lay there awhile, her mind too busy to let her relax into sleep right away. She worried that Arliss's accident was *not* an accident, but a deliberate attempt on the woman's life. An'gel found the coincidence of this event too great after the deliberate — and successful — attempt on Sarinda's life.

What was behind all of it? She worried over that until, at last, she fell asleep from exhaustion.

An'gel and Dickce were on their way to the hospital a few minutes before eight that morning. About a half mile past the driveway to Ashton Hall they saw the place where Arliss's car had evidently gone into the ditch. To judge by the deep gouges in the turf, An'gel thought, the wreck had been horrendous. She uttered another quick prayer for Arliss.

"She went off the road less than a minute after she turned onto the highway," Dickce said.

"Yes, and that strikes me as odd," An'gel said. "This stretch of road is perfectly straight for nearly a mile here. What made her run off the road?"

"A deer maybe?" Dickce tightened her grip on the steering wheel.

"Maybe," An'gel said.

They found Hadley, looking exhausted and hollow-eyed, asleep in the waiting room near the ICU. They hesitated to wake him, but Barbie Gross and Lottie MacLeod entered the room only moments behind them. Lottie went straight to him and shook him awake before anyone could stop her.

Hadley sat up and yawned. He rubbed his face, and after a moment he focused on them. "Good morning," he said, his voice hoarse.

"Poor man, you've been here all night, haven't you?" Barbie sat down on one side of him, Lottie on the other. Barbie patted his leg, and Lottie stroked his shoulder.

Hadley looked at Barbie and Lottie in turn before he stood up and walked a couple of feet away. He turned and gazed at An'gel and Dickce. "It's been a hellish night."

"How is she?" An'gel asked. She and Dickce seated themselves near him.

"Holding her own." Hadley rubbed a

hand across his eyes. "Lord, I need coffee and a hot shower." He yawned. "Sorry. I told the doctor and the nurses that I'm her stepbrother, otherwise I was afraid they wouldn't tell me anything."

"Has anyone called her sister in Jackson?" Barbie asked.

"I did," Hadley said. "She's on her way. She ought to be here any minute now."

"Does the doctor think she'll make it?" Lottie asked.

"It's touch and go," Hadley said. "She has multiple broken bones, and she hasn't regained consciousness yet." He glanced at his watch. "At least, not that I've heard. Last time I talked to a doctor was about two o'clock."

"I'm going to get you some coffee," Barbie said. "I'll be back in a few minutes." She left the waiting room. Hadley called his thanks belatedly after her.

"Do you have any idea when the accident happened?" An'gel asked.

"Must have been shortly after ten thirty," Hadley said. "We had dinner at Ashton Hall, and then we watched a movie. She left right about ten thirty." He shuddered. "It must have happened within five minutes or so after she left, and I think she was lying there in the wreckage for a good half hour before someone saw it and reported it."

"Thank the Lord someone did see it and called 911," Lottie said. "Poor Arliss. It's a wonder she didn't die on the spot."

"Did she hit a deer?" Dickce asked.

Hadley shook his head. "Not that I know of."

"She was probably drunk," Lottie said. "Poor Arliss does have a weakness for drink. We've worried about her a lot, driving after she's had too much."

"That wasn't the case last night," Hadley said, his tone sharp as he walked over to Lottie and glared down at her. "So put that right out of your mind. We had a couple of glasses of wine with dinner, but that was all. She was not drunk, do you hear me?" His voice rose on the last few words until he was almost shouting at her.

Lottie shrank back in her seat. Her lip trembled, and she started crying.

Hadley sighed and sat down beside her. He put his arm around her and patted her awkwardly on the knee. "I'm sorry, Lottie. I'm exhausted and upset. I didn't mean to hurt your feelings or frighten you."

Lottie cried for a moment longer, then pushed Hadley away. "I'm okay." She dug in her purse for tissues and dabbed at her eyes.

Hadley got up and moved toward An'gel and Dickce. "Right after we hear from the doctor again, I think I'd better run home and have a shower. Try to get myself together." He paused for a deep breath. "Will y'all stay here until I get back?"

"Of course," An'gel said. "I think that's a good idea. Make sure you eat something, too."

Hadley nodded. "I had a sausage and biscuit from the hospital cafeteria when it opened at six, just to keep me going for a little while. I could use something more substantial."

Barbie returned with the coffee, and Hadley accepted it with a smile of thanks.

An'gel waited until he'd had a few sips before she posed the question that had been troubling her ever since she and Dickce had seen the site of the accident.

"If Arliss hadn't had too much to drink, and she didn't hit a deer, why did she run off the road?"

Before anyone could respond, Kanesha Berry walked into the waiting room. "Good morning, everyone." She approached Hadley. "Mr. Partridge, how is Mrs. McGonigal?"

"Holding her own, the last I heard," he said.

"Good." Kanesha nodded.

"Do you have any idea what caused the wreck?" An'gel asked.

Kanesha again nodded. She glanced at each person in the room before she responded.

"I'm pretty sure she was deliberately run off the road."

CHAPTER 20

An'gel felt sick to her stomach, even though she had been expecting this news. She could see her own shock mirrored in the faces of her sister and her friends.

"Hello, everyone, sorry we're late," Reba Dalrymple said as she walked into the waiting room, her son Martin right behind her. "We were having car trouble this morning, otherwise we'd have been here half an hour ago."

An'gel stared at Reba in shock. Car trouble?

"How is Arliss?" Reba said. "Oh, hello, Deputy Berry." She hesitated. "What's wrong? Why is everyone staring at us like that?"

"Good morning, Mrs. Dalrymple," Kanesha said. "Mr. Dalrymple. What kind of car trouble were you having?"

An'gel felt the tension in the room as they all waited for Reba's answer.

"Dead battery," Reba said, still obviously puzzled. "We had to ask our next-door neighbor to jump us off. Why are you so interested in that? What's going on here?"

"Right before you and Martin came in," An'gel said, "Deputy Berry informed us that she's pretty sure someone deliberately ran Arliss off the road."

Reba paled. "Oh my Lord. How horrible." She glanced around the room, and then she apparently figured out why they had all been staring. "Surely you didn't think . . . ?" Her voice trailed off. She found an empty chair and dropped into it.

"You certainly couldn't blame us for wondering," Barbie said tartly. "You walk into the room talking about car trouble right after we hear that terrible news."

Martin moved to stand beside his mother and laid a hand on her shoulder. "Mama would never do something crazy like that." He laughed. "She has really bad night vision, anyway."

"Do you?" An'gel asked before she stopped to think.

Martin blinked at her. "What? Do I have bad night vision?" He shook his head. "No. Why?"

Reba glared at An'gel. "Martin would never do such a thing. He never even left

223

the house last night. How dare you imply anything of the sort, An'gel Ducote."

"If Miss An'gel hadn't asked, I was about to," Kanesha said. "Look, folks, I don't know what's going on here. First, Miss Hetherington dies under suspicious circumstances, and now Mrs. McGonigal is severely injured in what appears to be a deliberate attempt on her life. I swear to you, I will get to the bottom of this, and the person responsible is going to be prosecuted to the fullest extent of the law."

Despite her cool professional manner, Kanesha was furious. An'gel knew her well enough to see that. She didn't blame her. These cold-blooded actions sickened her. Who was behind them? And why?

"If you'll excuse me now," Kanesha said into the dead silence that followed her last words, "I need to find Mrs. McGonigal's doctor. Under the circumstances, I am going to insist that no one other than immediate family be allowed access to Mrs. McGonigal. The police department and the sheriff's department will be taking turns guarding her until this matter is resolved." With that, she nodded, turned, and left the waiting room.

An'gel looked around the room to gauge reactions to Kanesha's parting words.

Everyone seemed stunned, and that was to be expected. She did not see anything she could interpret as fear, however.

She exchanged an uneasy glance with Dickce, and she knew her sister was thinking the same thing. One of the other five people in the room was the murderer. But which one?

They waited in silence for several minutes, though An'gel could see the others were restless, casting sly looks at one another. The tension was palpable.

A young man in scrubs and a white coat strode into the room. He stopped for a moment, then approached Hadley. "Mr. Partridge, if I could have a word with you, please."

Hadley nodded. "Of course, doctor, but whatever you have to tell me, you can tell everyone here. We're all concerned about Mrs. McGonigal."

"Very well," the doctor said. "She is still in a coma, and her vital signs are mostly steady. But she faces a long recovery once she's out of the coma. Her injuries are extensive, and there is a possibility she will not be able to walk again or have the use of her upper limbs." He paused. "I'm sorry, I know the news is not encouraging, but we are hoping for the best." He turned and left the room.

"Oh dear Lord," Barbie said as her eyes filled with tears. She hung her head, and Lottie, seated next to her, wrapped her arms around Barbie and hugged her tight.

An'gel felt her own eyes filling. The thought of her friend, always so vibrant, left paralyzed was shocking. She would pray that Arliss might defy the doctor's prognosis and be able to walk and laugh again. She knew, however, that if Arliss survived the immediate threat to her life, her will to live would be strong. They would all have to do everything they could to help her.

Hadley walked out of the room without a word to anyone, though he did glance at An'gel and Dickce. An'gel tried to read his expression. He was obviously deeply upset, but there was something else there, something she couldn't quite put a finger on. Perhaps it was rage.

That was her predominant emotion, now that the first shock of the doctor's words was passing. Rage against the sick, cold-hearted, lost soul who had done this thing.

Was this attempt at murder connected in some way with Callie Partridge's disappearance? At the moment An'gel couldn't figure out how it might be. She had a hunch that there was a connection, she and Dickce simply had to find it.

Right now, though, she had to think of other matters. She looked around the waiting room. The first thing to do was to clear this room and send people home.

"I think you all should go on home," An'gel said in a firm tone. "It's obvious that we can do little for Arliss at the moment except pray, since we won't be allowed to see her. Her sister ought to be here soon, and she doesn't need a crowd of people to deal with when she arrives. Dickce and I will stay here until she comes, but the rest of you should go."

Barbie, her face blotched with red from crying, stood. "You're right, An'gel. Come on, Lottie. Let us know if you hear anything."

An'gel nodded. Lottie rose obediently at Barbie's words and followed her friend out of the waiting room. An'gel turned to Reba and Martin. Before she could speak again, Reba rose from her seat.

"Come along, Martin. We have to go buy a new battery for the car." She nodded in An'gel's direction before she departed. Martin shambled after her, staring at his phone as he went.

"Thank goodness you got them to go," Dickce said quietly. "I couldn't stand to look at any of them, knowing that one of them has to be responsible for this."

"I couldn't stand looking at them either," An'gel said. "We have a cold-blooded killer as a friend, and it makes me ill to think about it."

Arliss's younger sister Frances and her husband, Bill, turned up a few minutes later. An'gel and Dickce told them, as gently as possible, the truth of what had happened to Arliss. Frances and Bill were stunned, as the sisters expected, and they looked a little fearful. An'gel couldn't blame them.

"Please call us if there is anything at all we can do for you." An'gel gave them a card with the sisters' contact information. She and Dickce left the couple after sharing a brief prayer with them for Arliss's recovery.

"I hate leaving them alone like that, in that cold waiting room," Dickce said as she and An'gel walked out of the hospital.

"I know," Angel said. "Under the circumstances, however, I think it's best. Though we've met them a few times over the years, they don't really know us. They can't be sure one of us isn't responsible for the current situation. They really can't afford to trust any of Arliss's so-called friends until this is cleared up."

"I suppose not," Dickce said. "That's horrible to contemplate, though."

"Yes, it is." An'gel unlocked the car and climbed into the driver's seat. She was in no mood for her sister's driving at the moment.

They drove home to Riverhill in silence. When they entered the kitchen, they found Benjy, along with Peanut and Endora, talking with Clementine.

"How is she?" Clementine asked the moment she saw them.

An'gel shared the news of Arliss's condition. Clementine shook her head. "I'll be praying for her."

"She's going to need all our prayers," Dickce said.

"You both need hot coffee and food," Clementine said. "Y'all set yourselves down there at the table, and I'll have something ready for you in a minute."

"I'll get the coffee for you," Benjy said.

"Thank you," An'gel said. "Coffee and food would be good."

Peanut came to her and rubbed against her legs. She sat at the table, and he put his head in her lap. She stroked it, and he gazed up at her lovingly. She felt better for his attention.

Endora hopped into Dickce's lap the moment Dickce sat. An'gel could see that her

229

sister found the cat's attentions as soothing as she did Peanut's. Benjy set cups of coffee in front of each of them, and they both thanked him.

A little while later, An'gel pushed back her empty plate. "Thank you, Clementine. I hadn't realized how hungry I was. Dickce and I rushed off to the hospital without even any coffee."

"I know." Clementine frowned. "You shouldn't be doing things like that. Can't go neglecting yourselves. Not going to help anybody by doing that."

An'gel nodded. "You're right." Clementine fussed over them occasionally like they were her children. At times like this, An'gel appreciated her concern.

"Thank you," Dickce said. "I feel much better after that." She turned to Benjy. "What are you up to today?"

"Now that y'all are back, I thought I would go to the public library," he said. "I want to see whether they have the old phone books, like you and I were talking about. See what I can find through their databases."

"That sounds like an excellent plan," An'gel said. "If you can't find what you need there, let me or Dickce know, and we can call Charlie Harris and ask him to help you. I believe this is one of his days to work at the archive at the college."

"Thanks, I'll do that," Benjy said. "Is it true that he takes his cat to work with him?" He glanced at Peanut and Endora and laughed. "I can just imagine taking these two with me and trying to focus on work."

"When they're older, perhaps." Dickce favored the pets with an indulgent smile. "They're still young, practically like children in kindergarten. They'll be more settled before long."

"To answer your question, yes, Charlie does take Diesel to work with him," An'gel said. "Diesel has better manners than some people I know. He's a very well-behaved cat." She frowned at Endora. "This little miss could take a few lessons from him."

"Endora is a very good girl most of the time," Dickce said, a touch indignantly. "She's still kittenish, and you can't blame her for her occasional high spirits."

Benjy laughed. "Whenever Peanut gets in trouble, she's usually the ringleader. Will you mind looking after them while I'm in town?"

"Not at all," Clementine said. "If Miss An'gel and Miss Dickce are too busy, they can keep me company."

"Thanks," Benjy said. "In that case, I'm

231

going to grab my backpack and laptop and head to the library." He patted the dog and the cat on their heads, gave all three women a quick peck on the cheek, and then he was out the back door.

The phone rang a moment later, and Clementine answered. "Yes, they're right here." She looked at An'gel. "It's Kanesha."

"I'll take it," An'gel said. Clementine gave her the handset. "Hello, Kanesha. Do you have any news about Arliss McGonigal?"

"Nothing new, Miss An'gel," the deputy said. "She's still holding her own. The reason I called, though, is to tell you we have a preliminary report from the professor at the college."

An'gel gripped the handset tighter. "What's the verdict?"

"He says the remains are definitely not *old bones,* as he called them. They're too recent. So I suspect we have probably found Callie Partridge."

CHAPTER 21

An'gel felt a sudden great wave of sadness. She had more or less been expecting this news ever since they found the remains at Ashton Hall. But now that she heard it from Kanesha, it finally began to sink in. Callie Partridge was dead.

"An'gel, what is it? You look like you're going to faint," Dickce said, obviously alarmed.

An'gel drew a deep breath. "I'll tell you in a minute," she said to her sister. To Kanesha, she said, "How long do you think it will be before we know for sure?"

"That depends," Kanesha said. "If we had medical or dental records to check against, it might be sooner. But given how long ago this probably happened, those might not be available. All we have to go on at the moment is that the remains are those of an adult female, and that diamond and emerald ring has been identified as belonging to

Mrs. Partridge."

"I see," An'gel said. "Thank you for the update. We'll keep this to ourselves, of course."

"Good. We won't be releasing that news yet," Kanesha said. "I need to talk to Mr. Partridge again to see what he can tell us about his sister-in-law. Who her doctors were and so on."

"I can tell you that," An'gel said. "Elmo Gandy was her doctor. I don't know about her dentist, though."

"Thank you, Miss An'gel. I'll be talking with you later, I'm sure." Kanesha ended the call.

An'gel gave the handset back to Clementine.

"It was about Callie, wasn't it?" Dickce asked.

"This can't go any further than this room," An'gel said. Dickce and Clementine nodded. "Yes, it was about Callie. The expert they consulted says the remains were definitely not from an old burial. They're too recent."

"So we know where Callie was now, these past four decades," Dickce said. "I kept hoping, maybe foolishly, that it wouldn't be her we found."

"I know," An'gel said. "I wanted to think

234

she was alive and happy somewhere."

"How old do you think she was when she died?" Dickce asked. "I'm thinking she was close to thirty."

"That sounds about right," An'gel replied. "I know she was several years younger than Hadley and probably nearly fifteen years younger than Hamish. I think he was about a year older than me."

"How long's it going to be before they know for sure who it is?" Clementine asked.

"It could take weeks, if not months," An'gel said. "They'll be trying to find dental and medical records for her, because those could give them the information they need."

"Elmo Gandy should be able to help, then," Dickce said.

"He should be able to," An'gel said. "I hope they can identify her quickly so she can be given a proper burial."

Dickce yawned suddenly. "My goodness," she said. "I guess after that good breakfast, I'm feeling sleepy."

"We both had an interrupted night," An'gel said. She tried to resist but she couldn't help yawning either.

"I think y'all better go upstairs and take a little nap," Clementine said. "Nothing you can do right now anyway, might as well get some rest."

"I think you're right." Dickce stood. "I suspect I'll be dragging this afternoon if I don't rest now." She looked at the cat nestled in her arms. "Endora, would you like to go upstairs with me?"

Endora, thus addressed, stirred and looked up at Dickce. She yawned, then meowed. "I'll take that as a yes."

An'gel rose to follow her sister out of the kitchen. Peanut woofed at her. "I suppose you want to go with me?"

Peanut wagged his tail and woofed again. "Come along, then."

She paused at the door to turn back and speak to the housekeeper. "Did Benjy say whether he would be back in time for lunch?"

Clementine nodded. "Said he was going to have lunch in town. He's expecting to be at the library a good part of the day, he said."

An'gel thanked her and headed for the stairs. Peanut loped ahead. Dickce was already on the landing above her when she started up. She heard her sister's door close when she was halfway to the top. An'gel proceeded up the stairs where she found Peanut waiting at her bedroom door. She opened the door and followed him in, thinking about Benjy's research at the library.

She hoped he could find some kind of clue that might lead them to Coriander Simpson. If Callie's former housemaid was still alive, she might know something that could shed light on what happened at Ashton Hall all those years ago.

An'gel changed into a gown and climbed into bed. Peanut, after circling one spot several times, curled up at the corner of the bed near her feet, and went to sleep.

An'gel was tired, but she wasn't expecting to fall asleep right away. Her mind felt too busy to allow her to relax enough. She kept picturing Arliss in a hospital bed, hooked up to the Lord only knew how many wires. She prayed that Arliss would recover and not be left paralyzed. She also prayed that Kanesha would soon get to the bottom of these vicious attacks and expose the guilty person.

Before long she drifted off, hazily aware of the dog's gentle breathing. She came out of a sound sleep sometime later when she heard her cell phone ringing insistently on the bedside table. Still groggy, she picked it up and peered at the caller's phone number. The name attached to it was L. B. Turnipseed. That brought her completely awake.

"Hello." She identified herself and waited for Mrs. Turnipseed to respond. Peanut looked at her reproachfully for being awoken. He put his head down and watched her while she talked.

"I reckon you know who this is," the woman said.

"I do, Mrs. Turnipseed," An'gel replied. "I trust you're doing well this morning."

"I am, but that ain't why I'm calling," Mrs. Turnipseed said, her tone harsh. "I been thinking about what you and your sister were saying to me yesterday, and I reckon I might have remembered a thing or two after y'all jogged my memory."

An'gel felt her pulse quicken. She had been right. The former housekeeper did know something. "I'm glad to hear it. My sister and I would be happy to come and visit with you again to hear all about what you've remembered."

"I was pretty sure you would," Mrs. Turnipseed replied. "There's others that are pretty interested in what I have to say, too. What I'm wondering, though, is who's going to be the *most* interested and grateful to hear it."

An'gel wanted to tell Mrs. Turnipseed that she and Dickce weren't about to stoop to bribery, but she knew that the woman likely wouldn't talk to them unless they made it worth her while.

"I'm sure we could come to a mutually satisfactory arrangement," An'gel said, trying to keep the distaste from her voice.

"I'm sure we can," Mrs. Turnipseed said.

"Can you give me a little hint about what you've remembered? My sister and I are busy this afternoon, and if we're going to have to rearrange our schedules, we want to be sure it's going to be worth the trouble." They had no plans for the afternoon, but Mrs. Turnipseed didn't need to know that.

"I don't know," Mrs. Turnipseed said. "I got things to do myself." She fell silent for a moment. "Well, I reckon it won't hurt to tell you this much. Let's just say I might've had to go back to Ashton Hall to pick up something before I went to my sister's, and I could have seen something one night. Something that certain parties didn't know I saw."

An'gel wished she was close enough to grab the woman and shake her hard. Had she really been a witness to what happened to Callie? There was only one way to get the whole story, she supposed. She took a deep breath before she responded.

"That sounds promising. What time should my sister and I call on you?"

"How about four o'clock?" Mrs. Turnipseed said. "And bring cash." She ended the call.

An'gel set her cell phone on the bedside table and leaned back against the pillows. She wondered whether she should let Kanesha know about the phone call. If she did, Kanesha would probably tell her and Dickce not to go. She really wanted to talk to Mrs. Turnipseed, however, and they could always tell Kanesha afterward.

She hesitated when she thought about actually giving the former housekeeper money. The woman was obviously greedy. How much would she want? What if she demanded an exorbitant sum, say ten thousand dollars? Or twenty?

There was no way she and her sister were about to hand over that kind of a bribe. Perhaps they could get out of her what they needed to know without actually giving her much money. They could say they couldn't raise that much cash with only a few hours' notice. Instead they could offer her a thousand and promise to give her the rest in a few days' time.

What are you thinking?

An'gel realized the situation could easily spin out of control. She also realized that Mrs. Turnipseed could be playing a danger-ous game. What *certain parties* was she talk-

240

ing about?

If the woman planned to put the bite on the person responsible for putting Callie in the ground at Ashton Hall, that person might not take kindly to the attempt at bribery. Mrs. Turnipseed could be putting her own life at risk.

An'gel frowned. What was it that Mrs. Turnipseed had said? *There's others that are pretty interested in what I have to say, too.*

That could mean Mrs. Turnipseed had called someone else before she called An'gel.

An'gel snatched up her phone and speed-dialed Kanesha's cell. That other person could already be on the way to make sure Mrs. Turnipseed didn't talk to anyone else — ever.

The call went immediately to voice mail. An'gel waited for the tone, her anxiety growing. "This is An'gel Ducote. Mrs. Turnipseed just called me. She's trying to get money out of me in exchange for information. I'm afraid she's already talked to someone else. If she really knows anything, I think she's in danger. Please send someone right away to check on her." She ended the call.

Peanut stirred, no doubt alarmed by her tone. He crawled closer to her and laid his head on her leg. He whined, and she patted his head. "Nothing for you to worry about, handsome boy."

An'gel dialed the sheriff's office. She told the operator she had left a message for Kanesha and stressed the urgency of her call. She gave the gist of her message to Kanesha to the operator, and the operator promised that the deputy would be informed right away.

An'gel set her phone down on the bedside table. She stared down at the dog, still obviously uneasy because of her own agitation. She rubbed his head to calm him and at the same time to calm herself. She had done all she could for Mrs. Turnipseed.

No, I haven't. She grabbed her phone again and looked at the list of calls. She found Mrs. Turnipseed's number and called it back. She let the phone ring at least fifteen times, but there was no answer. Frustrated, she put the phone down again and went back to petting the dog, trying to keep her fears for Mrs. Turnipseed's safety at bay. She could only pray that the sheriff's department or the police department could get to the woman in time to prevent another death.

CHAPTER 22

As she continued to stroke Peanut's head, An'gel debated whether to share her fears with Dickce. After a moment's reflection she decided there was no need to wake her sister. Dickce would find out soon enough. One of them ought to have a few more restful moments while she could.

An'gel glanced at the clock. Nearly eleven thirty. Later than she expected. "I might as well get up and get dressed again," she told Peanut. He seemed happy enough to remain on the bed while she changed clothes and went into the bathroom to brush her hair and check her makeup.

Peanut hopped off the bed when she opened the bedroom door and trotted across the hall to Dickce's room. He whined and scratched at the door. Moments later the door opened, and Endora walked out. She rubbed her head against Peanut's and meowed. An'gel watched them with a bemused smile. She had never seen a cat and a dog behave like best friends, but these two shared a strong bond.

"Did you get any rest, Sister?" Dickce asked as she stepped out of her room. "I had a good nap."

"I did," An'gel said, "until I was woken by a phone call." She proceeded to tell Dickce about her conversation with Mrs. Turnipseed and her own calls to urge Kanesha to ensure the woman's safety.

"I have a bad feeling about this," Dickce said as she and An'gel walked downstairs, preceded by their four-legged companions.

"I do, too," An'gel said. "I hope that foolish, venal woman doesn't come to any harm over this." She stared down at the phone in her hand. "Surely Kanesha will call soon and let us know what's going on."

"She will," Dickce said. "I don't know about you, but I'm thirsty. Let's go to the kitchen and get something to drink."

An'gel agreed. Peanut and Endora had taken off for the kitchen the moment they reached the bottom of the stairs. The sisters found them getting treats from Clementine.

"You're spoiling them rotten," An'gel said.

Clementine laughed. She gave Peanut and Endora each another tidbit. An'gel thought it was boiled chicken.

"They're still growing," the housekeeper said. "They need to eat a little extra now and again."

"As long as now and again isn't three or four times a day," An'gel said wryly. She accepted a glass of ice water from her sister and drank half of it. "That hit the spot."

"What time you reckon y'all be wanting lunch?" Clementine rinsed her hands at the sink and dried them with a hand towel.

"How about one o'clock?" An'gel said.

Dickce nodded. "That sounds good. What are we having?"

"Salad, vegetable soup, and cornbread," Clementine replied.

"That sounds perfect for a chilly day," An'gel said. "We'll have it in the parlor, I think." She and Dickce refilled their glasses and left the kitchen. Peanut and Endora remained with Clementine, no doubt hopeful for more treats, An'gel thought.

In the parlor they sat at either end of the sofa. An'gel felt disinclined to talk at the moment. Her thoughts remained focused on Mrs. Turnipseed, and she wouldn't rest easy until she heard from Kanesha. She prayed for the woman, that she would be found safe at home.

When her cell phone rang, An'gel almost dropped her glass. She set it down on the coffee table and pulled out her phone. After a glance at the screen she looked at Dickce and said, "Hadley's calling."

Dickce moved closer on the sofa as An'gel answered the call. She set it on speaker so her sister could hear. After an exchange of greetings, An'gel said, "How are you? Have you had any news from the hospital?"

"I'm doing okay, I guess," Hadley said. "I managed to get a couple of hours' sleep. I haven't heard anything from the hospital. I was hoping you might have."

"No, I haven't," An'gel said. "I gave Arliss's sister my number and I expect she'll call at some point to let us know how Arliss is doing."

"I hope so," Hadley said. "I just can't get my head around the fact that someone deliberately drove her off the road. I never expected this kind of thing when I decided to come home again."

"Your return does seem to have acted as a catalyst of some sort." An'gel hoped her candor wouldn't offend Hadley, but getting at the truth behind these attacks was more important than bruised feelings.

"Yes, I suppose it has," Hadley replied. "Excuse me a moment, An'gel."

An'gel heard another voice in the background. A female, she thought, perhaps

Hadley's housekeeper.

Hadley confirmed that moments later. "Sorry about that," he said. "My housekeeper came to let me know one of the workmen has questions. I'm afraid I'll have to go in a moment because they're at a standstill until I respond. If you hear anything from the hospital, please let me know."

"I will," An'gel said, frustrated that the conversation was being cut short. She wanted to press Hadley further. "I know this is an imposition, because you're busy there, but could Dickce and I come by this afternoon sometime? I think we really need to sit down and discuss a few things."

Hadley didn't answer right away, and for a moment An'gel thought he'd already hung up. Then his voice sounded in her ear. "If you'll give me a couple of hours to deal with things here," he said, "you'll of course be welcome. Does that work for you?"

"It does," An'gel said. "We'll see you around two, then." She ended the call and set her phone down on the coffee table.

"What are these *few things* that you want to talk to Hadley about?" Dickce asked.

"You remember what I said to him about his return serving as a catalyst of some sort?" An'gel waited for Dickce's nod before she continued. "Things were quiet before

Hadley returned. Suddenly, here he is, and Sarinda's dead. Arliss is in the hospital in critical condition. Remains are found at Ashton Hall. Remains that we now know are of fairly recent origin, and not an ancient burial. They're all connected to Hadley in some way. The question is, how?"

"That's all fairly obvious," Dickce said. "What is it you expect to learn from Hadley?"

"I want to know what was going on forty years ago that could have led to all this," An'gel said. "Hadley was messing around with someone. Barbie, Lottie, Reba, Arliss, Sarinda, perhaps even all of them. Sarinda and Arliss are out of the picture though, and that leaves Barbie, Lottie, and Reba. Is one of them so determined to have Hadley she's willing to kill to get the others out of the way?"

"You've left two names off your list," Dickce said, her tone bland.

"Who are you talking about?" An'gel asked, confused.

"You and me," Dickce replied with a mischievous smile. "As I recall, we both found Hadley sinfully attractive. For a while there he seemed to be paying a lot of attention to you, and you weren't doing anything to discourage him." She giggled. "I was pretty jealous, if you want to know the truth. He never flirted with me the way he did with you. The question is, how far beyond flirtation did you go?"

An'gel stared at her sister, momentarily speechless as long-suppressed memories came flooding back. She felt the heat of a flush stealing over her face, and she wanted to get up and walk out of the room. Instead she remained seated and tried to will those memories away.

"Don't worry," Dickce said. "I'm not going to press you for details. Your expression just now tells me enough."

An'gel's phone rang, and she snatched it up, thankful for the distraction. She recognized Kanesha Berry's number.

After a quick exchange of greetings, Kanesha said, "I don't have good news, I'm afraid. When we reached Mrs. Turnipseed's house, we found it empty. The police department is talking to neighbors to see if any of them saw something, but at the moment we don't have anything. There was no sign of a struggle, and her car is gone. She might have gotten scared and left on her own."

"I hope so," An'gel said. "But there is a possibility that she was forced to leave, I presume?"

"Yes," Kanesha replied. "We have to

249

consider that, and we will be looking for her. I'll be in touch when we know more." She ended the call.

An'gel set the phone down again and regarded her sister. She repeated what Kanesha told her.

"Presumably she had a friend or a family member she could go to," Dickce said. "We'll simply have to hope that is what she's done."

"Instead of being abducted and taken somewhere to be murdered." An'gel shuddered. "I didn't care for her but I certainly wouldn't wish that on anyone."

"Surely one of the neighbors saw *something,*" Dickce said. "There's nothing we can do for her at the moment except pray." After a brief silence she continued, "Now, back to Hadley."

An'gel tensed. She didn't want to be subjected to an inquisition by her sister. She didn't want to lie to Dickce, but neither did she want to tell her the complete truth. There were some memories she didn't wish to share, even with her sister.

Dickce smiled. "Like I said, I'm not going to press you for details about what went on between you and Hadley. You can stop looking so apprehensive."

"Thank you," An'gel said, greatly relieved.

She wouldn't put it past Dickce, however, to bring the subject up again in the future. "Hadley is going to have to come clean, there's no way around it. I hate to say this, but I think he knows exactly what happened to Callie and how she came to be buried in the garden at Ashton Hall."

"I suspect you may be right," Dickce said. "I hate to think that about Hadley, though."

"If he's covering up for his brother's crime, I suppose I can understand it, at least in part," An'gel said. "Though the greater part of me knows he shouldn't have let his brother get away with murder."

"No, he shouldn't have," Dickce said. "But what if Hamish didn't kill Callie? He certainly couldn't have killed Sarinda, or driven Arliss off the road. Unless you think there are two murderers, Hamish forty years ago, and someone else now."

"That's certainly a possibility," An'gel said. "But what I can't figure out, if that's the case, is why the murder and attempted murder now? Hamish is dead, and what harm could there be, really, if it became known he murdered Callie?"

"It would tarnish the family name, certainly," Dickce said, "but would Hadley kill for that reason?"

"I just don't know." An'gel frowned. "I

think Hadley is the key to all this, though."

"Even more reason for us to try to pin him down on everything he knows," Dickce said.

An'gel heard a muffled ringing. "Is that your phone?" she asked.

Dickce reached into the pocket of her skirt and retrieved her phone. "Benjy," she said after a glance at the screen. "Have you found anything?"

An'gel watched as Dickce's eyes widened in what appeared to be shock. "What is it? What did he find?"

CHAPTER 23

Dickce held up her hand to quiet her sister. She wanted to be sure she heard everything Benjy had to tell her. Once he finished, she said, "Oh, that's wonderful, Benjy." She paused for a moment. "No, come on home when you're done. We'll work out then what our next step is."

She could see that An'gel was fairly bouncing with impatience on the sofa when she ended the call and tucked the phone back into her skirt pocket.

"Well?" An'gel said.

Dickce smiled. "He's such a clever young man. He found a lead on Coriander Simpson."

"Don't just sit there grinning," An'gel said when her sister failed to continue. "Give me the details."

"Benjy figured that Coriander Simpson was probably a unique name, and he was right," Dickce said. "He searched genealogical databases for birth records and so on, and he found one for her. Of course it had her parents' names listed, too. Then he looked at census records and some kind of online phone directory and found the address in Memphis where she grew up. He thinks her family still lives there."

"Did he find any other record of her?" An'gel asked. "Like a death or marriage record?"

Dickce shook her head. "Not that he said. I'm sure he would have mentioned it if he had. He's going to do a bit more research before he comes home."

"Call him back," An'gel said. "I think we need to act on this right now."

"What do you mean?" Dickce pulled her phone back out.

"I think we need to go to Memphis this afternoon. We can be there in less than ninety minutes."

"We can go to the address Benjy found and talk to whomever we find there," Dickce said. "Good idea. Wait a minute, though. What about Hadley? You were really determined to talk to him a few minutes ago."

An'gel frowned. "Yes, I do think it's important to pin him down." She thought for a moment. "Why don't you go talk to Hadley this afternoon? I'll go to Memphis and track down Coriander Simpson's family."

"No," Dickce said. "I have a better idea. You go talk to Hadley, since he's more likely to talk to you. You being a former flame of his and all." She grinned. The opportunity to needle An'gel was too good to pass up. "Benjy and I will go to Memphis and find the Simpsons."

For a moment Dickce thought An'gel was going to have one of her occasional temper fits. She did that sometimes when she didn't get her way. Evidently she thought better of it this time, though. After a brief hesitation, An'gel nodded. "All right. I'll talk to Hadley. You go to Memphis."

Dickce called Benjy and informed him of the change in plans. "He'll be home in about twenty minutes," she informed An'gel.

"Excellent." An'gel stood. "I'll go tell Clementine. We can all have lunch in the kitchen, and then you and Benjy can be on your way to Memphis."

Dickce watched her sister's retreating form and smiled. She was excited at the thought of the trip to Memphis. Usually when she and An'gel went someplace together, An'gel tended to take over, and Dickce ended up playing second fiddle. Not this time, though. Dickce loved her older sister, but she also appreciated an opportunity to accomplish a task without An'gel.

She thought for a moment about An'gel and Hadley. She knew there was a story there somewhere, but she didn't know exactly how far the flirtation between her sister and Hadley had gone. She understood why An'gel was reluctant to share details. They both had secrets of their own. Dickce smiled fondly whenever she thought of a certain young British aristocrat whose family she and An'gel had met nearly fifty years ago on an extended visit to England. Had she wanted to spend the rest of her life in England, Dickce had no doubt she could have married Nigel. She simply couldn't see herself as the lady of an English manor and a countess to boot. She preferred Riverhill to Nigel's drafty, moldering pile in Lancashire.

So let An'gel keep her memories of Hadley to herself. Dickce had never told An'gel all the details about Nigel. Dickce's smile broadened as she rose and followed her sister to the kitchen.

An hour later, Dickce and Benjy were on the road to Memphis, accompanied by

Peanut and Endora, safely anchored in the backseat of Benjy's car. He had insisted on driving, and Dickce didn't argue. They wouldn't arrive in Memphis as soon, but Benjy could use the experience of driving on the interstate highway and in a large city.

An'gel had objected to their taking the dog and the cat with them, but Dickce had disagreed. "We can't leave them for Clementine to babysit all the time," she pointed out reasonably. "She has other things to do, and I don't imagine she wants Peanut and Endora *helping* her. Nor would she want to coop them up in one part of the house while she's working in another."

When Clementine agreed, tactfully but firmly, An'gel ceased her protests. Peanut and Endora came along for the adventure.

As they sped north on the interstate, Benjy kept his attention focused on his driving. Dickce wished he would drive faster, but he set the cruise control on the speed limit, and that was that.

"What should our strategy be?" Benjy asked. "Are we going to show up on their doorstep and start asking questions?"

"I've been thinking about that," Dickce said. "Once we get to Memphis we can look for somewhere to stop near their neighborhood and call them. You put the address in the GPS, didn't you?"

Benjy nodded. "We shouldn't have any trouble finding the address. What are we going to say is the reason we're looking for Coriander Simpson?"

"That's the tricky part," Dickce said. "She could actually be living there now, though I think that would be too big a coincidence. I don't think it's going to be that easy to find her."

"You never know," Benjy said. "She may have no idea anyone from Athena is interested in her whereabouts."

"Maybe," Dickce said. "We'll have to see. Now, as to what we will tell her family." She thought for a moment. "We could tell her that Hamish Partridge had left her a small legacy, and we are helping his lawyer track her down."

Benjy shook his head. "I don't think that's a good idea." Peanut woofed, and Benjy and Dickce laughed. "I guess Peanut agrees with me."

"He usually takes your side." Dickce laughed again. "Why don't you think it's a good idea?"

"There's no legacy, as far as we know. We're making it up. If we do manage to find her, she's going to be upset when she discovers we were lying about the inheritance."

"Good point." Dickce sighed. "What do you think we should tell them?"

Benjy didn't respond until he had safely passed a slower-moving vehicle in front of them. Once the car was back in the right lane, he said, "Why don't we simply tell them that Hadley Partridge came home after his brother died, and he is concerned about his sister-in-law's whereabouts. We want to talk to Coriander Simpson to see whether she can tell us anything about that."

"That's what we should do," Dickce said. "I should have thought of that, instead of trying to come up with a more convoluted reason. Maybe I'm not as good at being Nancy Drew as I thought."

Benjy flashed her a grin and then returned his attention to the road ahead. "No one is as good at being Nancy Drew as Nancy was. No one else is as perfect."

Dickce chuckled. "I guess you're right. Still, good for you for coming up with the best plan." Peanut woofed again, and Dickce laughed along with Benjy.

Thirty minutes later they approached the outskirts of Memphis. Their destination was in the southeastern part of the city. They found a park a few blocks from the Simpson residence, and Benjy pulled the car up to the curb. "I'm going to take Peanut for a short walk," he said. "Just in case. You can call while I do that."

"Okay," Dickce said. "No, Endora, you have to stay with me."

Peanut whined when he realized the cat wasn't coming with them, but Benjy led him firmly away from the car. Endora meowed loudly three times before she settled down and started grooming herself.

Dickce picked up the piece of paper on which Benjy had written the phone number he found for the Simpsons. She took a couple of deep breaths before she punched the number into her phone.

A young-sounding voice answered after five rings. "Hello. This is the Simpson residence. Who's calling, please?"

"Hello, my name is Dickce Ducote. I am looking for Coriander Simpson. I need to talk to her about someone she knew many years ago."

"Hang on a minute," the young voice said. "I got to ask my great-granny."

Dickce waited for what seemed like five minutes but was probably less than one.

"As long as you ain't no bill collector, my great-granny says you can come talk to her. She don't like talking on the phone. She don't hear so good, even with her hearing aid turned all the way up."

Dickce smiled at the child's words. She — or he? — was probably no more than five or six, she reckoned.

"Please thank your great-granny," Dickce said. "You can tell her I'm not a bill collector. We'll be there in a few minutes."

"All right. I'll tell her." The phone clicked in Dickce's ear.

Benjy returned a couple of minutes later with Peanut. Dickce informed him of her successful phone call, and they headed to the Simpson house.

The neighborhood appeared to be an older one. Dickce judged that the houses were at least fifty or sixty years old. Most were in good repair, with neat yards, though a few could use some fresh paint. When Benjy pulled into the driveway of the Simpson residence, Dickce noted that the house appeared better kept than some of its neighbors on the street.

Dickce spotted a little girl on the porch. She was tiny, and Dickce revised her age downward to four. She had several short braids, each fastened with a colorful bow, and she wore sneakers and a bright yellow overalls and a red T-shirt under them. She waved at Dickce as she got out of the car.

261

"Good afternoon," Dickce said as she approached the porch. "I called a few minutes ago. Was it you I talked to?"

"Yes'm," the child said. "I'm Monique. I'll be five in three months. How old are you?"

Dickce was slightly taken aback. "I'm much older than four or five," she said.

Monique's attention was already diverted, Dickce realized.

"Is that your dog?" the little girl asked.

"Yes, that's Peanut," Dickce said. "Would you like to meet him?"

Monique nodded. "He can come in if he wants to. Great-granny likes dogs, too."

"Does she like cats?" Dickce asked. "I have a cat, too, and she's in the car with Peanut."

Monique frowned. "I don't think so. Great-granny don't like cats."

"All right," Dickce said. "The cat can stay in the car." Endora wouldn't be happy about that, but Dickce couldn't risk offending Great-granny.

"Excuse me a moment while I get Peanut," Dickce said.

"Yes'm." Monique nodded.

Dickce went back to the car and explained the situation to Benjy. He looked a bit disappointed but said, "That's okay. I'll stay here and keep Endora company."

"I'm sorry, but thank you." Dickce opened the back door. She took firm hold of the dog's leash and guided him out.

Monique appeared slightly fearful when Peanut approached. After a moment she extended a hand, and the Labradoodle sniffed it and then licked it. Monique giggled. "That tickles."

"Perhaps we should go in and say hello to Great-granny," Dickce said. Monique seemed so entranced by the dog she had forgotten the reason for Dickce's visit.

"Yes'm," Monique said. "Y'all come right on in. Great-granny's in here watching television."

Dickce and Peanut followed the little girl inside the house. The interior was as neatly kept as the outside, and there was a pleasant smell of furniture wax and vanilla. Monique led them through the first doorway to the right, and said, "Here they are" in a loud voice.

An elderly, white-haired woman, encased in a shawl and covered by a crocheted blanket, turned her head in the direction of the child's voice. Dark eyes gazed with curiosity through thick-lensed glasses. Dickce reckoned her to be in her late nineties.

"Good afternoon," she said, her voice surprisingly strong.

"Good afternoon, Mrs. Simpson," Dickce said. She moved forward and extended her hand. "My name is Dickce Ducote."

Mrs. Simpson shook Dickce's hand briefly. Like her great-granddaughter, however, she appeared more interested in the dog. "That's a beautiful dog you got there, Miss Ducote." She reached out to stroke Peanut's head. He woofed gently at her in response.

"Thank you," Dickce said. "He's sweet and friendly."

Mrs. Simpson continued to stroke the dog's head. "I miss having a dog. Can't rightly take care of one myself these days, and Monique is too little right now to help, though the Lord knows she's a blessing to me in every way."

Monique had disappeared, Dickce realized. Where had the child gone?

"Please sit down, Miss Ducote," Mrs. Simpson said. "I'm forgetting my manners. Now, Monique said you want to find my daughter, Coriander."

Dickce seated herself on a nearby chair before she replied. "Yes, ma'am. Many years ago she worked for a friend of mine, Calpurnia Partridge, down in Athena."

Mrs. Simpson nodded. "Yes, that's right.

She worked for Miss Callie's family here in Memphis before she married and moved down there. She wanted Coriander to come with her."

"That's what I'd heard," Dickce said. "I'm not sure if you're aware, though, that Mrs. Partridge disappeared forty years ago. Her husband died recently, and his brother has come back to Athena to take care of the estate. He didn't realize his sister-in-law was gone. We all thought, frankly, she had run away with him when he left Athena because she disappeared not long after he left."

"I didn't know all that," Mrs. Simpson said. "That don't sound like Miss Callie, though, running off after a man." She frowned. "But Coriander can't help you about that. She died a long time ago."

CHAPTER 24

An'gel hadn't wanted to argue with Dickce over who went to Memphis and who talked to Hadley. An'gel wasn't eager to tackle Hadley on her own, but she knew if she insisted that her sister do it instead, Dickce would press her hard for a reason. An'gel found it easier to give in to Dickce's plan.

As she drove the short distance to Ashton Hall, An'gel felt apprehensive on two counts. The first was the weather. The sky had begun to darken to the west not long after Dickce and Benjy departed, and An'gel feared another storm was moving in. She prayed her sister, Benjy, and the two pets would be safe at home before anything nasty threatened.

An'gel also felt nervous about her ability to wring the truth from Hadley. She knew all too well how good he was at evading any subject he didn't want to discuss. She was determined that today, however, he would answer her questions.

To her great annoyance she discovered that she was not the only visitor to Ashton Hall this afternoon. She recognized the two cars already parked near the front of the house. One car belonged to Lottie MacLeod, and An'gel reckoned that if Lottie was here, so was Barbie. The two women seemed to go everywhere together. The second car was Reba Dalrymple's, and An'gel figured Martin would have accompanied his mother. Reba rarely went anywhere without her son in attendance.

An'gel parked next to Lottie. After a glance at the sky she dug out an umbrella from the backseat to take with her. She rang the doorbell and waited.

And waited. She glared at the door. She rang the bell, longer and more insistently this time. Where was Hadley's housekeeper?

She was about to ring the bell again when the door opened to reveal Hadley, looking more than a bit harried and disheveled.

"Thank the Lord you're here, An'gel." Hadley drew her in and bestowed a kiss on her cheek. "They're driving me crazy. Maybe you can help me get them out of the house."

"What on earth is going on?" An'gel asked as she followed her host down the hall.

267

"Why are they all here?"

"They just showed up." Hadley spoke over his shoulder. "When I was growing up, people always called before they appeared on your doorstep. Apparently that's too old-fashioned for this group."

Why *had* they all come? An'gel wondered.

"At least they brought news from the hospital," Hadley said. "Arliss is still in a coma but she's stable. Some small progress." He opened the door to his late father's library and motioned for An'gel to precede him.

Four faces regarded her as she approached the center of the room. "Goodness," she said. "I had no idea you'd all be here when I made an appointment earlier in the day to call on Hadley this afternoon." She hoped they noticed the slight stress she laid on the word *appointment.*

"We simply invited ourselves." Lottie giggled. "We were sure Hadley wouldn't mind. We've all been dying to see the inside of Ashton Hall since he came back."

"I thought you said you visited Hamish frequently in his last months." An'gel found an empty chair near Lottie. "Surely you already knew what it looked like here."

Lottie sniffed. "Hamish had let things go pretty badly. I was sure Hadley would have everything cleaned up. I tried to get Hamish to let me find him another housekeeper, but he insisted that nasty Mrs. Turnipseed was just fine."

"I was about to go to the kitchen for drinks for everyone," Hadley said. "An'gel, what would you like?"

"Whatever everyone else is having is fine with me," An'gel said. She wondered why the housekeeper wasn't taking care of the drink situation.

Almost as if he had read her mind, Hadley said in an apologetic tone, "The beverage of choice seems to be coffee, and I'm afraid you'll have to put up with my attempts at using the coffeemaker. My housekeeper has come down with some kind of bug, and so I'm looking after myself temporarily."

"I'd be delighted to help," Barbie said crossly. "I told you I'm very good at making coffee."

"I appreciate your offer," Hadley said. "But I'll manage. I'm not going to put my guests to work. My mother would be spinning in her grave at the very thought." He flashed a brief smile. "I'll be back soon." He headed out the door.

An'gel wished she could go after him and try to get a few private words in the kitchen, but she knew that wouldn't fly. Instead she glanced around at her fellow guests. Reba appeared to be disgruntled over something, and An'gel suspected it was because she wasn't the center of Hadley's attention. Martin had his eyes fixated on his cell phone. Barbie also wasn't happy, but Lottie seemed to be in her own little world, as she often was.

"Hadley mentioned that there was good news about Arliss," An'gel said to break the silence. "Did one of you go by the hospital?"

"I did," Lottie said. "The sister and her husband were there, and I talked to them for a few minutes. I really would have loved to see Arliss, but they wouldn't let me." Lottie sighed. "She must feel terribly alone in that hospital room."

"She's in a coma," Reba said. "Has no idea where she is."

Lottie gazed at Reba for a moment. "You're right. I guess I forgot about that." Her gaze moved on from Reba and seemed to focus on the shelves above Reba's head.

An'gel wondered sometimes whether Lottie's occasional scatterbrained episodes were real or feigned. She suspected the latter. Lottie had an odd sense of humor, and An'gel wouldn't put it past her to behave like a ditz simply for the amusement value it afforded her.

"What brought you and Martin here?" An'gel asked Reba. "Were you dying to see the inside of Ashton Hall also?"

Reba cast a withering glance in Lottie's direction. "I know perfectly well what the inside of this house looks like. I visited Hamish regularly over the years, much more often than anyone else."

"I suppose you knew his housekeeper then?" An'gel asked.

"Of course. I've known Thomasina Turnipseed for years," Reba said.

Martin giggled suddenly. "Thomasina Turnipseed. Thomasina Turnipseed. What a name." He went back to staring at his phone.

Reba appeared not to notice her son's interruption. "Thomasina took excellent care of Hamish over the years. Why are you asking about her, An'gel? Don't you know her?"

"Not really," An'gel said. "Years ago Hamish rebuffed our attempts to visit him, and finally Dickce and I stopped trying. I hadn't seen Mrs. Turnipseed in over thirty years, I suppose, until the other day."

An'gel felt a sudden tension in the room, and she glanced quickly at each face in turn. She could read nothing in anyone's expression, however.

"You saw Thomasina?" Reba asked.

An'gel nodded. "Dickce and I wanted to consult her about something. Oddly enough, though, since we talked to her, she seems to have disappeared." She checked for reactions to that statement, and though she once again felt tension, she couldn't identify the source.

"Disappeared?" Barbie frowned. "What do you mean, disappeared? Did she run off with some man?"

An'gel shrugged. "All I know is that the police wanted to talk to her about the remains found here, and when they went to her house, she was gone. Nobody seems to know where she is."

Reba frowned. "She has no family to speak of since her sister died. There's a nephew, but he's most likely in prison still. Or again." Her lips contorted in a grimace. "He's a terrible man. I don't think Thomasina had anything to do with him, though."

"You must know her pretty well, to know all that," Lottie said.

"Her mother worked for us when I was growing up. Thomasina was younger than I, but I saw her frequently over the years until her mother passed away. And of course when she came here to work for Mrs. Partridge."

"Who are you all talking about?" Hadley asked from the doorway. He pushed a serving cart in front of him. Barbie hopped up to help him, and he rewarded her with a brief smile.

"Mrs. Turnipseed," An'gel said.

Hadley frowned. "Why on earth are you talking about her? Dreadful woman. Hamish gave her a lot of Mother's furniture for some reason, and I'm not happy about that." He poured a cup of coffee and handed it to Reba. "He could have given her plenty of other things to thank her for all her years of service here. Mother wasn't that fond of Mrs. Turnipseed, even though she was an exemplary housekeeper."

"That's terrible." Barbie passed coffee to Lottie. "Why would he do such a thing?"

"Because he knew it would make me angry, I expect." Hadley shrugged. "I was Mother's favorite, he was our father's." He brought An'gel her coffee. For Martin he had a chilled can of soda.

Hadley picked up his own cup and sat on the sofa next to Barbie, who scooted over toward Lottie to make room for him. Lottie frowned.

An'gel had her own ideas about why Mrs.

Turnipseed had ended up with the late Mrs. Partridge's furniture, but she wasn't about to share them with the group. Especially when she figured one of them was a murderer.

She wondered if she had done the right thing in mentioning Mrs. Turnipseed's supposed disappearance. One person in this room might know exactly where the housekeeper was right now. Or be impatient to track her down, if she had indeed fled of her own accord. An'gel hoped it was the latter. That would mean the woman was still alive and unharmed.

"I still think it was an awful thing for your brother to do." Barbie patted Hadley's knee.

Reba fixed Barbie with a withering stare. "Hamish had a perfect right to dispose of his property any way he saw fit."

An'gel was startled by Reba's vehement statement. Had Reba nourished an unrequited passion for Hamish? That was an interesting thought. If she had been as attentive to Hamish over the years as she claimed, she might have hoped to become the second Mrs. Hamish Partridge.

Had she now set her sights on Hadley? An'gel regarded her friend surreptitiously but she couldn't tell whether Reba was focused on Hadley or Barbie at the moment. She would have to be more observant.

"Yes, he did," Hadley said. "The only thing he couldn't dispose of as he wished was the house itself. By the terms of my father's will, if Hamish predeceased me without children, Ashton Hall came to me."

"As it should have," Barbie said. "Your father was obviously determined to keep Ashton Hall in the family."

"It's a pity, though, you don't have a child to leave it to." Lottie held out her cup for more coffee.

"Sadly, no, I don't," Hadley said. "I will have to make other arrangements."

An'gel heard the sadness behind his words, and she felt for him.

"You could always marry a woman with children," Lottie said.

Hadley looked pained at the notion, An'gel could see, and she didn't blame him. Lottie really was thoughtless sometimes.

"Don't be ridiculous, Lottie," Barbie said.

An'gel glanced at Reba and noticed an odd gleam in her eyes. An'gel had the strangest feeling, suddenly, that Reba wanted Ashton Hall for Martin.

Then she scolded herself for having such an absurd thought. Even if Reba somehow maneuvered Hadley into marriage, she doubted he would ever leave his family home to Martin Dalrymple. The house could fall down around Martin and he would never notice. Or care, An'gel suspected. Reba would have to be slightly deranged even to think such a plan could have any hope of success.

An'gel heard chimes that sounded like a cell phone. She knew it wasn't hers. The phone continued to chime. Hadley stood and reached into his pants pocket and retrieved his phone. He glanced at the screen and frowned. He appeared to hesitate, then put the phone back in his pocket.

"Excuse me, ladies," he said, "and gentleman. I'm sorry to have to do this, but an urgent task has come up that I need to take care of. I hate cutting our visit short, but I really have no choice."

"We certainly understand," An'gel said. She set her coffee cup on the tray. "These things happen. We'll get out of your way, won't we, girls?"

"Sure," Barbie said. "Come on, Lottie."

"Come along, Martin." Reba stood and glared at them all. An'gel could tell she wasn't happy about this turn of events.

An'gel wasn't happy either. She was annoyed with the other women for showing up unannounced and interfering with her plans to talk to Hadley about the past. She was also annoyed with Hadley, because she suspected he had arranged this to get rid of them all. He had been gone long enough making coffee to have asked someone to text him with an *urgent task.*

The other women and Martin preceded An'gel out of the library and down the hall to the front door.

"An'gel, hang on a moment," Hadley said in a low voice. "Can you stay behind until the others leave?"

An'gel nodded. She remained where she was while Hadley passed her to see the others out. Reba and Martin disappeared through the door. Barbie and Lottie were discussing something on the verandah, then An'gel heard Barbie call out Reba's name. At that point Hadley shut the door and walked back to her.

Before he could speak, there was a massive crash of thunder, and the rain came pounding down. An'gel was glad she had thought to bring an umbrella with her.

"I hope they all made it into their cars before the rain started," she said. "Though it would serve them right if they got wet."

Hadley smiled. "For showing up unannounced, you mean." He laughed when An'gel nodded. "You are wicked, An'gel, but that's one of the reasons I adore you."

An'gel felt uneasy at those words. Then she realized Hadley didn't mean them as a declaration. "Why did you ask me to stay behind?"

"I wanted to apologize for not being able to talk this afternoon," Hadley said. "With all of them here there was no way we could have a private conversation. And since something's come up that I need to deal with, I'm afraid I can't talk now that they've gone. I hope you understand."

"Certainly," An'gel said, though she still suspected that the situation he needed to deal with was manufactured to get rid of them all. "We do need to talk, though, and *soon.*"

"I promise we'll have time to talk," Hadley said as he escorted her to the door. "Perhaps tomorrow." He opened the door and peered out. "I hate to send you out in this."

An'gel looked outside. The rain seemed heavy, but the walk to her car was short, and she had an umbrella. "I'll be fine. It's only a short drive."

"If you're sure." Hadley gave her a quick kiss on the cheek. As soon as she was out on the verandah, he shut the door behind her.

She grimaced at the closed door, then

278

unfurled her umbrella. She managed to make it into the car without getting too damp, although the umbrella dripped on her. She sat in the car for a moment and watched the rain. The highway would be slick, but as she had said to Hadley, it was only a short drive.

She drove slowly, the windshield wipers on high, until she reached the end of the driveway. Visibility wasn't great, but she couldn't see any traffic on the highway. She turned onto it and drove toward home.

She was perhaps a hundred feet from the driveway to Riverhill when she felt an impact from behind, and her car went into a skid on the wet road.

CHAPTER 25

Coriander Simpson was dead.

For a moment Dickce couldn't take it in. She realized she should have considered the possibility, but she was shocked nevertheless.

"I'm so sorry for your loss," she said after a moment. "I had no idea."

"Thank you." Mrs. Simpson sighed. "So long ago, but sometimes it feels like just yesterday we got the news." She kept stroking Peanut's head, and he stared at her with his most soulful gaze. Dickce thought her hostess drew comfort from the dog's presence.

"Do you mind if I ask what happened?" Dickce said.

"Not at all," Mrs. Simpson replied. "I don't rightly know the details, but I can tell what I do know." She leaned forward in her chair and twisted her upper body so she could face the door. "Where is that child?"

She raised her voice. "Monique, honey, where are you?"

"I'm coming," Monique answered, evidently from the hallway, Dickce decided, because the words were pretty clear. A moment later Monique came into the room at a slow pace, her attention focused on the tall glass of iced tea she held. She walked up to Dickce. "This is for you, ma'am. I'm going back to get Great-granny's tea."

"Thank you, Monique," Dickce said as she accepted the glass. She was grateful that Peanut remained by Mrs. Simpson's side. She had feared he would, in his puppy-like enthusiasm, bound over to Monique and have tea and glass going everywhere.

The child giggled before she scampered out of the room.

"What a precious child," Dickce said.

"She is that," Mrs. Simpson said. "Now you go on and drink your tea. Monique will be back soon with mine."

"Thank you." Dickce took a sip of the tea and then another. "It's delicious." The tea was strong the way she liked it, and the sweetness was perfect.

"I'm glad you like it," Mrs. Simpson said. "Now, what was I going to tell you? Oh, yes, about Coriander. Like I said, I don't rightly know the details. We got a telegram telling us she was dead, and that was about it."

"My goodness," Dickce said. "That's strange. Where was she when she died?"

"Over in Europe," Mrs. Simpson replied. "I think it was in England. Now, I expect you're wondering how she ended up there when she'd never been anywhere except here and Mississippi before."

"Yes, I was wondering that," Dickce said when it seemed that Mrs. Simpson required a response. "She must have left the employ of Mrs. Partridge."

"She was planning to get married over there," Mrs. Simpson said. "A couple months before she quit working for Miss Callie and left the country she sent me a letter, telling me she'd done fell in love with a man, and he wanted to marry her. She didn't tell me who he was or even what his name was, but she promised she'd come home and bring him to meet me."

"Did she?" Dickce asked.

"No, she never did. After that, the next I heard was that telegram telling me she was dead."

Dickce found this story odd. There was something about it that simply didn't sound legitimate. She would have to tread carefully because she didn't want to upset Mrs.

Simpson.

"When exactly did all this happen?" Dickce wondered if Coriander had left Ashton Hall after Callie disappeared, or before. She couldn't remember Callie ever telling them that her housemaid had left her.

"It was forty years ago," Mrs. Simpson said. "Would you like to see the telegram? It's got the exact date on it."

"If you wouldn't mind, if it's not too painful," Dickce said, "I would like to see it."

Mrs. Simpson raised herself slowly from her chair. "You stay right there, sweet boy," she said to Peanut before she stepped past him. The Labradoodle obeyed.

Dickce sensed that any offer of assistance would be rebuffed, but she was ready in case Mrs. Simpson should falter. She gave Peanut a stern look, hoping he would be still until Mrs. Simpson was back in her chair.

Mrs. Simpson moved slowly to a desk that stood against the wall and opened the top drawer. She shuffled papers for a moment, then turned with a single piece of paper in her hand. She brought it to Dickce and resumed her seat. Peanut promptly laid his head on her knee, and Mrs. Simpson patted it.

Dickce stared down at the rumpled piece

of paper. The message was brief. And brutal, she decided. *Regret to inform you that Coriander Simpson was killed in an accident in London. Burial to take place here. Sincere condolences. H. Wachtel*

The name puzzled Dickce. She couldn't recall any people with that name in Athena, though there must have been someone. Where else would Coriander have met him?

She looked at the date. June fifteenth. The same year that both Hadley and Callie disappeared from Athena.

Dickce returned the telegram to Mrs. Simpson. "Did you ever hear from this H. Wachtel again?"

Mrs. Simpson shook her head. "Not another word." She sighed. "I couldn't even bring my baby home to bury. She's over there, and I don't even know where."

Dickce felt the woman's grief, and for a moment she couldn't speak. Finally she found her voice again. "Thank you for sharing this with me, Mrs. Simpson. I can only imagine how painful this is for you, and you have my deepest sympathies."

Mrs. Simpson smiled briefly. "Thank you, ma'am."

"I can tell you that your daughter must have left Athena around the same time that Callie Partridge did, but other than that, I don't know anything. I've never heard of the person who sent the telegram." Dickce shook her head. "I know there's no comfort in that, but if I find out anything more, I will come back and tell you."

"Thank you," Mrs. Simpson said.

"Here's your tea, Great-granny," Monique said. The child's quiet approach and sudden words startled Dickce, and she barely missed knocking over her own glass.

Mrs. Simpson accepted the glass and drank. Dickce decided she had taken enough of her hostess's time. She finished her own tea and handed the glass to the hovering child. She thanked her again and rose.

"Mrs. Simpson, I appreciate your time, but I'd better get back on the road for home." She pulled one of her calling cards from her purse and handed it to her hostess. "If there's ever anything I can do for you, please call."

Mrs. Simpson thanked her and held out her hand for Dickce to shake. "I hope you can find out what happened to Miss Callie," Mrs. Simpson said. "She was always good to my daughter."

"I'll let you know, I promise." Dickce held out her hand toward Peanut. "Come on, boy, time to go home."

Peanut whined and looked up at Mrs. Simpson. She rubbed his head twice more and told him he was a sweet boy. Then he seemed satisfied and ready to go with Dickce.

Monique showed them to the door. She gave Peanut a quick hug and a pat on the head, and he returned her gestures with a couple of licks to her face. She giggled, and Dickce said good-bye.

Peanut jumped into the backseat, where Endora greeted him with several loud meows and a swipe at his head. Peanut barked at her, and that seemed to satisfy the cat. Once Peanut and Dickce were both settled, Benjy started the car and backed carefully out of the driveway. Dickce looked back to see Monique still on the porch, waving at them. She waved back until they were out of sight.

As Benjy navigated their way back to the highway, Dickce shared with him the details of her visit with Coriander Simpson's mother. She concluded by saying, "There's something fishy about that story and that telegram."

"I think you're right," Benjy said. "You can't remember anybody named Wachtel from Athena, you said."

"No, I can't," Dickce replied. "But the

name is oddly familiar for some reason. I must know it in some other context." She shook her head. "Right now I can't recall it. Hopefully it will come to me later."

Benjy chuckled. "I usually remember things in the shower, for some reason."

Dickce smiled. "Maybe I should take a shower when I get home and see if it helps."

They were silent until they reached the highway south. "I can't wait to tell An'gel about all this." Dickce checked her watch. "It's only a quarter to four. I wonder if she's still talking to Hadley." She fished out her cell phone and speed-dialed her sister. She listened briefly, then said, "Give me a call when you get this message, Sister." She laid the phone on the seat beside her.

"I'm thinking about the timing of Coriander's departure," Benjy said. "She obviously left Athena not long after Hadley Partridge. If we accept the fact that the remains that we found belong to Mrs. Partridge, then Coriander probably left before Mrs. Partridge died. Does that sound reasonable?"

Dickce thought this over for a moment. "It seems reasonable, but we really can't be sure when Coriander left. She might even have left before Hadley. We know she was dead by the fifteenth of June, two weeks after he says he left. She had to have a few

287

days to get to London somehow, and she could have gone straight to Memphis with this Mr. Wachtel and boarded a plane for England."

"True," Benjy said. "Too bad we don't know where Mrs. Turnipseed is, or we could ask her when Coriander left."

"I only hope we get the chance to talk to her," Dickce said. "For all we know she could be lying dead in a ditch somewhere."

CHAPTER 26

An'gel had always prided herself on her reflexes, that hers were like those of a much younger woman. They served her well a split-second after she felt the impact of another car and her own vehicle began to skid on the wet road. She kept control of the car and managed to avoid going into the ditch. She didn't try to look behind her to see the car that hit her. Instead, the second her car was mostly under control again, she floored the accelerator and aimed for the driveway to Riverhill.

If the car tried to follow her up the driveway, An'gel would have to come up with a plan to keep from getting hit again. She prayed that the other driver would think twice about following her any farther.

Seconds later An'gel reached the entrance to the driveway. She slowed just enough to enable her to turn in, then jammed the accelerator again and sped toward the house.

Now she glanced into the rearview mirror. With great relief she saw that the road behind her was clear. She kept up her speed, however, until she reached the house. She slowed as she pulled around to the back and put the car into park. She sat there a moment, the motor still running, and craned her neck around to make sure the other car hadn't followed her after all.

She didn't see anything. She sat in the car a few seconds longer, then she opened the door, grabbed her purse, and ran to the back door, forgetting her umbrella. She jerked the door open and stumbled inside. With shaky hands she shut the door and locked it. She pushed her soggy hair back from her face.

"Lord have mercy, Miss An'gel, whatever is going on? You look like the devil himself is after you." Clementine's eyes fairly popped out of their sockets, or so it seemed to An'gel. "And look at you, dripping wet."

"I'm okay," An'gel said, her breath still ragged. "Need to sit down though." She made her way shakily to one of the chairs around the kitchen table and dropped into it.

"You need a nip of something," Clementine said. "I'll get you some whisky. And a towel."

An'gel nodded weakly. She concentrated on getting her breathing and her heart rate back to normal. As soon as she did, she was going to call Kanesha Berry and report the attack. She wondered briefly why the attacker hadn't followed her off the highway, but she was grateful he hadn't, whatever the reason.

Clementine quickly returned with both a large towel, which she wrapped around An'gel's shoulders, and a healthy tot of whisky. An'gel downed the whisky in one gulp and felt the warmth begin to spread. She pulled the towel more tightly around her.

"I must look a mess," she said with a weak smile. "Thank you, Clementine."

"You surely do," Clementine said. "What on earth is going on?"

An'gel gave the housekeeper a brief explanation. "Now I need to call Kanesha and tell her about this. It's too late to find the lunatic, but she needs to know what happened."

"Soon as you're done with that, you need to get right on upstairs and out of those wet clothes." Clementine shook her head. "Can't have you coming down with a cold."

"No, certainly not." An'gel smiled briefly. She retrieved her cell phone from her purse and speed-dialed Kanesha's cell. The call went to voice mail, and An'gel left a terse but coherent message about her ordeal before she went to change.

Twenty minutes later she was back downstairs, dressed in dry clothing, her hair restored to its usual state, and grateful to find that Clementine had fresh coffee waiting.

"Who do you think was trying to run you off the road?" Clementine asked.

"I'm not sure," An'gel said. "It has to be somebody who was at Ashton Hall this afternoon, since it happened right after we all left. Barbie Gross and Lottie MacLeod were together in Lottie's car, and Reba Dalrymple was with her son Martin. I didn't really get a look at the car that hit me, though, so it could have been either pair."

"Why would any of them want to run you off the road?" Clementine shook her head. "Don't make no sense to me."

"To me either," An'gel said. "It has to have something to do with what happened at Ashton Hall forty years ago. That's all I know at the moment. We've got to figure this out."

Her cell phone rang, and she saw that Kanesha was returning her call.

"How are you, Miss An'gel? Were you hurt

at all?" Kanesha sounded angry, An'gel thought.

"I was a bit shaky for a while afterwards," An'gel said. "I feel fine now, though I might be sore tomorrow."

"I'm thankful you're okay," Kanesha said. "Did you get a look at the car that hit you?"

"No, I didn't. It all happened too fast, and all I could think about was getting away from whoever it was." An'gel shuddered. For a moment she felt the terror she had experienced right after her car got hit.

"Tell me again where you were before this and what led up to the attack."

An'gel gave the deputy a summary of her visit to Ashton Hall and explained who else was there. "They all left ahead of me," she concluded. "So one of the cars could have been waiting for me to get on the highway. It was raining, and I didn't see anyone, but there are a couple of side roads nearby where they could have been waiting."

"I've already sent someone to investigate," Kanesha said. "With the rain, though, I'm not sure they'll be able to find anything. How badly was your car damaged?"

"I don't know," An'gel said. "I haven't looked at it yet. To be honest, I haven't really thought about it until now."

"Leave it as it is for now," Kanesha said.

"There'll be someone there a little later on to have a look at it. In the meantime we're going to be checking with Mrs. MacLeod and Mrs. Dalrymple to see if they have any damage to their cars."

"Then we'll finally know who's behind all this crazy behavior." An'gel felt relieved. This might soon be over, and then they would know who was responsible for Sarinda's death and Arliss's accident.

"That's what I'm hoping," Kanesha said. "Then maybe we can find out why. I have to go now, Miss An'gel. You take care of yourself, and I'll be back in touch soon."

"Thank you," An'gel said. "I'm really looking forward to hearing that this is all over." She said good-bye and ended the call. She set the phone down on the table. As she did so, she suddenly felt exhausted. The ordeal had taken a toll, and she realized she needed to rest.

"I think I'm going to stretch out on the sofa in the study for a little while," she told Clementine. "At least until Dickce and Benjy get home from Memphis."

"That's a good idea," Clementine said. "I'll let you know when they're back."

An'gel thanked her and headed for the study. She retrieved a blanket from a cabinet and then stretched out on the sofa. She

294

covered herself with the blanket, got her head comfortably situated on a pillow, and moments later was sound asleep.

"I thought we'd never make it through all that rain," Dickce said as Benjy turned off the highway onto the driveway at Riverhill. "You drove us safely through, and I'm thankful for that."

Benjy smiled briefly. "I am, too. I'm ready to be out of the car, though, I can tell you that. It feels like we've been on the road all day."

"I know. Thank goodness the rain finally stopped," Dickce said. "Peanut and Endora are restless, too. I can't wait to tell An'gel what we found out in Memphis." She frowned. "I wonder why she didn't call me back, though. Surely she's not still at Ashton Hall with Hadley. I hope nothing's wrong."

They drove around the house and approached the garage. Dickce spotted their car where An'gel had left it. She gasped. "Oh my Lord, look at that. The car's been hit. I hope An'gel is all right."

The moment Benjy had his car stationary in the garage, Dickce was out and headed for the house. "I've got to find out about Sister," she said.

She left Benjy to deal with Peanut and

Endora, and she hurried to the kitchen. She found Clementine inside preparing their dinner.

"Clementine, where's An'gel? Is she okay?" Dickce said. "What happened to the car?"

"She's okay," Clementine said. "She's taking a little nap in the study." She explained what happened, and then repeated it moments later when Benjy came in with the animals. Peanut and Endora made a beeline for Clementine and greeted her like they hadn't seen her in months. The housekeeper spoke quietly to them and gave each a few rubs on the head.

"Thank the Lord she wasn't hurt." Dickce collapsed into the chair Benjy hastily pulled out for her. Clementine handed her a cup of coffee, and Dickce took it gratefully.

"Somebody from the sheriff's department was here a little while ago," Clementine said. "He looked at the car and took pictures of the damage. I didn't wake Miss An'gel, though. She needs to rest."

Dickce shuddered. "I'm sure she does. How terrified she must have been, though. She could have ended up in the hospital like poor Arliss McGonigal. Surely the police or the sheriff's department can find the car that caused these accidents pretty soon."

"I surely hope so," Clementine said. "How was the trip to Memphis? Did y'all find out anything?"

"We found the Simpson house," Benjy said. "Coriander's mother still lives there."

"I talked with her," Dickce said after a sip of coffee. She shared the news of Coriander's death with Clementine.

"That poor girl, killed like that on her honeymoon." Clementine closed her eyes for a moment. When she opened them again, she asked, "Who did you say she married?"

"A man named Wachtel," Dickce replied. "I can't recall anyone by that name from Athena, though the name sounds familiar for some reason."

"No folks I know of by that name," Clementine said. "Must've been somebody here just a short time, I reckon."

"Maybe so," Dickce replied.

"I'm going to look up the name," Benjy said. "It's too bad we don't have the first name, instead of only an initial. Having a whole first name would make it easier. Still, I might be able to find something."

"What are y'all talking about?"

Dickce started at the sound of her sister's

voice. She got up and hurried to An'gel. "Are you okay, Sister?" She gave An'gel a quick hug.

An'gel gave her a wan smile. "My back is getting stiff. I have a feeling it's going to be sore tomorrow. My neck, too."

"You need a hot shower and some aspirin," Dickce said. "Thank the Lord it's not worse."

"Amen to that," An'gel replied. "I'll go up and take a shower in a few minutes. First, though, I want to hear all about what you found out in Memphis."

Dickce escorted her sister to a chair, and Peanut came to greet An'gel. He whined, and she rubbed his head. Endora came near her, meowed, and then hopped into Dickce's lap. An'gel smiled and continued to give Peanut the attention he craved.

Dickce gave her sister a report of the conversation she'd had with Coriander Simpson's mother. An'gel did not comment until Dickce finished.

"That's a strange story," she said. "I wish we knew more about this Wachtel person."

"So do I," Dickce said. "Clementine doesn't remember anybody by that name, either."

"I'm going to see whether I can find out anything about him," Benjy said. "I might get lucky, but without more to go on, I might not find anything."

An'gel's phone rang. Dickce took it from her hands. "Let me answer this," she said. "You still look tired." She glanced at the screen.

"Hello, Kanesha, this is Dickce. An'gel is here with me," she said.

"Is she doing okay?" Kanesha asked.

"A little stiff, but otherwise okay," Dickce replied.

"Glad to hear it," Kanesha said. "I've got some news for y'all. We've checked the cars belonging to Mrs. MacLeod and Mrs. Dalrymple."

"Which one of them tried to run An'gel off the road?" Dickce asked.

"Neither of them," Kanesha said.

Chapter 27

An'gel held out her hand. "Give me my phone. I'm perfectly capable of talking to Kanesha."

"All right then, Miss Grumpy Pants." Dickce thrust the phone at her.

"Hello, Kanesha. This is An'gel. What were you telling my sister?"

"I hope you're doing okay, Miss An'gel," Kanesha said. "I told Miss Dickce we checked both Mrs. MacLeod's and Mrs. Dalrymple's cars, and they were intact. No damage."

"How bizarre." An'gel was stunned. She had been so sure one of their cars would have been the one trying to force her off the road.

"We also checked Mr. Partridge's car," Kanesha said. "It is also intact."

"Then who on earth was it, do you think?" An'gel said.

"It's entirely possible it was a hit-and-run

300

by a stranger," Kanesha said. "We'll have to keep that in mind. It's a huge coincidence, though, after what happened to Mrs. McGonigal."

"It certainly is," An'gel said. She was thankful to know that Hadley hadn't been the one who hit her. Perhaps it was just a coincidence after all. The road was slick, and visibility was reduced.

"We'll be on the lookout for a vehicle with a damaged front end," Kanesha said. "We still haven't identified the vehicle that forced Mrs. McGonigal off the road."

"I hope you can identify it soon," An'gel said. "Have you made any progress in the search for Mrs. Turnipseed?"

"Nothing new to report," Kanesha replied. "Sorry, Miss An'gel, but I've got to go. Y'all stay safe now, all right?"

"We'll do our best," An'gel said, her tone wry.

"Well, what else did she tell you?" Dickce said when An'gel put down her phone.

"She said they checked Hadley's car, and his isn't damaged either. Kanesha said to keep in mind the possibility that it was merely a coincidence and not connected to the other incidents at all." An'gel frowned. "The conditions weren't great, so someone who wasn't paying attention could have

301

come up behind me and not realized I was there."

"Did you remember to turn the headlights on?" Dickce asked. "That car is gray, and in the rain it's hard to see if the lights aren't on."

"I don't remember," An'gel said. "I was preoccupied when I got in the car, and I may have forgotten the lights."

"If you did, it's no wonder somebody ran into you." Dickce frowned. "You've got to be more careful, Sister."

An'gel could have sworn she heard a snicker, but she wasn't sure of its source. Both Benjy and Clementine were looking down at their hands when she checked.

"That's rich, coming from you," An'gel said, her temper flaring. "Considering you drive like you're trying to get away from a stampeding herd of elephants all the time."

Peanut whined, and An'gel realized she and her sister were on the verge of one of their rare arguments. She knew her sister was worried about her, because the outcome of the accident could have been so much worse.

"Sorry, Dickce." An'gel reached over and patted her sister's arm. "I guess I'm still a little off balance from the accident." Endora swatted at her hand, and An'gel drew it back quickly.

"Apology accepted," Dickce said.

"What did Deputy Berry have to say about Mrs. Turnipseed?" Benjy asked.

"Nothing new to report," An'gel said. "I can only hope that, in this case, no news is good news."

"No telling about that woman." Clementine sniffed. "She's liable to be up to anything."

"I sure would like another chance to talk to her," An'gel said.

"I hope you won't bring her inside this house." Clementine looked determined. "Don't need that bad stuff coming in here."

An'gel and Dickce exchanged a swift glance. They had rarely heard their housekeeper speak so harshly of anyone. An'gel hastened to assure Clementine that she wouldn't talk to Mrs. Turnipseed at Riverhill unless there was no other way.

"Provided, of course," Dickce said, "she's not dead in a ditch herself somewhere." She shivered. "I shouldn't have said that. I said it when we were on the way home from Memphis, and then we get here and find out you could have ended up in a ditch."

"The Lord was looking out for Miss An'gel," Clementine said. "Now it's my turn. Dinner will be ready soon. Why don't y'all go on and get washed up?"

"That sounds like a good idea to me," Benjy said. "It's been a long time since lunch." He stood. "Come on, guys, time for us to go." He picked up Endora from Dickce's lap, and Peanut followed him as he went to the kitchen door. "Stopped raining, at least. I'll be back soon as I get the guys settled. I'll put the car in the garage, too."

"We'll set the table," An'gel told the housekeeper.

Clementine nodded. "Thank you. I'll bring the food along shortly."

An'gel and Dickce left the kitchen. They took turns washing up in the downstairs powder room before they went into the dining room. They began to lay the table while they chatted.

"If that car hitting you wasn't a coincidence," Dickce said, "who do you think could have been driving the car?"

"It happened too soon after we all left for any of the others to get home, find another car, and come back." An'gel frowned. "And Hadley's car was undamaged. I think surely whoever hit me sustained damage to their car, so that lets Hadley off. Who else is there?"

"I know this may sound odd," Dickce said, "but the only other person connected to this that we know of is Mrs. Turnipseed."

"Why would she try to run me off the road?" An'gel asked.

"I don't know," Dickce said. "She's just the only other person I can think of."

"Unless there's a Mister or Miss X," An'gel said. "Someone we don't know about yet who is involved somehow."

"That hardly seems likely," Dickce said.

An'gel sighed. "I know, but it seems about as likely as Mrs. Turnipseed."

"She as good as told you that she was actually at Ashton Hall when Callie left," Dickce said. "She must have seen something or she wouldn't have tried to get money from us."

"I agree." An'gel stood back and admired their handiwork. "Perhaps she put the bite on the person she saw then, and that person has forced her to help them now. Are you thinking something like that?"

"Pretty much," Dickce said. "Only I wonder what kind of inducement that person is using. Threatening to kill Mrs. Turnipseed if she doesn't go along with them, or offering a huge bribe. Which might it be?"

An'gel thought about that for a moment.

"Actually there's another possibility. Make that two possibilities. The first is that Mrs. Turnipseed has been behind everything all along. The second one is that the person behind it has equally damaging evidence against Mrs. Turnipseed."

"I like that second one," Dickce said. "We don't have much to go on, based on our only recent encounter with Mrs. T, but I think she's probably a nasty piece of work. I wouldn't put much past her."

"Me either," An'gel replied. "And you heard what Clementine thinks of her. She's usually the soul of charity, but when she doesn't like someone, it means that person is horrid."

Benjy entered the dining room bearing a large bowl of salad. Clementine was right behind him with the serving cart.

"Something sure smells wonderful," Dickce said.

"Chicken tetrazzini and garlic bread," Benjy said with a happy grin. "Man, I can't wait to dig in." He set the salad on the table.

Clementine set chilled bowls at each place. She put the large casserole dish on a trivet on the table and then set the garlic bread near it.

"Looks wonderful," An'gel said. "We'll clean up. You go on home."

Clementine nodded. "See you tomorrow."

Conversation was sparse as the three ate their meal. After his second helping of the chicken dish, Benjy pushed back from the table a little. "I think I'm completely stuffed."

"I am, too," Dickce said. "Although I keep thinking I want another piece of garlic bread."

"There's only the one left," An'gel said. "If Benjy doesn't care for it, go ahead."

Dickce glanced at Benjy. He shook his head, smiling. Dickce picked up the slice of toasted bread and took a bite out of it.

"While my sister munches in peace," An'gel said, "what are your plans for tomorrow, Benjy?"

"I'm going to continue my research," he replied. "I'll probably work some tonight. I want to see if I can track down this H. Wachtel person. I thought I might also try searching English newspaper archives to see if I can find anything on Coriander Simpson's death."

"Excellent. I hope you can find something," An'gel said. "If you can't, it won't exactly prove that Coriander didn't die in England, of course."

"No, but a negative result will tell us something," Benjy said. "I might have to

307

pay to get into some of the archives. Is that okay?"

"Certainly," Dickce said. "Use your credit card." They had given him his own card recently, but he was careful about using it unless he discussed it with them first.

"Thanks." Benjy stood and began to clear his side of the table.

"We'll take care of the rest," An'gel told him. "You go on and see if Clementine left anything in the fridge for dessert." She winked. "Then go and research."

Benjy laughed. "I shouldn't eat anything more, but Clementine's desserts are hard to resist. I guess I'll say good night then."

An'gel and Dickce both wished him good night, and he left the dining room humming.

"It's wonderful to see the change in him since we first met him three months ago," Dickce said. "He's become so much more confident, and he smiles a lot."

"Having a home, good food, and people who actually support him and pay attention to him has made a huge difference." An'gel smiled. "I'm glad you talked me into making him our ward."

Dickce picked up her glass and stared into it. An'gel waited. She knew Dickce had something on her mind, but there was no point in rushing her.

After a moment, Dickce said, "I've been thinking about that, having him as our ward. We use that term, but there's really nothing legal behind it to define the relationship." She paused. "I want to adopt him." She held up a hand toward her sister. "And before you tell me that's a ridiculous idea, a woman my age adopting anyone, I'm pretty determined about this."

"I'm not going to say it's a ridiculous idea," An'gel replied. "I've been thinking about it myself. We have no direct heirs, and when we're gone, I want someone who will appreciate Riverhill to have it and take care of it. I think Benjy could be the right person for that."

"I do, too." Dickce smiled, obviously relieved by her sister's words. "I'm so glad you agree."

"My only stipulation is that we wait until Benjy has been with us a year," An'gel said. "We need more time to get to know him, and he to know us. At the end of a year, we can sit down and talk about it. Will you agree to that?"

"I suppose you're right," Dickce said. "I know I shouldn't be too hasty with a decision like this." She thought for a moment. "Okay. A year it is, but I'll hold you to it."

An'gel laughed suddenly. "We're certainly optimists, aren't we? At *our* age, talking about what we'll do nine months from now." She sobered. "Still, I think it's best that we wait."

"Agreed." Dickce stood and began to gather dirty utensils and plates to take to the kitchen.

An'gel knew her sister was bothered by the mention of their ages, but they had to be realistic. They were both in excellent health, but so many things could happen to change that, and quickly. She'd had a lucky escape today, thank heavens, and she didn't care to think about how bad it could have been.

She forced her thoughts away from that subject. Time to focus on something else. She thought about Callie Partridge and how easily — or so it seemed — she had slipped from their lives. They hadn't questioned it among themselves, at least not seriously. Gossip had quickly provided an answer, but as it turned out, not the correct one. Callie had lain in a grave at Ashton Hall all these years.

An'gel was struck by an odd thought. There were two women missing: Callie and Coriander. What if those weren't Callie's remains they'd found? What if they'd belonged to Coriander instead?

CHAPTER 28

An'gel followed as Dickce pushed the serving cart, now laden with the remains of their
dinner, dirty plates, and utensils, back to
the kitchen. Could she possibly be right?
she wondered. She debated whether to
share her idea with her sister. Dickce might
think she was being foolish to think such a
thing. After all, An'gel thought, what motive
could there have been to murder Coriander
Simpson?

She continued to play with the idea in her
mind while she and Dickce rinsed the dishes
and put away the meager leftovers of the
chicken tetrazzini. When they finished their
tasks, Dickce declared she was going to the
front parlor for a glass of postprandial
brandy.

"Sounds good," An'gel said. "I'll join you
in a minute."

Dickce looked at her oddly but didn't
question her. The moment she left the

room, An'gel picked up the kitchen phone and punched in a number.

"Good evening, Elmo," she said when the elderly doctor answered. "How are you doing?"

"Tolerable, just tolerable," Gandy replied. "How about your lovely self, An'gel?"

"I'm doing fine." An'gel moved over to the table and sat. Elmo could be long-winded sometimes, and she felt tired. "I hope you won't mind my calling, but there's something weighing on my mind. I'm hoping you can help me with it."

"What's that?" the doctor asked, sounding concerned. "Your sciatica acting up again?"

"No, that's not bothering me, thank heavens," An'gel said. "No, what I wanted to talk to you about is Callie Partridge."

"What about her?" Gandy said.

When An'gel didn't immediately respond to his question, the doctor went on. "This is about the remains found up at Ashton Hall, isn't it?"

"Yes," An'gel said. "Ever since we found them, Callie has been weighing heavy on my mind. I just wondered if you were able to help the sheriff's department identify them."

"Unfortunately, I haven't. I suppose it's all right to tell you this, but Callie, you see,

313

had never broken any bones to my knowledge, and there was no evidence of broken bones in the remains. So that was a washout. The remains are approximately the size Callie was, about five foot seven, but that's not positive proof. That anthropologist from the college thinks the woman was roughly the same age as Callie was when she disappeared, but he can't say precisely how old she was."

"What about dental records?" An'gel said.

"They're trying to track down her dentist. He left town a good twenty-five years ago, and he was in his early sixties then, if I'm remembering correctly. Her records may no longer be available."

"That's frustrating," An'gel said. "At this rate we may never know for sure who was buried in that grave."

"If they can track down a member of Callie's family and get a good sample, a DNA test will provide the answer," Gandy said.

"True," An'gel said, "but who knows how long that could take?" She debated whether to share her idea that the remains might belong to Coriander Simpson. She decided the notion was a bit too farfetched and would only complicate matters at this point. She would have to think about it more before she discussed it with anyone else.

"Thank you, Elmo," she said. "I appreciate you answering my question. I know you must think I'm being a busybody."

Gandy chuckled. "Not at all, my dear. We're all concerned about this."

An'gel thanked him again and ended the call. She realized Dickce would be wondering why she hadn't come to the parlor for her brandy. She'd better go, she decided, before Dickce came looking for her.

"What took you so long?" Dickce asked the moment she entered the parlor.

"I had a phone call I wanted to make." An'gel headed for the liquor cabinet and poured herself some brandy. She took the snifter and joined her sister on the sofa.

"I see." Dickce sipped at her brandy. "And this was a call you couldn't make with me listening in, I gather?"

"Not really," An'gel said, slightly annoyed at her sister's snippy tone. "If you must know, I called Elmo Gandy to ask him whether he had been able to help identify those remains as Callie Partridge."

Dickce leaned forward. "What did he say?"

"There was no conclusive evidence. No broken bones, and Callie had never broken any, to his knowledge. Approximately the

315

right age and height, but that's it, really." An'gel stared at the amber liquid in the snifter before taking a sip.

"What about dental records?" Dickce asked.

An'gel repeated the doctor's words. "The only hope, really, is DNA testing, if they can find a member of Callie's family."

"They ought to be able to find someone," Dickce said. "I don't recall Callie ever saying anything about a brother or a sister, but surely there's a cousin around somewhere."

"I believe she was an only child," An'gel said. "We'll have to hope for a cousin. If anyone would know, Hadley should. I'm sure Kanesha has already talked to him about it."

"No doubt," Dickce said. "Changing the subject here, but have you called the insurance company about the car?"

An'gel shook her head. "No, I haven't. Frankly, it went clean out of my mind until you mentioned it. I'll call in the morning. We'll have to get the report from the sheriff's department anyway, and we can't do that until tomorrow."

"I didn't really take the time to look at the damage," Dickce said. "The moment I saw it all I could think about was you. Now it's too dark to see that good."

"I'm deeply thankful it was still drivable." An'gel downed the rest of her brandy. "Otherwise, well, I don't want to think about the otherwise."

"No, let's not." Dickce rose and held out her hand. "How about a little more brandy?"

An'gel gave Dickce her snifter. "Perhaps a bit more. Thank you."

When Dickce returned with the brandy she said, "Another change of subject. Do you remember what Coriander Simpson looked like?"

An'gel thought for a moment, tried to dredge up a clear memory of the young woman. All she got was a hazy picture of an attractive woman with short hair and café au lait skin. She shared the meager description with Dickce.

"That's about the best I can do," Dickce said. "I do remember, though, that she was slender, like Callie, and about the same height." She paused for a sip of brandy. "Maybe I should have asked Mrs. Simpson for a picture of her I could borrow. I didn't think about it at the time, though."

"She might have thought that it was a strange request," An'gel said.

"You're probably right."

"I wonder if there are any pictures of her

at Ashton Hall," An'gel said. "We might ask Hadley."

"What reason could we give for asking for a picture of a former housemaid?" Dickce asked.

"Good point." An'gel thought for a moment longer, then felt foolish as a memory surfaced. "*We* have a picture of her. I just remembered."

"We do?" Dickce said. "Why do we have a picture of her?"

"From that big party we had here that last Christmas before Hadley left and Callie disappeared. Don't you remember?"

Dickce nodded. "Now that you mention it, I do. Didn't Coriander Simpson come over to help Clementine supervise the caterer's staff that evening?"

"She did," An'gel said. "The question is, where are the picture albums from back then? You packed a bunch of them away, didn't you, about fifteen years ago?"

"I did," Dickce said. "I know exactly where they are, too. Unfortunately, we can't get at them tonight."

"Why?" An'gel asked. "Where are they?"

"In the Athena College archives," Dickce replied. "That particular Christmas party was a fund-raiser for the library. They needed money for something — can't remember now what it was — and we hosted the event. Eulalie Estes asked me for them, and I didn't see any need for us to keep them."

"I'd forgotten it was a fund-raiser," An'gel said. "I guess we'll have to go by the archives tomorrow and visit with Charlie and Diesel and get a copy of any picture we can find with Coriander in it."

"After we get the car to the body shop," Dickce said. "It's always fun to visit Charlie and Diesel."

"That takes care of our morning," An'gel said. "I think we need to talk to Hadley in the afternoon. I know Kanesha has probably already questioned him more than once, but she probably didn't ask him everything I plan to."

"Do you think we ought to tell her what we're doing?" Dickce said. "She might prefer that we keep our noses out of this."

"We're simply going to be talking to an old and dear friend about memories from the past," An'gel said. "I can't see the harm in that. Besides, I think we're more likely to get Hadley to open up to us than Kanesha is. He's hiding something, I'm almost sure of it, and I intend to find out what it is. If it helps put an end to this situation, then

Kanesha will be happy to have the information."

"Hadley's more likely to open up to *you,* you mean," Dickce said.

An'gel didn't care for the mischievous glint in her sister's eye. She wished Dickce would give up trying to needle her about Hadley. She was tired of it, and she was having a hard enough time suppressing certain memories without Dickce's teasing to keep them resurfacing.

"I'm feeling tired. I'm going up to bed." An'gel rose. "Would you mind taking my snifter to the kitchen?"

"Not at all," Dickce said. "You have had an unusual day, and I'm sure you're ready to put it behind you. Go on up, and I'll make sure everything is locked up for the night."

"Thank you, Sister." An'gel appreciated how sweet Dickce could be when she wasn't feeling her best.

She climbed the stairs slowly. She could feel the stiffness in her back and knew it might be worse in the morning. Her neck was a bit sore as well. She decided a nice hot soak in a tub with Epsom salts might be exactly what she needed to help with her back. Their mother had always sworn by Epsom salts for a variety of issues, and over the years An'gel and Dickce had realized the benefits of their mother's advice. With her plan in mind, An'gel headed straight for her bathroom to begin filling the tub.

The next morning An'gel felt only a slight stiffness when she awoke, and she hoped a hot shower would soon put that right. The soreness in her neck had diminished a bit, but if it persisted she would probably have to have it x-rayed, she realized.

She called their insurance agent at eight o'clock, and he promised to have everything taken care of. He would contact the sheriff's department in case they wanted someone at the body shop to examine the car further before repairs began.

By nine o'clock, An'gel and Dickce were finished at the body shop. Dickce drove them to Athena College in the rental car the insurance agent had arranged for them and parked near the antebellum home that served as the offices of the library's director as well as the home of the rare book collection and college archives.

They stopped to chat briefly with Melba Gilley, the director's administrative assistant, before continuing upstairs to the archive. An'gel had called Charlie Harris from the body shop to make sure he would be available and that he would have time to help them find the pictures they sought.

An'gel knocked on the open door, and Charlie Harris looked up from his desk. His face broke into a wide smile as he rose and came around the desk to greet them. Right behind him came Diesel, his Maine Coon. Diesel was Charlie's constant companion, and An'gel and Dickce were as fond of the cat as they were the man.

"Miss An'gel, Miss Dickce, this is such a pleasant surprise," Charlie said. "It seems like ages since we've seen you. You're both looking well."

He had two chairs already arranged for them, and in his usual courtly fashion, he made sure they were seated comfortably. Diesel had to warble for each of them in turn and have his head scratched. His greetings completed, he stretched out on the floor between their chairs.

"It has been ages, Charlie," An'gel said. "You're looking well, and Diesel looks as handsome and spoiled as ever."

Charlie laughed. "We're doing fine, and we're both glad to see you. What can we do for you this morning? You said you needed to look at some pictures you gave to the archive back in Miss Eulalie's time, I believe."

"Yes, they're pictures from a fund-raiser at Riverhill that we held for the library's benefit. Eulalie asked for the pictures fifteen years ago, though the party actually took place four decades ago."

"I see," Charlie said. "I've been looking through our records, and I'm pretty sure I know where the photographs are. Miss Eulalie kept excellent track of everything. If you don't mind waiting a few minutes, I'll go next door and retrieve the box."

"We don't mind waiting at all," An'gel said. "I'm sure Diesel will be happy to keep us company."

At the sound of his name the cat chirped and meowed, and An'gel and Dickce smiled.

"I'll be right back." Charlie strode from the room.

The sisters took turns rubbing Diesel's head and back while they waited.

"I hope we're not misremembering about those pictures," An'gel said. "Surely there's one of Coriander among them."

"Bound to be," Dickce said.

Charlie returned a couple of minutes later with an archival box. He set it on his desk and removed the lid. From inside it he pulled out a smaller box of an appropriate size for photographs.

"There are four of these, each with about

forty to fifty photographs," he said. "They're all pictures from that fund-raiser, according to Miss Eulalie's notes."

"That sounds about right," Dickce said. "The photographer was snapping pictures constantly."

"Why don't you let each of us have a box to go through," An'gel said. "Shouldn't take us long to find what we're after."

Charlie gave them cotton gloves to put on. The gloves would protect the photographs from any oil or other residue on their fingers.

An'gel settled her box in her lap and cautiously began to go through the photographs. At first the process was awkward, but she quickly got used to the gloves. She had to resist the temptation to linger over certain pictures, especially those that brought back particular memories. She forced herself to focus.

Moments later, Dickce said, "I've found her." She brandished a photograph. "Here's Coriander Simpson."

CHAPTER 29

"Let me see." An'gel held out her hand for the photograph.

Dickce held on to it a moment longer, staring at the image, before yielding it to her sister.

An'gel let it lie flat on her palm as she examined it. The setting was the kitchen at Riverhill, and the subjects were two women, their housekeeper Clementine and another young woman whom An'gel recognized as Coriander Simpson. They stood together near the stove, smiling into the camera. Both women wore red in honor of the season, and Coriander stood a couple of inches shorter than Clementine.

"She was a lovely girl," An'gel said. "She looks about twenty-five here."

"I found another one," Dickce said. "Here she is with Callie. Now that's interesting."

"What do you mean?" An'gel asked.

Dickce thrust the picture at her, and

An'gel took it and laid it over the first one. Callie Partridge and Coriander Simpson stood together in conversation near the staircase at Riverhill. Each was in profile as she faced the other. What struck An'gel immediately was that they appeared to be the same height. Then, as she continued to examine the picture, she noticed that their hairstyles were similar. Callie was about the same age as Coriander, and they were both beautiful young women.

"I see what you mean." An'gel looked up at Charlie, who was regarding her and Dickce with interest. "Is there a way we could have copies of these pictures?"

Charlie nodded. "I can scan them and email them to you."

"Excellent," An'gel said. "We'd appreciate it." She handed him the two photographs.

"Here's one more," Dickce said. "Scan this one, too." She gave the one she held to Charlie.

"What's that one?" An'gel asked.

Charlie passed it to her, and An'gel examined it. The composition was almost exactly the same as the one she had just seen, of Callie and Coriander. In this photograph, they also stood in profile near the staircase, but now An'gel could see Hadley Partridge standing nearby, to the left of Coriander.

He was gazing at the two women, and An'gel couldn't decipher his expression or be sure which woman was the object of his focus. She gave the photograph back to Charlie to scan.

"If you'll excuse me a few minutes, ladies," Charlie said, "I'll turn on the scanner and have these ready to email to you right away." He nodded toward a machine that stood on a desk nearby. He walked over to it, sat down, and began to work.

"It's odd how Hadley is looking at them, don't you think?" An'gel said.

Dickce nodded. "I can't quite figure out his expression, but it certainly seems intense."

"We'll have to ask him," An'gel said. "I just wonder, though, if he'll tell us the truth."

"I think he was really in love with Callie despite what he told us," Dickce said.

"You may be right," An'gel said.

They waited in silence after that for Charlie to finish his work with the photographs. Diesel continued to nap quietly between their chairs.

"All done." Charlie came back to them with the photographs, and Dickce replaced them in the box. "I've emailed them to both of you. The scanner is high resolution, so

327

the pictures should be really clear for you, depending on your computer monitor or your phone screen."

"Thank you, Charlie, we really appreciate your help," Dickce said.

"I'm sorry we can't go into more detail about why we want these pictures," An'gel said.

Charlie grinned. "I'm betting they have something to do with the remains found at Ashton Hall." He resumed his seat behind the desk and continued to grin at them.

"How on earth did you hear about that?" An'gel said. "It hasn't even been in the local newspaper."

Charlie pointed down at the floor, and An'gel looked at him, puzzled. Then the light dawned.

"Melba, you mean." An'gel shook her head. "How that woman finds out everything that's going on in Athena is beyond me."

"She has a network that rivals the CIA," Charlie said. "She told me about it this morning when I mentioned to her that you were coming to see me."

"Maybe we should ask her if she knows who those remains belong to," Dickce said in a jesting tone. "Wouldn't surprise me if she does."

"I do want to have a word with her," An'gel said. "I guess we couldn't expect the news not to spread. It simply amazes me, though, how quickly things get around."

"I asked her how she found out about it," Charlie said. "She told me she heard it from one of the ladies from the garden club. I think the name was Gross. Not anyone I know."

"Barbie," An'gel and Dickce said in unison. It didn't surprise An'gel that Barbie was going around talking about the remains. She and Lottie always liked to have "tidbits" to share.

An'gel thanked Charlie again for his assistance, and they chatted a few more minutes with him. They also made sure to give Diesel attention, and he thanked them with more warbles.

On the way out of the building they stopped to speak for a moment with Melba.

"I ran into Barbie Gross at the grocery store," Melba said in answer to An'gel's question. "I hadn't seen her in a while, and we talked for a few minutes. She told me about the discovery of those bones up at Ashton Hall." Her eyes gleamed. "I'll bet they're all that's left of that Mrs. Partridge. I remember my mama talking about how she just up and left her husband and went after his brother."

Dickce started to speak, but An'gel laid a warning hand on her sister's arm. Anything they told Melba would likely be all over town by nightfall unless they swore her to secrecy. Melba talked a lot but she did honor anything told to her in strictest confidence.

"That's what everyone thought at the time," An'gel said. "Now that Hadley is back, though, he says it didn't happen. In fact, he seemed to be surprised when we told him that Callie went away soon after he did."

"Guess that makes sense," Melba said. "Especially if that was Mrs. Partridge in the ground. So who do you think killed her? Her husband? I'm betting it was him. Mama always said there was something a little odd about him."

"It's a possibility," Dickce said. "But it's up to the sheriff's department to figure it out. First, though, they have to identify the remains."

"If anyone can do it, Kanesha Berry can," Melba said.

"Yes, you're right about that," An'gel said. "Well, Melba, we've enjoyed visiting with you, but Sister and I had better get going. You take care now."

330

Melba bade them good-bye, and An'gel led the way out of the building and back to the car.

"At least we know what the woman on the street thinks about all this." Dickce buckled her seat belt and then inserted the key in the ignition. "Where to next?"

An'gel didn't respond right away, and Dickce had to ask her again.

"Sorry, I was thinking," An'gel said. "I've had an idea. Why don't I call Barbie and see if she'll meet us for coffee and a pastry at Helen Louise's bistro? I think we need to talk to her about Hadley and what she might have been up to with him forty years ago."

"Sounds like a plan," Dickce said. "Call her, and even if she can't join us, we can still have that coffee and pastry." She put the car in gear and headed for the town square.

An'gel pulled out her phone and found the number in her contacts. Moments later she was speaking to Barbie.

"We're in town this morning on business," An'gel said. "We're heading over to Helen Louise's bistro for coffee and a pastry, and we thought it would be fun if you could join us. Can you?"

"Love to," Barbie said. "What a nice

331

surprise. I'll be there in two shakes." She ended the call.

"She's coming," An'gel said. "Now if we can only get her to tell us what we want to know."

Dickce found a parking space near the entrance to the bistro, and when the sisters walked inside, Helen Louise Brady, the owner, looked up from the cash register and smiled. She came around from behind the counter to greet them.

"Miss An'gel, Miss Dickce, how lovely to see you. I hope you've both been well." Helen Louise gave them each a quick hug.

An'gel had to look up slightly when she returned Helen Louise's greeting. The bistro owner was around six feet tall, a striking woman with dark hair and a sense of elegance about her, even in her work clothes and baker's apron.

"We're doing fine," An'gel said. "We thought we'd have lunch here. A friend is going to join us. Barbie Gross. Do you know her?"

"Yes, I do. She's a regular." Helen Louise escorted them to the table she reserved for special guests. "What would you like to drink?"

"Water for now, I think," An'gel said. "What is the special today?"

"Chicken cassoulet," Helen Louise replied. "I can promise you it is *vraiment délicieux,* even if I prepared it myself." She smiled broadly.

"I don't think I've ever had anything here that wasn't *vraiment délicieux,*" Dickce said with an answering smile.

"Sounds perfect to me," An'gel said. "I agree with Sister. The food here is always *magnifique.*"

"Merci beaucoup, Mesdames," Helen Louise replied with a tilt of the head. "Cassoulet for two, then. Anything besides water to drink?"

"I'll have a glass of whatever wine you think appropriate," An'gel said, and Dickce echoed her.

"Barbie ought to be here soon," Dickce added.

"I won't serve the cassoulet until I know what she wants," Helen Louise assured them. "I'll be back in a moment with water for you."

Right after An'gel and Dickce received their water with slices of lemon, Barbie breezed in. She spotted them immediately but paused on the way to the table to speak to another customer — an older man, quite distinguished looking, An'gel thought. She didn't know him, though.

Barbie, dressed in a silk warm-up suit and sneakers and sporting pearls around her neck and on her ears, sat down across from An'gel. She stuck her purse on the vacant chair to her left.

"I'm so glad you called," she said. "I was getting bored. Lottie had something she just had to do, and I didn't feel like TV or a book. I've been feeling so restless lately, all these odd things happening."

"I know what you mean," An'gel said, rather mendaciously. She and Dickce rarely ran out of things to do and so were seldom bored.

"Yes, these terrible things." Dickce shook her head. "First Sarinda, and then Arliss. Makes you wonder, doesn't it?"

"There's a lunatic out there." Barbie shivered. "I'm surprised the police or the sheriff's department hasn't tracked him down yet. Surely they can find the person who ran Arliss off the road."

"They are looking," An'gel said. She debated whether to mention her own experience to Barbie. She decided she would, simply to gauge the reaction.

"As a matter of fact, I had a similar experience," An'gel said. "To what happened to Arliss, that is."

"Seriously?" Barbie's eyes fairly popped.

"When?"

"Right after we all left Ashton Hall yesterday afternoon," An'gel said. She thought Barbie's astonishment wasn't feigned.

Helen Louise came to the table then with water for Barbie, who also decided on the cassoulet for lunch, along with wine. "Just bring the bottle," she told Helen Louise.

Barbie turned back to An'gel. "Exactly what happened? Why aren't you in the hospital?"

An'gel gave her a quick summary of the incident. After she finished, she waited for Barbie's reaction.

"Are you sure it wasn't simply a coincidence?" Barbie asked. "Seems to me if the person who hit you really wanted you in that ditch, he would have tried again."

"It's entirely possible," An'gel said. "I'd much rather think that than think someone was trying to kill me."

Helen Louise arrived with their servings of cassoulet before they could discuss the subject further. For several minutes all three women concentrated on the delicious dish.

An'gel ate about half of hers before deciding she had eaten more than enough. The rest could go home with them. "This is superb, but I think I've had enough for now." She picked up her wineglass and finished off the contents.

"Yes, it is. I think I'm about done, too," Dickce said. An'gel noticed Dickce had about half of hers left as well.

Barbie showed no signs of stopping. An'gel could see that there was little of her cassoulet left, and she seemed determined to finish it. She caught An'gel's glance and grinned.

"I'll burn it off on the tennis court," she said. Three more bites, and she was done. She refilled her wineglass and drank half of it at one go.

Barbie was certainly a woman of healthy appetites, An'gel thought. Now that Barbie was full of wine and cassoulet, and hopefully in a somewhat mellow mood, An'gel decided to ask a question.

"Did you have an affair with Hadley before he left town forty years ago?"

CHAPTER 30

Barbie had been about to drink more wine when An'gel posed her question. She set the glass on the table and laughed, nervously, An'gel thought.

"Gracious, you certainly don't mess around, An'gel," Barbie said. "Why on the Lord's green earth are you asking me such a question?"

"Because of the bones we found at Ashton Hall," An'gel said. "Something terrible happened there, and the roots of that and the terrible things that have happened here recently all connect to the past. The common denominator in all this is Hadley Partridge."

Barbie stared at her as if dazed. She licked her lips and started to speak. No sound came out. She took a breath and tried again. "Why should me having an affair with Hadley back then — and I'm not saying I did, mind you — why should that have anything

337

to do with the rest?"

"Because," An'gel said, pausing deliberately, "someone is evidently so desperate to have Hadley that she's been willing to kill for him. Forty years ago, and again now."

Barbie emitted another nervous laugh. "That's crazy. The man is incredibly attractive, even now, and he oozes charm like nobody's business. But kill in order to have him?" She shook her head. "That's nuts."

"To a sane person, yes," An'gel said. "But to someone whose reason is warped, whose passion is out of control, it's not. I have tried to come up with some other explanation for everything that's happened, and I always come back to this." She stared hard at Barbie. "Did you have an affair with Hadley back then?"

Barbie held up her hands. "All right, I give. I'll tell you the whole pathetic story. I *didn't* have an affair with him, but I would have given just about anything to get him into bed with me back then." Her mouth twisted in a grimace of distaste. "My husband was good for maybe once a week, if you know what I mean. And not all that exciting even then. He cared more about hunting and fishing than he did about having an intimate relationship with me. I was ready for the first really good-looking man who came along. The minute I met Hadley, he was the one I wanted and thought I had to have." She picked up her glass and drained the rest of the wine. When she set the glass back on the table, her hand shook a little.

"But Hadley didn't return your lust, as it were?" An'gel asked, hoping she didn't sound bitchy. She wasn't comfortable hearing such details of another woman's private life, but there wasn't any way around it, she figured. She'd have to listen in order to get the answers she sought.

"No, he didn't." Barbie stared at the wine bottle and, after a brief hesitation, picked it up and emptied its contents into her glass. "I was devastated at the time. I got over it, though, and found consolation elsewhere." She sipped at her wine.

"Did you have any idea at the time why Hadley wasn't interested?" Dickce shook her head. "You were a beautiful young woman. I'm really surprised he didn't respond."

Barbie laughed, bitterly this time, An'gel thought. "I don't know. At the time I thought he might be gay. But after he turned me down flat, I caught him in a compromising position with someone else."

"Who?" An'gel and Dickce asked in unison.

"Reba Dalrymple," Barbie replied. "Go figure. She had about as much sex appeal as a toaster, but I caught them in a major clinch. Neither of them seemed to be in a hurry to let go, either, from what I could see."

"Where was this?" An'gel asked. "And when was it, do you remember?"

"Only too well. It was at that Christmas fund-raiser you and Dickce hosted about six months before Hadley left town. They were in one of the bedrooms upstairs at Riverhill."

"Heavens," An'gel said faintly.

Dickce snorted. "An'gel won't ask you, but I will. Were they wearing any clothes?"

"Yes, fully clothed," Barbie said. "They weren't on the bed, mind you, but they might have ended up there. I don't know. I shut the door and scurried back down the stairs. I decided I would wait and use the powder room downstairs. I'd gone up there, you see, looking for another bathroom and opened the wrong door. Obviously." She knocked back more wine.

"If I were you, I'd go track Reba down and have a talk with her," Barbie said. "And while you're at it, you might as well go see

Lottie." She shook her head. "My so-called best friend, then and now, was also hot to get Hadley into bed. Her husband was my husband's hunting and fishing buddy, if you'll recall, and she was as eager for attention as I was."

"Good grief, it's like *Peyton Place,*" Dickce said, "except it's all about one man. Did Lottie have any success with Hadley, do you know?"

Barbie shrugged. "She would never say, one way or the other. She seemed pretty hung up on him, even after I told her what I'd seen at your Christmas party. I had a hard time believing Hadley was really interested in Reba, frankly. I thought for sure the reason he was resisting my nubile young charms was Callie. I still think she was the one he loved. I saw him and Callie and that maid of hers, the one with the weird name, out and about several times in out-of-the-way places. I guess they took her along to make it look respectable." She flashed a smile. "This was while I was out hunting for other prey, you understand."

"I can't believe I didn't know any of this was going on," An'gel said. "If you had any inkling, Sister, you never said a word to me about it."

Dickce frowned. "To be honest, I had

picked up a little hint here and there, but I never mentioned it" — she flicked her gaze toward Barbie and back again — "because I knew you hated to hear gossip like that."

An'gel understood. Dickce had protected her from hearing these things until An'gel was able to deal with her own feelings toward Hadley. She smiled briefly, and Dickce winked.

"If you want to get to the truth of the matter," Barbie said, "Hadley is the only one who can tell you what was really going on."

"Yes," An'gel said. "We plan to talk to him."

"What about Sarinda? And Arliss?" Dickce asked, looking directly at Barbie. "They were around at the time. Was either of them involved with Hadley? Or did either of them want to be?"

Barbie shrugged. "Arliss had just gotten divorced from hubby number one, hadn't she? I imagine she was on the prowl then as much as she is now." She paused briefly. "Or I guess I should say, as much as she was before the accident. With Sarinda, well, who really knows? You know what they say about still waters."

Dickce nodded. "I keep thinking about the way she jumped up and basically threw herself into Hadley's arms the last time we saw her. That was such an odd thing to do, even as much as we know she liked attention. I think she must have had feelings for him."

"Wouldn't surprise me," Barbie said. "We were all circling around him in the old days like he was the last man on earth." She snorted. "Handsome, rich, and charming. He had it all. Still does, frankly. Why is it that men only get sexier as they age, and we women get treated like we're ready for the slag heap?"

"I haven't been sitting on any slag heaps lately," An'gel said in a tart tone, "and I don't imagine you have been either. Most of that's nothing more than Hollywood bullhockey, and you know it."

Barbie grinned. "That's one of the reasons I get such a kick out of you, An'gel. You're one tough broad."

An'gel laughed. "If that's all anyone can think of to put on my tombstone, I guess I wouldn't mind. I've had to be. Most women have to be if they're going to get anywhere in this world."

"Ain't that the truth." Barbie downed the rest of her wine. "Well, girls, it's been, well, not exactly fun, but you know what I mean. I need to get going. Supposed to play tennis later on with Lottie, if she remembers to show up this time." She rummaged in her purse and came up with a couple of twenty dollar bills. She dropped them on the table and stood. "That should cover my part of the tab. See you later, girls."

An'gel and Dickce watched as Barbie headed for the door. An'gel was concerned that Barbie was a little inebriated, but she seemed fine. When the door closed behind her, An'gel turned to her sister.

"What do you think? Was she telling us the truth about her and Hadley?"

Dickce shrugged. "I think so, but we can't really know for sure, can we? She seemed genuine when she told us Hadley wasn't interested in her."

Helen Louise came to the table to clear away their plates. "How was the cassoulet?"

"Superb, as always when we dine here," An'gel said. "You are so talented."

Helen Louise grinned. "Thank you, Miss An'gel. I'm simply doing what I love. I'm not sure why I ever bothered going to law school first."

Dickce smiled. "Because your parents wanted you to have a profession in which you could support yourself. They would be so proud of you now, even though you gave up the law."

"I'd like to think so," Helen Louise said.

"Thank you, Miss Dickce. Now, let me get all of this out of the way. Did you save any room for dessert?"

"Not today," An'gel said. "You have fed us all too well."

Dickce nodded. "As much as I'm tempted by the thought of your desserts, I have to agree."

Helen Louise, arms loaded with plates and cutlery, said, "I'll be back in a moment with your check. Thank you, ladies."

Five minutes later An'gel led the way out of the bistro to the car. Dickce got behind the wheel and prepared to crank the car. While An'gel was buckling her seat belt, a cell phone chirped.

"Mine, I think." Dickce pulled it out of her purse. "Yes, a text message. From Benjy." She stared at the screen for a moment. "Oh, that sly man."

"Who are you talking about?" An'gel asked. "What did Benjy say?"

Dickce looked up at her sister. "Benjy was trying to track down the H. Wachtel from the telegram to Mrs. Simpson. He couldn't find anyone who might plausibly be the same person. He got curious about the name Wachtel, however, and dug into it. It's German, and it means *quail* or *partridge*."

"That sneaky devil," An'gel said. "So *Had-*

345

ley sent that telegram?"

"It seems that way," Dickce said.

An'gel thought for a moment. "You saw the telegram, and I didn't. Was there anything on it that indicated it truly came from London?"

Dickce looked pensive. "No, not that I can remember. I'd have to look at it again to be sure, though. What are you getting at?"

"Only that the *H* could be Hamish and not Hadley," An'gel said.

"Why would Hamish have sent a telegram, purporting to be from London, saying that his maid was killed in an accident there? It doesn't make sense."

"Not much about this whole situation does," An'gel replied, her tone grim.

"If Hadley sent it," Dickce said, "do you think Coriander Simpson ran away with him and was tragically killed? Was Hadley in love with her?"

"I don't know," An'gel said. "It's certainly possible. Remember, Barbie told us she had seen the three of them — Hadley, Callie, and Coriander — in public together away from Athena. She thought Coriander was there to provide a screen for Hadley and Callie. But what if Callie was there to provide a screen so Hadley and Coriander could be together?"

346

An'gel waited for Dickce's response. The idea made sense to her, but she wanted to know what her sister thought.

"I suppose that's a possibility," Dickce said. "If Hadley was truly in love with Coriander, they couldn't have been open about it without causing quite a stink forty years ago. You know what people in this town are like, even now when we see interracial couples more often."

"And what *Hamish* was like," An'gel said. "He might have had a stroke on the spot if *he'd* ever found out about them."

"Would have served him right." Dickce sniffed. "But, look here, if Coriander went to England with Hadley and was tragically killed there, and Callie was lying in the ground at Ashton Hall all this time, why the heck is someone trying to knock off the members of the garden club board forty years later?"

"My guess is frustrated passion," An'gel said. "One of those women must have been so fixated on Hadley all these years that, now he's come back, she's trying to make sure she has no competition. I know that might sound crazy but, frankly, I think one of them is crazy as a betsy bug."

"Warped by unrequited love." Dickce shrugged. "I suppose it happens. If that's the case, though, whoever the deranged one is, she's done a great job of hiding it all these years."

An'gel nodded. "Yes. I'm betting on either Lottie or Reba. I don't think it's Barbie."

"Maybe," Dickce said. "I'm still not so sure you're right about the motive. Maybe it's something else entirely."

"I don't think so," An'gel said. Why was Dickce so hesitant to agree with her? She hadn't come up with any other reasonable motive. "We won't get anywhere, however, if we don't talk to Hadley and force him somehow to come clean. Only he can tell us who he was really in love with."

"Ashton Hall then?" Dickce asked as she put the car in reverse.

"Ashton Hall," An'gel said and settled back for the ride.

Fifteen minutes later Dickce pulled up in front of the Partridge ancestral home.

An'gel saw workmen clearing away the downed tree, while others worked on clearing underbrush from outlying flower beds and the edge of the woods that separated Ashton Hall from Riverhill.

"Things are definitely looking better, don't you think?" Dickce asked.

"Yes, but there's still a long way to go if Hadley's going to have everything ready for the spring garden tour." An'gel stepped out of the car and shut the door. She waited for Dickce to join her before they proceeded up the walk to the front door.

An'gel rang the bell, and they waited. She rang it again and held her finger on it for several seconds. Moments later the door swung open, and Hadley stood there.

He flashed a brief smile but did not step back from the open door. "Good afternoon, An'gel, Dickce. As always, it's lovely to see you, but I'm afraid I'm really swamped at the moment. Can't we talk later?"

An'gel glared at him. She wasn't going to be put off by these tactics. Hadley ought to know her better.

"No, we can't talk later." An'gel pushed against the door, and Hadley stepped back, his expression one of resignation. "We have to talk to you, and it has to be now. I don't care what else is going on, it can't be as

349

important as what we have to discuss." She walked into the entry hall with Dickce right behind her.

"Really, An'gel," Hadley protested, "this is high-handed, even for you. I can't imagine you have anything to discuss that calls for forcing your way in here so rudely."

"You shut that door, Hadley Partridge," An'gel said. "Three women are dead, one is missing, and another one is barely hanging on to life, and it's all due to you. So don't you tell me I'm being high-handed. You get yourself into that parlor and start talking to Dickce and me. We have to stop this craziness before someone else gets killed. Do you understand me?"

An'gel was ready to snatch Hadley bald-headed, as her mother used to say to her and Dickce when she was aggravated with them. Hadley stared at her as if she were a complete stranger, but after a moment's hesitation, he nodded. "All right." He led the way into the front parlor.

An'gel was right behind him, and Dickce brought up the rear. Hadley indicated they should be seated, and An'gel chose the sofa. Dickce sat beside her. An'gel stared pointedly at Hadley until he took a seat in an armchair across from them.

"Why is it you think I'm somehow responsible for all this?" Hadley asked. "I didn't harm Sarinda, and I surely didn't run Arliss off the road."

"You were always too good-looking and too charming for your own good and anybody else's," An'gel said, trying hard to hold on to her fast-fraying temper. *The most eligible bachelor in Athena.*" She snorted in a most unladylike manner. "I hate to admit it now, but even I fell for those so-called charms of yours. Briefly."

Dickce coughed, and An'gel turned her head to glare at her sister. She suspected that Dickce was covering up a laugh. She turned her focus back to Hadley, who was sitting there looking like a juvenile who'd just been caught smoking or doing something else inappropriate.

Hadley opened his mouth to speak, but An'gel wasn't done yet.

"You went around playing fast and loose with women's hearts, and consorting with married women," An'gel said. "Your parents raised you better than that, and you know it. Your mother spoiled you rotten, but even she didn't want to see you running around with other men's wives. Especially your brother's."

Hadley tried to speak again, but An'gel was on a roll. "I know you've told us you

351

weren't in love with Callie, but that doesn't mean she wasn't in love with you. The same thing goes for Barbie Gross, Lottie MacLeod, Reba Dalrymple, Arliss McGonigal, and poor Sarinda Hetherington. And then there's Coriander Simpson. What about her, Hadley?" An'gel finally paused for breath.

"What about her?" Hadley asked. "What do you mean? She was my brother's servant, Callie's maid. What does she have to do with anything?"

An'gel knew by the way he'd tensed up the moment she mentioned Coriander's name that he was lying to her now. He knew exactly what Coriander had to do with everything.

"You're still trying to lie to us even now," An'gel said. "I swear to you, if you don't start acting like the man your daddy and mama raised you to be and start telling us the truth, I'm going to, well, I don't know exactly what, but it's going to hurt like hell, I know that much."

An'gel felt Dickce's hand on her arm, and she realized she was getting too worked up. She had lost control of her temper, she realized, because she'd been on the point of getting up and slapping Hadley for all she was worth. She made herself take several deep breaths, but she kept her eyes locked on his.

Hadley must have read the determination in her gaze and in her words. He held up his hands even as his shoulders slumped in obvious resignation.

"All right, An'gel, you win," he said. "I'll tell you anything you want to know."

An'gel wanted to say, *It's about damn time,* but refrained. Instead she said, "Let's start with Callie."

"I loved her with all my heart." Hadley sighed. "She was my dearest friend, my sister. I wasn't in love with her. I didn't want to steal her away from Hamish. But she fell in love with me. Hamish wasn't tender, he wasn't romantic, he wasn't understanding. You know what he was like. But he loved Callie, too, in his way. He was devastated when he realized how she felt about me." He paused for a moment. "I loved my brother, and I hated to see him in pain. That's why I left and didn't come back until after he died. I hoped my being gone would help Callie and Hamish somehow rebuild their marriage."

"It evidently didn't work," An'gel said. "If that truly was Callie we found out there under the tree, something went badly wrong after you left."

"I have no idea what happened after I left," Hadley said, his expression devoid of emotion. "I thought by cutting myself off completely, I'd done the best thing I could for us all. I never spoke to my brother again."

"Do you think Hamish killed Callie?" Dickce asked.

"Who else would have done it?" Hamish replied. "He must have struck her in a rage, it happened accidentally. You know what a temper he had. Then, instead of calling the authorities, he decided to bury her and pretend to everyone that she had run away to be with me. I never knew it until I came back."

That sounded truthful, An'gel thought. "I agree that Hamish is the most likely suspect in Callie's death. But we have Sarinda's death and Arliss's accident to account for. Hamish wasn't responsible for those."

"No," Hadley said. "I don't understand what is going on with that."

"I have a theory," An'gel said. "I'll explain it in a minute. First, though, tell me, did you ever have affairs with any of the garden club board members?"

Hadley looked pained. "I hardly like to talk about what happened so long ago, especially when the other parties aren't around to give their consent."

"We understand that," Dickce said, "but you can't afford such niceties of behavior now. Lives are at stake."

"I suppose you're right," Hadley said. "Okay, then. Yes, I did have brief flings with a couple of them. Barbie Gross and Lottie MacLeod."

An'gel exchanged a swift glance with Dickce. Barbie had lied to them after all, despite being so convincing earlier.

An'gel turned back to Hadley. "What about the others? Reba, Sarinda, and Arliss?"

"Sarinda was very sweet," Hadley said. "I was pretty sure she was infatuated with me, but I simply wasn't interested in her. Arliss, who'd divorced her husband not long before I left, was doing her best to get me into bed, but as attractive as she is, I wasn't interested in her either. She was fun to flirt with, but that was as far as it went."

An'gel felt a moment of sadness for Sarinda, who had never married. Had that been because of Hadley? she wondered.

"What about Reba?" Dickce asked.

Hadley grimaced. "She was married and had a child, and frankly I never found her that attractive. She was after me, though I did my best to discourage her. She even trapped me once — I believe it was at Riverhill, actually — in a bedroom and tried to force me into, well, you know."

"We do know, actually," An'gel said. "Barbie Gross saw you, and she told us about it this morning."

Hadley looked startled. "I remember thinking at the time that somebody opened the door, but Reba was so determined that I didn't have time to see who it was. I had to concentrate on getting her to understand I wasn't interested."

"Tell us more about Lottie and Barbie," An'gel said.

"They were definite mistakes," Hadley said. "You're right, I was raised better, and I knew better than to get involved with married women. The problem was, I was trying to avoid commitment, and they seemed like ways to accomplish that. The thing with Barbie consisted of maybe three encounters, shall we say? We parted quickly by mutual agreement."

"And Lottie?" Dickce prompted.

"That was a bit more than three encounters," Hadley said. For a moment, An'gel thought he was actually blushing. "Let's just say that Lottie was on the aggressive side, okay? And she wasn't easily discouraged. It didn't take me long to realize I'd made a huge mistake getting involved with her, and breaking it off wasn't easy. She wanted to divorce her husband and marry me. She wasn't happy when I told her there was no way that was going to happen." He shuddered. "I don't know who was worse, her or Reba. They were both nightmares, in a way. Reba kept pestering me, even after that incident at Riverhill."

An'gel felt sure now that her theory was right. One of those three women — Barbie, Lottie, or Reba — was behind the murders and the attempts on Arliss and herself.

"There's one more woman unaccounted for," Dickce said. "Coriander Simpson."

Hadley didn't appear so surprised by that name this time, An'gel thought. Before he could respond to Dickce, however, a voice from the doorway captured their attention.

"I believe I can explain that."

CHAPTER 32

An'gel turned to see a tall, striking woman in her sixties advancing into the room. White hair, cut short and styled attractively, framed a face with flawless café-au-lait skin. She was dressed comfortably in black slacks and a white blouse.

Hadley rose quickly and went to her side. "Why didn't you stay upstairs, honey?" He appeared distressed.

The woman kissed his cheek. She ignored his question. She looked straight at An'gel and Dickce. "I'm Coriander Simpson."

"My wife," Hadley said.

Coriander took Hadley's chair, and he stood, looking ill at ease, beside it. She looked up at him fondly. "Relax, love, it's all going to be just fine."

He touched her shoulder briefly, and An'gel could see that he adored her.

"We're delighted to know that you're alive," An'gel said. "And the heartiest congratulations to you and Hadley."

"Thank you," Coriander said. "I know this must come as quite a shock to you. Not only my being alive, but also being married to Hadley."

"In a way," Dickce said. "An'gel had already figured out that it was you Hadley was probably in love with forty years ago."

Coriander nodded. "He was, though he didn't want to admit it for a while. He wasn't so good at committing to one woman back in those days." She laughed and looked up at him. "Fortunately for me, he got over it."

"I visited with your mother," Dickce said, her tone cool. "Either she's a prize-winning actress, or she really believes you died forty years ago."

Coriander closed her eyes for a moment. When she opened them, tears began to flow. "Mama doesn't know I'm still alive. I wasn't even sure if she was either. She'll soon be ninety-eight. Tell me, how is she?"

"She looks well," Dickce said. "She still grieves for you."

An'gel couldn't blame her sister for being blunt with Coriander. Mrs. Simpson had obviously made a deep impression on Dickce, and even though she hadn't met her, she could understand some of the pain

Mrs. Simpson felt.

"Perhaps you should go see her," Dickce added. "Before it's too late."

Hadley pulled a handkerchief from his pocket and handed it to his wife, who was now crying softly. She mopped at her tears and nodded. "I know it was a terrible thing to do to Mama," she said. "But at the time it seemed best to make a complete break. We didn't think we'd ever come back here, you see."

"It was my idea," Hadley said. "I had to talk her into it, and I've regretted it often. We never really expected to come back to Athena, and we thought we might as well protect them from the backlash they could face because of an interracial marriage." He glanced at his wife. "I know Hamish would have reacted badly."

"My daddy would have, too, God rest his soul," Coriander said. "He never would have understood, although Mama might have come around eventually. I thought about them every day since." She blew her nose into the handkerchief. "Once we sent that telegram, there was no going back."

Hadley smiled at his wife. "We'll go see your mother tomorrow, okay?"

"I think you should try to contact another member of the family first," Dickce said.

"Break the news to them, and let one of them tell your mother before you simply appear on her doorstep."

Coriander nodded. "You're right. I'll see if I can get ahold of one of my brothers. They're going to be upset, too."

"Why didn't you tell us the other day you were married?" An'gel asked. "When we first saw you at the garden club board meeting. Why all the secrecy now?"

Coriander said, "I was pretty sick when we first arrived. Had a terrible case of the flu that I must have picked up on the plane, or right before we left England. I was in no condition to meet anyone. It's only in the last couple of days I've felt halfway human again. I suppose you were trying to protect me, weren't you, honey?"

Hadley nodded. "I didn't want a lot of people turning up here when you were ill. I knew there could well be a circus once people found out we're married, and have been all these years."

An'gel had her own ideas about why Hadley hadn't told them he was married. He might sugarcoat it for his wife, but An'gel would bet he wasn't eager to confront anyone over the fact that his wife was African American.

Coriander caught An'gel's gaze and widened her eyes. An'gel realized that was Coriander's way of saying she understood Hadley's reluctance.

"Now that I'm feeling good again," Coriander said, "I'm ready to face Athena, I suppose. I know it's going to be hard for some people to accept, even now, but they'll simply have to deal with it. Their problem, not ours. After all we've been through, I'm not going to put up with their ignorance."

"Exactly," An'gel said. "Your marriage is your business and nobody else's."

"Up to a point," Dickce said.

"What do you mean?" Hadley asked, obviously startled.

"The current situation," Dickce replied. "If An'gel is right about the motive behind the murder and the attempted murders, Coriander could be in danger once the parties concerned find out about your marriage."

Coriander frowned up at Hadley. "What's going on here? You've obviously been keeping things from me. You never said anything about murder."

"I know," Hadley said. "I'm not going to apologize for not telling you about it all before now. You were too sick, and I didn't want you fretting. I didn't realize, frankly, that you could be in danger, though, until

An'gel forced me to face facts."

Coriander turned to An'gel. "What facts are we talking about?"

"The women of the Athena Garden Club board," An'gel replied. She named them for Coriander, who nodded to indicate she remembered them all. "One of them, I think, is obsessed with Hadley. Obsessed to the point that she will try to remove any obstacle standing in her way. She's already pushed Sarinda down the stairs to her death and run Arliss off the road. She even attempted to do the same to me, I think, although there's a possibility that was simply a coincidence."

"The point is, once she finds out Hadley has a wife, she could very likely target you," Dickce said.

"That sounds like the plot of a movie." Coriander shivered. "A creepy, scary movie."

"I'm afraid it may all be too true." An'gel looked straight at Hadley. "Have you told her about what we found in the garden?"

He shook his head. "Not at the time. She was really sick then, and I didn't want to worry her. I told her last night."

"I don't understand it," Coriander said. "I know Hadley thinks his brother killed Callie, but I can't believe he did. He loved her, and he had never raised his hand to her in all the time I worked for her. He had a temper and even broke things sometimes, but I don't think he would ever kill her."

Coriander sounded completely sincere, and An'gel had no doubt she believed Hamish was innocent. An'gel reserved judgment still.

"Then if Hamish didn't do it, who did?" Dickce asked.

"Track down that nasty woman who was housekeeper here," Coriander said. "Mrs. Turnipseed. She hated Callie with a passion because she fancied herself as Mrs. Hamish Partridge. If anyone killed her, that old witch did."

"Mrs. Turnipseed was in love with Hamish?" Hadley asked. "Are you sure?"

"Absolutely," Coriander said. "I caught her once in their bedroom, lying on the bed with one of his suits. She was stroking it and talking to it like he was there in the bed with her." She shook her head. "It was sickening."

"Did she know you saw her?" An'gel asked, fascinated by what Coriander had told them.

"I don't think so," Coriander said. "She always treated me like dirt, and I didn't notice any difference after that."

"Did you tell Callie?" Hadley asked.

"I wanted to," Coriander said. "I just couldn't, though. I know she complained to Hamish about the woman several times and wanted him to fire her, but he wouldn't. She seemed to have some kind of hold over him." She laughed suddenly. "She couldn't force him to marry her, though, even after Callie disappeared." She looked at An'gel and Dickce. "She didn't, did she?"

"I don't think so," An'gel said. "If he had, it was a deep secret. Otherwise he would have had to admit that Callie was dead."

"If he didn't kill Callie, and someone else did, then why didn't he call the police?" Coriander asked. "It doesn't make sense that he wouldn't, if he didn't do it."

"That's one of the reasons I'm inclined to think he probably did," An'gel said. "Though I wonder how it's connected to recent events."

"You were still here for a few days after I left and before you joined me in New York," Hadley said to his wife. "Did you see or hear anything that might have a bearing on Callie's death?"

Coriander frowned. "The afternoon I left the weather was pretty bad. Thunderstorms and heavy rain. I thought we weren't going to make it to Memphis for me to catch the plane to New York in time." She paused. "I left by the back door. I'd arranged with a man I knew in town to give me ride to Memphis. He was waiting around back when I came out. It was pouring rain by then, and I got soaked getting into the car with my suitcases. When he drove around the front to head for the highway, I saw a car there. I don't know who it was, though, but I remember thinking I heard somebody at the front door. Mrs. Turnipseed always answered the door, and I was happy she wasn't there in the kitchen when I left."

"I wonder who it was," Dickce said.

"Can you remember anything about the car?" An'gel asked.

"Let me think about it a moment," Coriander said. After a brief silence, she spoke again. "I think it was black, or some other dark color. Probably a four-door. That's all I can recall. It's been so long I'd almost forgotten about it."

An'gel looked at Hadley. "Do you have any idea whose car it was?"

He shrugged. "Who remembers what kind of car another person had forty years ago? I barely remember my own. I sold it in Memphis before I left for New York, but that's neither here nor there." He paused. "It sounds like a sedan, of course, and everybody was driving one back then. Reba was, and I'm pretty sure both Barbie and Lottie were, too. The color I have no idea about."

"That's not so sinister in itself," An'gel said after a moment's reflection. "Visitors came to Ashton Hall regularly, didn't they?"

"Not all that often, no," Coriander said. "Hamish didn't like company all that much. In fact, he used to complain to Hadley about the women who would show up here unannounced. Didn't he?"

"Yes," Hadley said. "I didn't encourage them to come here, they simply showed up. I tried to explain that to Hamish, but he didn't believe me."

"It's a fatal attraction you seem to have," An'gel murmured, "at least for some women." She shook her head before she focused on Coriander. "What about the few days after Hadley left and before you went to join him? Were there any unexpected visitors?"

"I'll have to think about that for a minute," Coriander said. "The more I'm trying to recall things from then, though, the easier it seems to be getting. Yes, I'm pretty sure that both Reba Dalrymple and Lottie MacLeod turned up, looking for Hadley. They both insisted he'd failed to keep a date with them, but I thought they were both lying.

They had made it up as an excuse to see him."

"Did you talk to them yourself?" An'gel asked.

Coriander shook her head. "No, Callie did, although she told me about it."

"Did she know that you and Hadley planned to run away together?" Dickce asked.

"Yes, we told her," Hadley said.

"How did she take the news?" An'gel said.

Coriander looked troubled. "She was heartbroken, even though she knew it was for the best. I knew she was in love with Hadley, but she knew he didn't return her feelings. She was talking about going away herself, at least for a little while, to sort things out."

"Did she tell anyone else that?" An'gel asked.

"She might have," Coriander said. "She was pretty low right after Hadley left. She might have told someone she was going away for a while."

"If she did, that person might have assumed she was going to join Hadley," Dickce said. "What story did Hamish and Callie give about Hadley leaving?"

"Not anything, really, other than that he was on an extended trip," Coriander said.

"Neither one of them wanted to say that he wasn't planning to come back. Hamish thought he left because of Callie, and in a way he did, I suppose. I wasn't going to tell him, and Hadley certainly didn't, that it was because of me."

"And almost everyone in town thought Hadley *did* leave because of Callie," An'gel said. "I'm sure that Callie's murderer thought that, too, and blamed her for Hadley's going away."

"You mean to tell me someone murdered Callie because I left town and they thought she was the reason?" Hadley asked.

"I do," An'gel said. "Now we simply have to figure out who it was." Before she could elaborate further, she heard her cell phone ringing. "Excuse me, I need to check this." She pulled it out of her purse and glanced at the screen. Kanesha Berry's name came up.

"Hello, Kanesha," An'gel said. "Any news?"

"Yes," Kanesha replied. "We found Mrs. Turnipseed and her car. She was dead inside, and the car's front end was damaged. I think she was the one who tried to run you off the road."

CHAPTER 33

"Oh, my heavens," An'gel said. "That's terrible. I was hoping she was still alive. Are you sure she's the one who tried to run me off the road?"

"Reasonably sure," Kanesha replied. "We can't say for certain until we can test and match the paint samples we found on your car and hers. I'm pretty confident, though, that we've found the right car."

"Where did you find her?" An'gel asked. She could see that the others were curious but she wanted to get all the details she could from Kanesha before she shared them.

"In her own garage," Kanesha said. "We're not exactly sure when she returned, or how she got by us, but a neighbor on the street behind her reported seeing lights around one o'clock this morning. We didn't hear about this until a couple of hours ago, however."

"How strange," An'gel said. "Do you know yet how she died?"

"We're pretty sure she was knocked unconscious and then strangled," Kanesha replied. "I'm hoping the witness who saw the lights can tell us something more that will give us a lead on who's responsible."

"I hope they can, too," An'gel said. "In the meantime, though, I think you really need to come out to Ashton Hall. There's new information that could help."

"Such as?" Kanesha said, her tone sharp.

"We found Coriander Simpson, for one," An'gel said. "Now, I know you're probably going to be aggravated we didn't tell you sooner, but the story is a bit complicated. If you can come out here now, we can tell you everything. Coriander is here with us now. She's actually Hadley Partridge's wife."

For once in her life, Kanesha must have been struck speechless, An'gel decided, as she waited for the chief deputy to respond. Finally Kanesha said, "I'll be on my way in a few." She ended the call.

"Tell us what all that was about," Dickce said.

An'gel shared what Kanesha told her about the death of Mrs. Turnipseed. When she finished, there was stunned silence for a moment.

Coriander looked up at Hadley. "I think maybe we should tell Ryan that he and Belinda and the boys should stay in Memphis until the murderer is caught."

"Good idea," Hadley said. "As soon as I know their plane has landed, I'll text him and tell him to call me before they leave the airport."

"Who are Ryan and Belinda and the boys?" An'gel asked, although she suspected she already knew.

"Our son and his wife, and our grandsons, Simon and Derek," Coriander replied. "They live in London, and they're on their way here for a visit."

"This will all be theirs someday," Hadley said. "If they decide they want to keep it and move here, of course." He looked down at his wife. "We're planning to stay here. That's why I'm investing time and energy and money in this house and grounds."

"I'm delighted to hear it," An'gel said. "You belong here."

"Me, too," Dickce added. "It will be wonderful to see children here at Ashton Hall."

Coriander laughed. "They're not precisely children. Simon will soon be seventeen, and Derek is fifteen."

"Young people then." Dickce smiled.

"I take it that Deputy Berry is on her way here?" Hadley asked.

"Yes," An'gel said. "She needs to know everything you've told us, and I'm hoping she will have other information she hasn't shared. Maybe that way she can figure out who's behind everything. Maybe even who really killed Callie."

"While we wait for her," Coriander said, "why don't I make some tea? I think we could all use it right about now." She rose from the chair.

Hadley smiled. "We've become accustomed to it. Tea as the antidote to everything. I frankly could use something a lot stronger, but tea will do. How about we all go to the kitchen and have it there? Cory made some fresh scones this morning."

"Sounds fine to me," Dickce said. "Come on, An'gel."

"I'll never say no to tea and homemade scones," An'gel replied as she rose from the sofa.

An'gel had barely finished her first scone when the doorbell rang. Hadley left the room to answer it.

"Will the deputy be offended if we talk to her in the kitchen?" Coriander asked.

"Not at all," An'gel said.

"Good. I'll get another cup out for her."

Coriander walked over to the cabinet.

Hadley returned with Kanesha Berry, and he quickly made introductions between his wife and the deputy. Coriander stared at Kanesha for a moment. "I believe I knew your mother," she said. "Azalea Berry, isn't she?"

Kanesha nodded. "Yes, that's my mother."

"I hope she's doing well," Coriander said. "She was always such a gracious person and very kind to me when I saw her."

"She's doing fine," Kanesha said. "I'll let her know you asked about her." She turned to greet An'gel and Dickce. "I don't mean to be rude, but I have a lot going on. I really need to hear what all you have to tell me."

An'gel knew that Kanesha was feeling the pressure of the investigation and was not bothered by her abrupt manner.

"Why don't you sit down and have a cup of tea and a scone, and we'll tell you everything as quickly as we can."

Kanesha didn't respond for a moment. "All right. I could use a little caffeine, frankly."

Hadley held out a chair for her, and she nodded before taking it. Coriander placed tea and a plate with two scones on the table in front of her.

An'gel said, "It all started with Dickce and

me trying to trace Coriander Simpson." She gave Kanesha a quick summary of Benjy's efforts and Dickce's visit with Coriander's mother. "We thought she really might have died in England, but as it turned out, we were wrong." She looked to Hadley and Coriander to take up the story now.

Hadley explained the reasons he left Athena and all that ensued, from his own knowledge, after that. Coriander then shared with Kanesha what she knew about the other women who were in love with Hadley, and about the car she had seen the day she left Ashton Hall to join Hadley in New York.

Kanesha had consumed both scones and two cups of tea by the time she heard all the information that An'gel, Dickce, Hadley, and Coriander had to share. Now they all waited to hear what she had to say in response.

Kanesha pushed the empty plate away and regarded them all with her habitual unreadable expression.

"Well?" An'gel said. "Does any of this help you figure out who the killer is?"

Kanesha nodded. "I believe so, but I do have one question for you. I think I know who it is, but tell me, is one of these women left-handed?"

An'gel looked at Dickce and frowned. "As I recall, both Lottie and Reba are left-handed, aren't they?"

Dickce nodded. "Yes, they are."

Kanesha muttered something under her breath, and An'gel thought she knew what it was. She didn't blame the deputy.

"I presume whoever killed Mrs. Turnipseed was left-handed?" An'gel said.

"Yes," Kanesha replied, "and I figured the chances were that only one of these ladies was a lefty. Now you tell me two of them are."

"At least that eliminates Barbie Gross," Dickce said. "I'm glad. I really like her."

"My vote is for Reba," An'gel said. "After all, she knew Mrs. Turnipseed rather well. She told us so herself. If Mrs. Turnipseed trusted the person who killed her, who was that more likely to be? Reba, I think."

"That makes a lot of sense," Dickce said.

"I agree," Kanesha said. "But we don't know for sure that Mrs. Turnipseed was working with someone she might consider a friend. I suspect she was being paid by someone. She was living well beyond the means of a retired housekeeper."

"How do you know that?" Coriander asked. "Surely you haven't access to her bank account so quickly."

376

"No, I don't," Kanesha replied. "I'll just say that we found plenty of things at her house that were way too expensive. She had a lot of antique furniture for one thing, antiques that looked like better quality than what she might have inherited from her own family. I knew of them. They weren't people who could afford such things."

"Some of them came from Ashton Hall," Hadley explained. "My brother left her most of the furnishings from my mother's bedroom and sitting room."

"That would account for most of them," Kanesha said. "It still doesn't explain the rest. Your mother didn't have an early seventeenth-century oak coffer, did she? Or an oak settle from roughly the same period?"

Hadley shook his head. "No, she didn't. We didn't have them anywhere in the house, unless they were purchased after I left. Frankly, though, I can't see my brother buying them. They would have been too old. He didn't care for anything before Regency."

"I see," Kanesha said. She glanced at An'gel and Dickce, obviously aware of their curiosity. "I watch shows about antiques when I'm off, and I've learned to recognize different periods and styles." She smiled briefly. "My one hobby."

"So you think Mrs. Turnipseed was black-mailing someone?" Dickce said.

"Yes, I believe so," Kanesha replied.

An'gel said, "I know Lottie's husband left her quite well off. Reba, on the other hand, has always seemed to be strapped for cash."

"Maybe because Mrs. Turnipseed has been blackmailing her for years," Dickce said. "They certainly used to have money, at least as long as her husband was alive. After he died, I thought she spent most of her money on keeping Martin happy with gadgets and cars."

"Do you think my brother murdered his wife?" Hadley asked.

Kanesha shrugged. "Hard to say at this point. Frankly, I have to assume he did, unless someone else confesses to it. The fact that he didn't report her dead or missing is suspicious. We have very little to go on in her case, unfortunately."

"I see." Hadley closed his eyes for a moment. Coriander laid her hand on his and squeezed it.

"I think it's likely that either Reba or Lottie killed Callie," An'gel said. "And I'm betting that Mrs. Turnipseed saw it happen, or else saw enough to figure it out. Then she blackmailed the killer."

"And when Hadley came back, either Reba or Lottie was so determined to have him, she went after the women who showed open interest in him." Dickce went on to explain about Sarinda's reaction to Hadley at the garden club board meeting and the fact that Hadley had been seen in town with Arliss.

"I feel so bad about that," Hadley said. "Arliss wasn't trying to seduce me, at least not that I could tell. She told me she was planning her first trip to London and wanted me to tell her about all the things she should see and where she should stay."

Coriander exchanged an amused glance with An'gel, as if to say, *He's still naive when it comes to women's motives for anything.*

"That's as may be," An'gel said. "The result was, however, that Arliss got run off the road and is now fighting for her life."

"I have some news on that," Kanesha said. "I know you'll be happy to hear she's improving, and the doctor is more hopeful that she'll be able to recover. Perhaps not completely, but better than expected."

"That *is* wonderful news," Dickce said.

"Thank the Lord," Hadley said. "I feel responsible for her being in the shape she is."

"Nonsense," An'gel said. "The person

who ran her off the road is responsible, not you."

"I agree, dear," Coriander said. "You aren't at fault for the actions of a lunatic."

Hadley didn't look convinced, but he would have to wrestle with his feelings of guilt, An'gel knew. In his place she would probably feel the same.

"How are you going to figure out which one of them is responsible?" Coriander asked.

Before Kanesha could respond, An'gel said, "I have an idea that might help get this over with quickly."

Kanesha looked at her, one eyebrow raised. "And what is that idea, Miss An'gel?"

"I know you don't like interference in your investigations," An'gel said. "But you have accepted our help in the past, and I think in this case we can help bring things to a close before anyone else gets hurt."

"Yes, I understand that." Kanesha frowned, and An'gel could see that her patience was wearing thin. "What is this idea?"

"We flush out the killer." An'gel leaned forward. "You have deputies here in the house, ready to arrest her. Dickce and I will each call one of them, ostensibly to gossip and share what we've found out, that Hadley is married. I'm thinking that news might make her so angry she'll storm over here and try something. Your men will be on hand, and they can arrest her then." She sat back in her chair and waited for reactions.

"The person would have to make a direct attack against either Mister or Mrs. Partridge," Kanesha said. "That's a big risk, and they would have to be willing to take it before I could even consider consenting to that kind of scheme."

An'gel looked at Hadley and Coriander. "What do you say?"

"Absolutely not," Hadley said. "In Cory's case, that is. I'm willing to be the bait, but I'm not going to allow her to be."

"Excuse me, Mister Partridge," Coriander said, her voice a little sharp, "you're not going to *allow* me? Is that so?"

Hadley's expression turned even more stubborn, An'gel thought, as he regarded his wife.

"This is no time to talk about being equal partners," he said. "This is your life we're talking about."

"It's also *your* life," Coriander replied. "I'm not all that eager to see you put yourself in danger, you know." She turned to An'gel. "Tell me, what do you think would enrage this woman more, seeing me or Hadley, or the two of us together?"

An'gel hated to say it, because she figured Hadley would never forgive her. "You two together."

"Then that's how we'll do it, or not at all." Coriander picked up the teapot. "I'll make more tea for all of us."

CHAPTER 34

Hadley yielded to his wife's determination, and that surprised An'gel a bit. She admired Coriander for her courage, and said so.

Coriander thanked her and continued her preparations for another pot of tea.

An'gel turned to Kanesha. "So what do you say?"

"I'm not fond of the idea," Kanesha said. "But it could resolve things quickly. At present, it could be weeks before we have enough information to make an arrest." She paused for a moment. "Okay, I'm in. Let me call for some backup first. I need to get them in place before you make those phone calls." She turned to Hadley. "Is there somewhere we can hide the patrol cars?"

"There's room in the garage behind the house," Hadley said. "We have only one car there at the moment, a rental, and there's space for three more."

"Good enough." Kanesha stood. "I'll just

step into the other room to call, if you don't mind." She strode out of the kitchen but was back in less than two minutes.

"Everything is set," she said. "I'm going to move my car now. Will you come with me, Mr. Partridge?"

"Certainly," Hadley said and followed her out of the kitchen.

Coriander came back to the table and resumed her seat while she waited for the water to come to a boil. "I have to say, you two seem remarkably cool about all this. I'm a bit jittery myself, but I'm going to see it through. But do you really think this woman might try to kill me? Or Hadley?"

"It's a distinct possibility," An'gel replied. "You're the more likely candidate, unfortunately. She would have to get rid of you in order to have Hadley for herself, you see."

Coriander nodded. The kettle whistled, and she rose to attend to it. Over her shoulder she said, "This is certainly not what I expected to be dealing with when we came back to Athena. Prejudice, certainly, but not a deranged person fixated on my husband."

"There will be prejudice from some people, even now," An'gel said. "I'm sorry about that, for your and Hadley's sake."

Coriander brought the teapot back to the

table and resumed her seat. She poured more tea for the three of them, then set the teapot aside. "It's not anything we haven't faced already," she said. "I dealt with it growing up because my mother was black and my father was mixed race. I can stand anything they throw at me."

"I believe you can." Dickce smiled. "And brava to you. Once all this is settled we look forward to meeting your family."

"Thank you," Coriander said. "I'm not sure what they're going to think of Mississippi, although Hadley and I have both talked about it often enough."

Hadley and Kanesha entered the kitchen through the back door and came to the table. Coriander refilled their teacups when they sat.

"My deputies will be here in under five minutes," Kanesha said. "I think it's okay to go ahead and make those calls, Miss An'gel, Miss Dickce."

An'gel nodded. "All right. Sister, will you call Reba, and I'll call Lottie?"

"Sure," Dickce said. "Doesn't really matter." She pulled her cell phone from her purse. "I'll go into the hall. You can stay here." She strode out of the room.

"Pour it on thick," An'gel called after her. She wasn't sure Dickce heard her, but she figured her sister knew what to say to Reba.

An'gel retrieved her own phone from her purse and found Lottie's name in her contacts. She tapped the call icon and waited for an answer. Kanesha, Hadley, and Coriander watched and waited quietly.

"Hi, Lottie, how are you?" An'gel asked, her tone bright and breezy. "I hope you're well."

"Doing fine," Lottie said. "What's up, An'gel? I'm supposed to meet Barbie in a few minutes."

"I won't keep you long," An'gel said. "I simply couldn't wait to call you. You'll never guess what Dickce and I found out. It's so juicy, you'll have a fit when you hear."

"Really? Do tell," Lottie said. An'gel heard the eagerness in Lottie's voice. She adored gossip.

"Well, Dickce and I dropped by to see Hadley a little while ago, and you could have knocked us down with a feather," An'gel said. She groaned inwardly at the cliche, but pressed on. "You'll never guess who opened the door."

"Who?" Lottie asked. An'gel thought she detected tension in that one syllable.

"His wife." An'gel paused deliberately too see how Lottie would react.

"I don't believe you," Lottie said. "Who is

386

she, some English woman?"

An'gel laughed. "Heavens, no. You'd never in a million years guess who she is."

"Who, dammit? Who is she?" Lottie was obviously agitated, whether from An'gel's teasing her by delaying an answer or from the very fact that Hadley was married. An'gel wasn't sure, but it was time to drop the bombshell.

"Do you remember Callie's maid? Coriander Simpson?" An'gel said. "She's Mrs. Hadley Partridge now."

"You have got to be kidding." Lottie snorted into the phone. "You're telling me that Hadley Partridge married his brother's servant? They'll kick him out of the country club for this. I can't believe it. Why'd he go and marry her?"

"For the same reason most people marry," An'gel said. "He loves her, and she obviously loves him. You should see them together. They make such a beautiful couple. She's every bit as striking as Hadley is handsome."

Hadley grimaced at her, and Coriander appeared embarrassed. An'gel couldn't help that. If Lottie was the killer, An'gel wanted to do what she could to get her worked up enough to show her hand.

"I've got to go," Lottie said abruptly. "Barbie's waiting. Talk to you later." The call ended.

An'gel set her phone on the table. "If that doesn't get her here — presuming she's the one we're after — nothing will."

Kanesha smiled. "Miss An'gel, you are even more devious than I ever suspected."

"I'll take that as a compliment, thank you very much." She shared with them some of what Lottie had said. Hadley laughed at the remark about his being kicked out of the country club.

"I couldn't care less about those old fogies," he said. "I hate golf anyway."

Kanesha stood. "I hear the squad car." She went to the back door. "Back in a moment."

Dickce returned to the kitchen. "Mission accomplished."

"How did she react?" An'gel asked.

"I was afraid she was going to have a stroke." Dickce shook her head. "I'm not going to repeat some of the things she said. Trust me, if she's the killer, she's bound to show up here in record time."

"The other deputies are here," An'gel said. She began to feel nervous. Would her plan work? Was she unnecessarily putting lives in danger? They would simply have to see how things played out.

Kanesha returned with three deputies. She discussed with Hadley where to have them wait, and they decided that she and two of her men would wait in the room next to the front parlor. There was a door between the two rooms, and they would stand there with it slightly ajar, ready to come in the moment they were needed. The third deputy would wait across the hall where he would be watching what happened when Hadley answered the door. He would move into place outside the outer door to the parlor once Lottie or Reba was in the parlor.

"We're going to be in the parlor with you," An'gel told Hadley and Coriander. She shot a defiant glance at Kanesha. "You'll have to lock us up somewhere to keep us out of there. Are you with me, Sister?"

"Absolutely," Dickce said. "We can cause a distraction if necessary. We both have mace in our purses, and we'll use it if we have to."

Kanesha looked resigned. "We don't have the time to argue this, and I'm sure not going to lock you and Miss Dickce up, Miss An'gel. I can't even imagine trying it." She paused. "Let's get everyone in place. No telling how quickly the killer will show up."

They all trooped out of the kitchen. Hadley showed Kanesha and her men into the library, the room next to the front parlor. Kanesha fixed the door how she wanted it. An'gel, along with Dickce and Coriander, seated themselves in the parlor. Hadley joined them moments later.

"I could use a drink," Hadley said. "Bourbon, anyone?"

"Not for me, honey," Coriander said. "You go ahead, though. Ladies?"

"No, thank you," An'gel said in unison with Dickce.

"I guess I'll hold off until after this is over," Hadley said with rueful smile. "I'll probably need it even more then."

A silence fell, and An'gel could feel the tension begin a slow rise. She was on edge, and she could only imagine how tightly strung were Hadley's and Coriander's nerves.

Twelve agonizing minutes passed as An'gel checked her watch every few seconds. Then they heard a car coming up the driveway, and it sounded like it was coming at a high speed. Hadley moved over to a front window and peered out. He winced as they all heard the sound of the car screeching to a halt. "She almost hit your car," he said to An'gel and Dickce. "Looks like Lottie MacLeod."

He headed for the front door while the women waited in the parlor. They all heard the sound of another car coming up the driveway, also at a high rate of speed. An'gel and Dickce shared a glance. What the heck was going on? Was Reba going to turn up as well?

An'gel got up and went to the window. She looked out just in time to see Reba Dalrymple's car make contact with Lottie MacLeod's. Reba climbed out of the car without even a glance at the damage she caused and made a beeline for the front door.

"Reba's here, too." An'gel hurried over to the doorway to the hall and peered out from behind the door. Hadley was admitting Lottie, carrying a large handbag, when Reba came barreling through the door. She knocked into Lottie, and if it hadn't been for quick reflexes on Hadley's part, both women might have crashed to the floor.

"What the hell are you doing here?" Reba jerked her arm from Hadley's grasp and glared at Lottie. Reba also carried a large handbag.

"I came to talk to Hadley about his unfortunate marriage," Lottie said. "Why the hell are you here?"

"The same reason," Reba said. She looked at Hadley. "What the hell were you thinking? Have you lost all sense of pride in your family's name and heritage? Why did you have to go and marry that slut of a maid?"

"That's exactly what I want to know," Lottie said. "Hadley, how could you? I've been here waiting all this time for you to come back to me. I thought you would have asked me to marry you by now. You're really naughty for not doing it but of course you can't now because you're married. That's a problem, but not one we can't solve."

An'gel was struck by Lottie's calm tone. The woman might have been discussing the weather or a favorite recipe.

"Marry *you*?" Reba shouted the words. "He's not going to ever marry you. He's going to marry me because I can give him a son. A son who will take care of Ashton Hall after he's gone. He's going to adopt Martin and make him his heir."

"The hell he is," Lottie said, still calm. "Why would he want to have that half-witted son of yours as his heir? No, that wouldn't do at all." She reached into her bag and pulled out a pistol. "No, that wouldn't do at all. I can give Hadley the son he's always wanted. And with that so-called wife out of the way, we can marry."

The moment Lottie pulled the gun from her purse, the deputy came out of the room across the hall. Hadley stepped back to get out of the way. He tried to push Reba away, but she resisted. The deputy tackled Lottie just as she fired her pistol at Reba. An'gel watched in horrified fascination as a patch of red bloomed on Reba's shoulder. Reba stared in shock at Lottie as the deputy bore her to the floor and wrested the pistol away from her. Then she began to crumple.

Hadley caught her in his arms and lifted her. He brought her into the parlor. Kanesha's other two deputies were in the hall with their fellow officer. An'gel watched as it took all three of them to handle Lottie. She fought them fiercely as they held her arms and tried to get cuffs on her. She kicked and screamed and tried to bite. The men were trying their best to subdue her without hurting her.

An'gel knew it was wrong of her but she itched to get out there and slap the heck out of Lottie. She wished one of the men would do it. They ought to coldcock her. That was the term, An'gel thought. Yes, coldcock her and stop all that carrying on.

They were being too gentle, and Lottie was fighting hard. An'gel moved quickly to her purse, pulled out her mace, and ran into the hall. She got as close as she could, and when she had a clear shot, she sprayed Lottie right in the face.

"Miss An'gel, what do you think you're doing?" Kanesha demanded.

An'gel could tell Kanesha was about ready to pick her up and shake her until her teeth rattled out of her head. She knew she was in the wrong, but Lottie had ceased fighting and was now crying and sputtering about the mace. The deputies were able to get the cuffs on her with no trouble now.

"I'm sorry," An'gel said, "but I'm not really sorry. They wouldn't stop her, so I decided to. Sometimes you simply can't treat a woman like a lady, and it takes another woman to treat her like the witch she is." She strode back into the parlor, her heart beating furiously from the aftermath of her actions. She dropped the mace in her purse and sat abruptly.

Dickce and Coriander were looking after Reba until an ambulance arrived. An'gel prayed they arrived in time. She hoped the bullet hadn't hit a vital artery.

Thank the Lord this is over now. Lottie was obviously completely crazy. *A woman her age thinking she could bear a child.* An'gel wondered how long she had been this way, and none of them suspected. She felt sorry for Lottie, and for Reba too. Both women had wasted years of their lives on unrequited passion for one man.

An'gel looked at Hadley. He watched helplessly while his wife and Dickce ministered to Reba. She had loved Hadley herself once, and she still was very fond of him. But was he worth all this? The destruction of several lives?

No, he wasn't, she decided. *No man was.*

CHAPTER 35

"I was never so surprised in my life," An'gel said. "I thought for sure after what happened at Ashton Hall that Lottie was the murderer."

"Me, too," Dickce said. "If it hadn't been for Reba's confession, though, she would have gotten away with it."

"Maybe not," Benjy said. He fed Peanut another tidbit, then gave one to Endora. "You said that her son talked to Deputy Berry at the hospital. Didn't he tell them he knew she'd killed Mrs. Turnipseed?"

An'gel didn't normally allow Peanut and Endora to be in the dining room while they ate, but tonight was an exception. Tonight was a celebration that the horrors of the past few days were mostly over.

"Yes, you're right," An'gel said. "But would Martin have sat there in court and testified against his mother? I don't know."

"I think that's why Reba confessed,"

396

Dickce said. "She didn't want Martin to have to go through that. Plus she thought she was dying."

"It might have been better if she had," An'gel said. "Though I have very little sympathy for her, frankly."

"I don't either," Dickce said. She picked up her wineglass and finished off the contents. She reached for the bottle and refilled her glass. "She killed three women, put another in the hospital with life-threatening injuries, and forced one of her victims to try to kill you."

"She either used Mrs. Turnipseed's car or had Mrs. Turnipseed herself run Arliss off the road," An'gel said. "I don't know which. That Turnipseed woman was a nasty piece of work."

"Why was she blackmailing Mrs. Dalrymple?" Benjy asked. "Did you find out?"

"I think it was because she knew Reba killed Callie," Dickce said. "What did Kanesha tell you about that? You haven't said."

An'gel sighed. "It's all so very sad. It took Kanesha a while to get this part out of Reba, but this is apparently what happened." She paused a moment. "You remember Coriander told us she saw a car in front of the house when she left for Memphis?"

Dickce nodded. "I've told Benjy all about that."

"That was Reba's car," An'gel said. "She had just found out that Hadley was gone, and she drove out to Ashton Hall to confront Callie. She was furious with her because she knew Callie was the reason Hadley had left. He was gone, and she was desperately in love with him. She found Callie and Hamish already having an argument over Hadley. Callie was allegedly pleading with Hamish to allow Hadley to come back, but Hamish wouldn't budge. Then Reba arrives and immediately starts screaming at Callie. She told Hamish that she knew Hadley and Callie had been having an affair — I think she was more than a bit unhinged back then, because I think it was a lie."

"Hamish probably went ballistic over that," Dickce said.

"He did," An'gel replied. "Reba said he was so enraged that he struck Callie and knocked her down, then he ran out of the room, crying. He thought he'd killed her because she struck her head."

"Didn't he?" Benjy asked.

"No," An'gel said. "Reba did. Callie was

in bad shape and might have died, I think, but Reba made sure she did. She picked up Callie's head and slammed it against the floor. Callie died then."

"So did Reba make Hamish think he'd done it?" Dickce asked, obviously appalled by the story. She had another sip of wine.

"She did, and she told him she would never tell anyone. She convinced him to bury Callie there at Ashton Hall. Everyone would think Callie had run away to join Hadley, and no one would ever know he killed his wife. Reba said she would make sure the rumor spread."

"That's sickening," Benjy said. "How could she do something like that? Especially since Hadley was long gone."

"I don't believe she really thought it through at the time," An'gel replied. "I don't think reality, such as it was with her, set in until much later. I think she was so obsessed with having Callie out of the way, she didn't realize Hadley wasn't coming back. She evidently had no idea that he was in love with Coriander instead, and that they were planning to be married and live abroad."

"Where does that Mrs. Turnipseed come into this?" Benjy gave the cat and the dog more tidbits, then held up empty hands to show them that there were no more. Peanut whimpered once, but Endora made her way to Dickce and leapt into her lap. Peanut stretched out on the floor beside Benjy and kept watch in case more treats should miraculously appear.

"I believe she saw what Reba did," An'gel said. "Reba wouldn't say for sure, but the woman had been blackmailing Reba for years. She also blackmailed Hamish, but she was shrewd enough not to ask for too much, evidently."

"Then Reba must have promised Mrs. Turnipseed something to get her help with running you and Arliss off the road." Dickce rubbed Endora's head and smiled at the resulting purr.

"She offered her more money," An'gel said, "though I don't think she really had much to pay her with by this time."

"Why did she kill Mrs. Turnipseed?" Benjy asked.

"Apparently after the woman tried to run me off the road, she demanded that she be allowed to live at Ashton Hall when Reba married Hadley." An'gel shook her head. "That was apparently too much, finally, and Reba decided she had to go."

"I just don't get how all these women were so obsessed with Hadley," Benjy said. "I guess he's good-looking, for his age, anyway, and I obviously didn't know him forty years ago. But it all seems whacked to me."

"It's whacked to me, too," Dickce said. "The heart wants what it wants, and with certain types of personalities, not getting what the heart wants can warp a person in strange ways."

"When we were young, women were reared with the notion that they couldn't have a complete and worthwhile life unless they married and had children," An'gel said. "That's nonsense, of course. It certainly was for Dickce and me, though we had our opportunities to change that."

"We sure did." Dickce smiled.

"For some women, though, this whole notion is so ingrained that they will go to great lengths to be married, even if they're not happily married. It doesn't make a lot of sense, I know, but that's the way it is."

"It's all very sad," Dickce said. "There's Lottie, locked away in the loony bin for probably the rest of her life. Reba is facing prison for murdering three women and trying to kill two more. So many lives ruined."

"I wonder how Martin will cope now that his mother is no longer there to look after him," An'gel said. "Perhaps he'll surprise us all and manage just fine."

"He'll have to get a job, for one thing," Dickce said. "I suppose he's smart enough with computers that he can find something."

"Let's hope so," An'gel said.

"You're going to have to find some new members for your garden club," Benjy said. "Or at least for your board."

An'gel and Dickce exchanged looks. "I hadn't thought of that yet," An'gel said.

"We can always ask Coriander to join," Dickce said with an impish grin. "That ought to liven things up."

"I daresay it will," An'gel replied. "I think she'd be better suited to it than Hadley. In fact, I think we should discourage men from joining altogether."

"Maybe we should simply exclude Hadley," Dickce said. "He was at the center of all the goings-on. With him out, things might settle down and operate smoothly again, like they did before he came back."

"We can only hope things will be quiet for a while," An'gel said. "We've got to get ready for the spring garden tour, and then there's the historical society meeting in Natchez. I've had enough of murder for now." She pushed back her chair and stood. "Now, who's for dessert?"

Peanut barked loudly, twice, and they all laughed.

The employees of Thorndike Press hope you have enjoyed this Large Print book. All our Thorndike, Wheeler, and Kennebec Large Print titles are designed for easy reading, and all our books are made to last. Other Thorndike Press Large Print books are available at your library, through selected bookstores, or directly from us.

For information about titles, please call:
(800) 223-1244

or visit our Web site at:

http://gale.cengage.com/thorndike

To share your comments, please write:

Publisher
Thorndike Press
10 Water St., Suite 310
Waterville, ME 04901